The
Marilyn Monroe
Connection

by
Crystal Jackson

BAITCAL
PUBLISHING

Crystal Jackson's literary journey began nearly a decade ago when she began documenting the 1500-year history of Pacoima, one of Los Angeles' oldest towns. Her critically acclaimed first book, "The Entrance: Pacoima's Story," is a 670-page encyclopedia of history about her hometown that drew rave reviews from educators and institutions nationwide.

Jackson, founder and president of the Pacoima Historical Society, consults and serves on advisory boards at Getty Center, Princeton University, UCLA, Los Angeles Public Library, and more.

Her impressive media credentials include appearances on major television and radio outlets such as ABC, CBS, NPR and numerous others.

Crystal Jackson is also an award-winning film producer whose movie, "PacoimaStories: Land of Dreams," won her a "Best Documentary" nomination at the Los Angeles Pan African Film Festival.

In 2022, she released her first historical fiction novel, "Not Colored," a series based on three generations of her family's female lineage, including her grandmother, who began working at the Los Angeles Police Department in 1945 and became the first woman to work in its detective unit.

"The Marilyn Monroe Connection" is Jackson's third book release, with a sequel scheduled to follow.

I began my writing career by focusing on my hometown of Pacoima, California, which had hundreds of amazing stories. It's a town whose history researchers have buried for decades. I realized early on that not only were these stories worthy but extremely fascinating.

The most surprising revelation was realizing my own family had historic relevance worthy of being told. These tales were not just local but national, yet they represented my small hometown. Stories that could educate readers as well as entertain and make jaws drop.

In 1982, I faced humiliation when news stories resurfaced about my father, exposing him of crimes after the District Attorney sought to reopen Marilyn Monroe's case. My father worked for the Los Angeles County Coroner's Office when she died and signed her death certificate under duress. He thought there should have been an inquest at the very least, but his boss told him to sign it or else.

While coping with the sadness and anger of discovering my father's criminal record, I decided to ask my mom to tell me everything. She described it as a dark and traumatic time. Losing their house and the personal distress was more than she could bear. The Monroe case stripped her of the life she always dreamed of, resulting in a divorce that left her numb. My mother also spoke about Marilyn's diary and revealed my dad brought it home. She believed it was at the center of everything. For the first time, I felt her pain when I looked into her eyes and decided some things were best left in the past.

After my father published his memoir in 2012, I had more questions because it was obvious their two stories needed to be merged. We spoke for many hours, and he shared intimate details about his life and Marilyn's case. This gripped my interest and set me on an unexpected path.

I wrote this novel because, in life, we seldom realize how things are connected. I'm a sucker for a good story, but it became more than that once I understood this situation better. It became the life of a brilliant man who fought for the truth even at a young age. But he eventually learned how the real world operates, a lesson that cost him dearly.

I also learned the depth of my parent's love because divorce is never easy, remembering only one argument between them when too young to understand. I walked down the stairs when we lived in the projects halting in the stairway when I heard their raised voices. Unsure whether to go back upstairs or proceed to the living room, I froze, having never experienced the two at odds. Little did I know, they were breaking up. Yet, despite growing apart, they had mutual respect throughout my childhood and even in my adulthood.

My father undoubtedly suffered irrefutable harm after Monroe's death. I don't know who killed her, nor do I want to. But like thousands of others, I'm convinced it was not suicide. This story lays out, in historical fiction form, my father's life and his experience working in the coroner's office. It includes his day-by-day discoveries after Monroe's body arrived on August 5, 1962, along with other high-profile cases he was assigned.

I was blessed to spend many hours with him as he shared his experiences while often trying to hide his pain. We had an extraordinary father-daughter relationship – one that I will always cherish.

Unexpectedly, my father passed away on January 6, 2021, from complications of Covid 19, and it pains me he's not here to see this book. He faced many skeptics from the onset that plotted to bury his truth. I don't think they knew or cared about his full story, but with me continuing this, the sacrifice he made will circulate to future generations and help secure that his journey, vision, and bravery were not all in vain.

Table of Contents

1 - Reflections

Frenchy sat on his uncomfortable jail bunk staring at a newspaper with Marilyn Monroe's photo, wondering how this blonde bombshell ruined his life. She was Hollywood's biggest star and lived in a world as far away from his as humanly possible, yet somehow their paths collided. However, what happened wasn't her fault. She was a victim, just like him.

When he walked into the Los Angeles County Coroner's office that fateful Sunday morning on August 5th, 1962, never in his wildest imagination could he have foreseen what would follow. The unfathomable chain of events that led to his current incarceration.

The size of the cell, coupled with its dreary grayness, was utterly depressing. Frenchy did not belong there and knew it. For God's sake, he was only 22 years old but felt more like fifty. *What if he never let anyone know about her diary? What did Dr. Noguchi's cryptic message mean?* But as he sat locked up only a few months after her death, his life was in shambles.

Perhaps fate would have spared him if he had just toed the line, but that's never been who he was, and the truth mattered. Getting assigned Marilyn's case and the responsibility of signing her death certificate was the pinnacle of his professional career. But dark forces at the coroner's office and beyond used it as his demise.

Putting the paper down, the putrid smell of body odor blew past his nostril, reminding him once again of his current situation. Footsteps and rattling keys approached his cell, and two jail guards appeared with devious smirks.

"Hey Joe, this is one of our celebrity inmates. His latest film was Invasion of the Body Snatchers. His role was snatching stuff from dead white people."

"I heard about him. He worked at the coroner's office. Didn't the newspapers call it the Ghoul case?"

"GHOOOUL !!!" voicing it like a ghost. "Well, let's see if this spook can make it out of here... Alive."

The two snickered, pleased with themselves, and scurried off.

The guards' words were alarming, causing Frenchy's pulse and heart rate to climb. Six months is a long time, and a lot can transpire between now and when he's released. If something happened to him, how would his family survive?

His thoughts drifted to Tipy, the woman he loved more than life itself. When he first met his bride-to-be, they were twelve. Tipy lived around the corner from his grandmother and was the most beautiful girl he had ever seen. Her pigtails, bright smile, and sassy personality were captivating from day one. She was always the one for him and always would be.

Wild thoughts of escaping permeated his mind while trapped in this tiny space, unable to see her. Frenchy laid back on his pillow and closed his eyes, drifting away to memories of his youth and those carefree days when the simplicity of life was golden. He reflected on how he became the man he was and what led to his inexplicable situation.

～～～～～～～

The pungent smell of eucalyptus trees mixed with rows of citrus saplings in a land of rocks and dirt consumed Frenchy's walk to San Fernando High School. It was 1956, and the life of this 16-year-old, while not particularly hard, was not easy. Frenchy was the nickname given to him since childhood. His mother said he had French in his lineage, even though the family was Negro, which always confused him.

Most of Frenchy's friends belonged to a club called "The Turks." Many used nicknames. Sammy was "Scratch," Romie was "Boppie," James was "Pudgy," and Johnny was "Skip." There was also "Grover," "Love," and others. They always hung out together at school, parties, and on the block.

Their families all migrated to Pacoima during the early fifties after land developers built the first Black suburb in the country. During that time, there was an acute housing shortage in Los Angeles. So, with segregation in mind, developers built "unrestricted" home lots on the northeast side of the suburban San Fernando Valley.

Members of the military received top priority for this newly built oasis. All the fathers were veterans of World War II, except for Frenchy, who barely knew his dad. He only remembered meeting him once at age four but never forgot that lingering image. It was an extremely awkward moment as this strange man in a zoot suit with wavy hair stared at him like visiting a giraffe in the zoo. He said hello but not much more.

The only remanence of his father's existence was a photo his mother kept of him standing by the railroad tracks that she would look at every night with sadness he never understood.

Being in a different situation than all his friends, Frenchy worked incredibly hard to conceal the lingering demons that haunted him. He was the only one without a father and subsidized his feelings with two antidotes, education and being cool. After shuffling around different schools most of his life, San Fernando High felt at home when he and his brother moved in with his grandparents.

Living in a house rather than an apartment, along with an abundance of friends also new to the area, he finally felt connected. The walk to school was about 45 minutes but seemed exceedingly fast because the guys were laughing, joking, and planning their next teenage adventure. The girls were with them, and it was like a party every day to and from school. When they left the Joe Louis Housing tracts, where they lived, the walk defied time, and their journey seemed a fun-filled blur. With mountain-lined hills nearby, the unforgettable smell of fields, trees, and country ambiance, resonated with the teens daily. Their old lives in the city were a distant memory as they crossed through the open lands, then followed the railroad tracks to La Rue Street, which led to the school.

The fellas did everything together and had a code 'Turks are one.'

"Hey, Frenchy, didn't you say your grandfather helped build the high school?" Boppie asked.

"That's what he told me," Frenchy replied, kicking a rock in the dirt.

"You think he could build us a clubhouse? We're gonna need a new spot."

"Why?"

"Moms said after I graduate this year, I have to go to college or get a job. Either way, no more hanging out."

As they continued their stroll, Frenchy's attention turned to Tipy, who was up ahead gazing adoringly at her boyfriend, Bobo. The two were holding hands, seemingly in a world of their own.

"Tipy," Frenchy shouted, glowering at them. "Tell your mom not to kick us out after your brother graduates."

Bobo placed his muscular arm around Tipy, letting his hand caress her back.   He was a buffed and in-shape 16-year-old who was also a bit arrogant and self-absorbed, something oblivious to her. Frenchy shot a venomous look of disapproval.

"You hear me, Tip?"

"Why would I do that? That's going to be the new girls clubhouse," Tipy smugly snapped.

"Oh, you gonna do us like that?" Love shouted out.

"Yep. The garage will be the palace for the Turkettes. We might give you passes to come visit us."

All the girls laughed emphatically at the thought.

"French…We really need to talk to your grandfather," Love sarcastically re-emphasized.

"Y'all betta be ready because before he builds it, he's gonna make us stack up all those rocks to clear space. So you cats will have to help."

"Shoot, I can't do that. I got new shoes on," Bobo smirked, causing an eruption of laughter.

Frenchy couldn't help but wonder what Tipy saw in Bobo. Although a Turk, his character was weak, with no actual substance. He just wanted to be a tough guy and wasn't right for her.

Tipy was the most popular girl in school. She always dressed well, maintaining the latest fashion, which included stylishly accessorizing her attire. Her chic short hair and smile made Frenchy's heart pound and each neuron fire endlessly.

Always trying to look cool, he usually wore a button-down shirt and khaki pants. Styling his thin, curly hair in a two-inch afro, the name Frenchy suited him perfectly. His Turk leather jacket helped him stand out as one of the in-crowd boys. All of the fellas wore theirs religiously, even if the temperature was sweltering.

When they arrived at San Fernando High, the atmosphere was energetic. Only a small number of Blacks attended the school, but enough to have a presence, nonetheless. Newer model cars owned by white kids lined the front of the school on O'Melveny Street. Skip was the only student in the Joe Louis Homes with a car, but he wasn't allowed to drive it to school. Nobody understood that because he could take it everywhere else. His parents said they didn't trust the white kids not to get jealous and do damage.

Although San Fernando was the most diverse school in the valley, the student population was overwhelmingly white. As a result, racial tensions were sometimes high, with Mexicans, Japanese, and Blacks feeling the brunt. However, unlike in the south, bigotry was rarely deadly. Still, black parents took precautions.

Frenchy watched Bobo kiss Tipy goodbye as she headed to class. A jealous sting engulfed the pit of his stomach with a burning sensation as he longed for her but couldn't show his hand.

"You got it bad, man," Grover said.

"I don't know what you're talking about," Frenchy replied, startled. "What do you mean?"

"Yo man, I saw the way you look at her. Why don't you just tell her how you feel?"

"Naw, she with Bobo."

"The way I see it, she should be with you," Grover touted before taking off to class.

High School was surprisingly easy for Frenchy. With a gift for test-taking and an analytical mind, he undertook a full load of extra classes and was on track to graduate early. Even in subjects where he rarely opened the textbook, he could still pass the exams.

Because neither of his grandparents could read, he handled all their paperwork at home. His mother, Ora, was well educated but lived in Los Angeles with her husband, who Frenchy loathed. However, despite the domestic issues and financial instability, she always made them study hard in grammar school and junior high.

When Frenchy arrived home from school, both grandparents were at work as usual. His brother Dennis, who was four years younger, usually went to their aunt and uncle's house a block away. Family was everywhere in Pacoima, and he loved them deeply.

His grandmother, who he called Mo, married his step-grandfather Tom a few years before buying their home. She was a widow when they met, and Tom took on the positive paternal role he needed at that time.

The house was quiet, so Frenchy began doing his homework. Suddenly, Dennis and younger cousin Printes came crashing in. They were always laughing about something. Being 12, they were into exploration, and Pacoima was a daily treasure hunt adventure.

"Hey, Frenchy, we're heading over to Hansen Dam to hunt some jackrabbits. You wanna come?" Dennis asked.

"Yeah, I need a lucky rabbit foot," Printes added. "The little bugger got away last time."

"Naw. Got homework to do."

"You ain't fun no more, bro," Dennis chided.

"He's probably just thinking bout that girl around the corner," Printes joked.

"I'm probably just thinking about coming over there and popping you in the head," Frenchy gently threatened.

"Come on, cuz, let's go," Dennis said. "We're gonna cut through old man Whiteman's land."

"Didn't he fire shots last time you were there? You know he doesn't want anyone on that hill by the airport."

"I ain't worried about that old man. He ain't trying to hit no one. He just wants to scare us." Dennis reeled back.

"Well, be careful. You know Mo won't like it."

"Catch ya later," the boys said as they headed out.

"Better be home before dinner."

As Frenchy was finishing his homework, Mo came home. She wore her hair in a bun and had thin-framed glasses. Despite her nervous personality, she loved and spoiled the boys to death. They could do no wrong in her eyes, and she took sole responsibility for their well-being.

Her only daughter, Ora, had lived a difficult childhood. When she was ten, her father died in a schoolhouse fire set by the KKK. He was a teacher and well respected by everyone. The horror and sadness of that tragic event changed them forever. Now 34, Ora had given birth to two children out of wedlock, something frowned upon in those days.

Her first love, and Frenchy's father, was a flamboyant musician playboy with many girlfriends. Freddy Grandison played with a jazz band that went around the country. They gigged in Detroit, Chicago, and numerous other venues. When he headed to Los Angeles, Ora made a calculated plan to visit her aunt, who lived in North Hollywood, with hopes of seeing him. After Frenchy was born, she suggested everyone pack up and move to Los Angeles because there was work, property, and very little racial violence compared to Louisiana.

"Hi baby," Mo greeted Frenchy.

"Hey, Mo-Mo."

"You gettin' your lessons done?"

"Yes, just finishing up."

"Where's Den at?"

"Him and Printes are out and about. I told them to be home for dinner."

"Are you hungry, baby?" Mo asked. "I can fix you a sammich to hold you over."

"You know I never turn down one of your sandwiches."

As Frenchy put his schoolwork away, Mo went to the kitchen

"Hey, baby. I need your help wit something," she said, returning with a plate. "I got a new job in G'anada Hills and needs help wit the bus."

"Sure. Mo-Mo. Do you have the address?"

"I have it right here in my purse. I don't want you to miss yo studies, though."

"Don't worry about that. I'll be back in school by recess. I'll go pick up the bus schedule and figure it out."

Mo handed Frenchy a small piece of paper with writing on it. Mrs. Wise 17559 Donmetz Street, Granada Hills, Ca 91344.

"Thank you, baby. I'm gonna start working there two days a week."

While eating his carefully made ham sandwich, Dennis and Printes burst through the door like wrecking balls. Then, looking at Frenchy's plate, eyes bulging, both simultaneously bellowed, "I want a sandwich."

Frenchy gave Mo a big hug.

"I'll be back," he tenderly said, kissing her cheek.

"Alright. I'mma make some bread puddin' tonight."

"You're the best!"

The next day Frenchy didn't go to school. Instead, he studied the bus route and guided Mo to her new job. They had to catch the bus on Van Nuys Blvd and San Fernando Road, about a mile up. A drug store called "The Hub" was on the corner, so Mo went in to get cigarettes, and Frenchy secretly grabbed a pack for himself. All his friends smoked, but he didn't openly let his grandparents know, although surely they suspected. Mo was unusually clairvoyant and tough to fool, despite her inability to read.

The two boarded a smoke-filled MTA bus that was nearly full. Frenchy studied the schedule to see the street name for their first bus transfer. Within minutes the driver was already making the announcement.

"Devonshire, the next stop."

Frenchy reached up and pulled the cord to let the driver know they were exiting.

"Come on, Mo. This is your first transfer. Remember this street name. Devonshire," Frenchy carefully explained.

"Devonshire," she slowly repeated in her southern dialect.

The two got off to catch another bus.

"This ride will be a little longer than the first. The next transfer is Balboa Blvd."

"Balboa? Lord have mercy. Whatever happened to numbers for street names."

"I don't know. San Fernando Mission Blvd is the last stop."

"Devonsho, Baboa, and San Fanando Mission?

"That's it," Frenchy smiled.

They got off on San Fernando Mission, and he patiently walked Mo to the address on Donmetz Street.

"This is the house."

The Wise house had a circular driveway and a well-manicured lawn with white lion statues lining the grounds. Frenchy stopped at the driveway and looked at his grandmother, knowing she would do fine.

"Do you want me to come back when you get off?"

"No, baby. I got it."

"Are you sure?"

"Baboa, Devonsho, den Van Nuys." she smiled. "Thanks, fo' helpin'. I'll get home just fine. You go on and get to school, baby. Your studies is important. See you tonight."

After giving her a big hug, Frenchy headed back to the bus. He respected his grandmother tremendously and knew her sensitivity to her formal educational challenges.

Born Minnie Estelle Lee in 1903, harsh racial circumstances forced her to work the cotton fields in Mississippi after only completing second grade. Frenchy had taught her to sign her name and how to read a few sight words. Occasionally, he would catch her staring at a newspaper, fixating on the pictures. Sale items seemed to catch her eye with images and numbers that allowed her inclusion in the mysterious world of literature, if only briefly. But he knew the lack of schooling could not measure her intellect.

Despite Mo's request, Frenchy decided to play hooky. He could have made it to school by morning recess but instead stopped in San Fernando to look around. There was a Sears department store and a Levi shop on the bustling strip mall.

Usually, when he and the guys would shop there, they would be followed, which made him very uncomfortable. They were not into stealing, and their parents usually paid decent allowances. Not to mention the punishment they would receive if caught would be brutal. Still, employees looked upon them as possible criminals.

He browsed the Levi establishment, which was small and cramped. Tables of folded jeans and a leathery smell consumed the building. The company had just released a new version of 501s, and Frenchy wanted to check them out. Many of the white students at school already owned a pair. These latest jeans featured a two-horse heavy-duty patch with "Levi Strauss & Co" and other cool words, which made them stand out.

The price of the Levi's was $6. It seemed a bit high, but he knew the pants were durable and would last long. He patted his pockets, feeling the coins jingle knowing it wouldn't add up to $6, so instead placed these popular new jeans on his bucket list.

By the time he got home, school was out. Frenchy was anxious to catch up on the day's events. Curious, he strutted eagerly to Love's house and found him standing in the front yard. Love's first name was Ron, but nobody called him that. Instead, he was known by his last. Intelligent with a relaxed, low-key demeanor, Love always had the scoop on the latest happenings.

"Hey, man. What's going on?" Frenchy greeted him.

"What's up?" Love grinned as they bumped hands. "You sick or something? Where were you today?"

"Naw, I ain't sick. I had to help my grandmother with something. So, what's the latest? What happened at school?"

"They at it again."

"Who?"

"White boys from Canoga Park."

"Who did they get this time?"

"They got some Mexicans and one of us."

"How bad?"

"The ese needed to go to the hospital. They had to take him all the way to County because no hospital here would treat him."

"What about the brotha?"

"He'll be alright. We gotta stop this. I guess they hung at James Restaurant until dark, then started bashing folks," Love explained.

"We gotta get organized and stop them. Let's call a meeting at Boppie's house tomorrow after school."

"I'll pass the word."

"Cool. I'll clear it with him."

"I heard something else through the grapevine," Love slyly blurted.

"What's that?"

"I hear Bobo is tappin' Betty."

"Who told you that?"

"A little bird. They said because Tipy ain't given it up."

"That's her best friend," Frenchy said, trying to conceal his emotions while churning inside.

"Yep. Someone saw them creeping. I ain't gonna say who, but it's a reliable source."

"That boy's a fool. Betty's cute and all, but what is he thinking?"

"His you know what, is getting in the way."

"How could Bobo do that with her best friend? What a punk-ass." Frenchy growled. "Let me know if you hear anything else."

"I ain't your personal spy-boy," Love jested. "I see that look in your eyes. If I were you, I'd be planning my next move."

"Man, you are trippin'. Let's figure out what we're gonna do about them white boys."

"Cool."

Frenchy scurried to Boppie's house, thinking about the scandal unfolding with Tipy. Realizing Bobo was blowing it, Frenchy knew biding his time was essential. His grandmother always said, 'what's done in the dark will eventually come to light.'

As he approached their house, Tipy and Bobo were flirting outside. Betty, who lived next door, was standing in her yard. Frenchy's eyes were thundery, knowing the two people she was closest to were betraying her. Betty waved hello when Frenchy passed by, so he reluctantly nodded.

Entering the gate, Frenchy acknowledged Bobo and Tipy, suppressing the hurricane brewing inside. He stopped by Boppie's bedroom window, right by the front door, and tapped lightly on the pane.

"Hey, Boppie. You in there?"

"Yeah."

"Come out for a second. I gotta shout at you."

"Hold on."

After a few minutes, Boppie emerged smiling.

"What's crackin', man? Where was you hiding out today?"

"That ain't important. Check this out. White boys are still jacking us. We gotta hold a meeting with the Turks and Saints. Can we do it over here?" Frenchy asked.

"The Saints?"

"Yes. They're jacking the Mexicans too. It's time for us to come together."

"Are you sure you wanna do that?"

"I got a plan."

"Alright, but it's gotta be right after school before Veda gets home. She's usually here by seven."

"Cool. We'll pass the word. Hey Bop, why do you call your mom Veda?"

"It's a long family tradition. Moms are called by their first name."

"I call my mother by her first name too. That's weird huh?"

The next day both the Turks and Saints assembled. The Saints were a club of English-speaking Mexicans who loved their customized cars, and many of them attended San Fernando. Frenchy, who was sergeant of arms for the Turks, took charge.

"Listen up, everyone, we can't let outsiders keep coming to our town and hurting our folks. I have a plan to send a strong message that we ain't no punks."

"My sister was attacked the other day. They told her she needed to go back to Mexico. She was born here!" one of the Saints angrily bellowed.

"They threw eggs at my little cousin while calling him the "N" word. He didn't even know what that meant," Pudgy added. "I'm so ready to "f" some white boys up."

"That's why we're here," Frenchy said. "Most of the Saints live on the other side of the railroad tracks, with us Turks on this side. We need a phone system to notify everyone the next time they head down here. So, let's all keep an eye out and call as soon as they are spotted."

"What kind of cars do they drive?" Kiko, the leader of the Saints, asked.

"My sister said it was a red 55 Ford Fairlane."

"Little cuz said a fancy greenish, teal car threw the eggs. He didn't know what kind."

"Well, that's a start. One thing we do know is they're white. With eyes and ears open, we can get them."

"Hey, they hang out at James Restaurant. We can ambush them there if we time it right," Grover surmised.

"That's perfect!" Frenchy said. "Let's set that as our spot. The only thing is we will stand out like sore thumbs. They don't even let us eat there."

"My grandma lives right by the tracks behind the restaurant. I can stake it out and call as soon as I see them there. They come all the time. Mostly loud and drunk."

"What's your name?" Frenchy asked.

"Julio."

"Alright, here's the plan. Julio calls Kiko and me as soon as he sees them there. Kiko, you get the rest of the Saints together, and I'll contact my guys. We meet up at Julio's grand-moms. Then while they're inside eating, we'll get in place. All you guys gotta bag up some rocks and have them ready. We need tons of them. I'll give the word when they come out, and it's on!"

"You think it will work?" Love asked.

"The key is the element of surprise. They won't know what's happening when those rocks start raining down, but they'll think twice about returning to Pacoima," Frenchy confidently replied.

With a plan in place, the teens dispersed to begin collecting rocks. There were plenty of open fields containing hundreds of them. They gathered their newfound ammunition for the next two days, which Skip stored in his trunk. Of course, their size had to be perfect, and it wasn't long before they weighed down his car, making it look like a low-rider vehicle.

A week later, the anticipated call came.

"Hey, Frenchy, they're here."

"Are you sure it's the same guys?"

"Si. Both of the cars are here. There are about seven or eight gringos."

"All right. Game on!"

Frenchy made several calls, and Kiko did the same. In no time, they assembled at Julio's grandmother's house. Both groups felt united for the moment. It wasn't that they were ever at odds, except for a few isolated incidents, but they typically kept to their own.

Skip's car pulled up, packed with teens and a loaded trunk of rocks. Boppie borrowed his mother's wheels, and another vehicle arrived full of ready-to-fight teens. They all gathered to assess how it would go down.

"We gotta surround them when they come out," Frenchy said. "Some of you line up on the rail tracks. Dump your rocks on the ground so you can get to them easily. We need guys hiding behind cars in the parking lot. Make sure they can't see you. And some more on the other side of the exit."

"Dang Frenchy, were you military in another life?" Grover asked.

"Naw. I read up on WWII. Having allies and the element of surprise works." he replied, laughing.

"Man, I tune out my pops when he talks about the war," Pudgy said.

"Well, I listen and like to read. There is a lot of helpful info out there. So, let's do this, fellas. Tonight, we are united."

When the white guys came out of the restaurant, Frenchy whistled. Immediately Kiko followed suit, and the relentless rock throwing began. One after another, stones hit the unsuspecting youth, leaving them befuddled. Windshields cracked, while screams rang every time someone got hit. Being ambushed, they didn't know which way to run or where to go. Most tried to get in or hide behind their cars, but the stones came persistently, banging with stark precision. The popping of metal and the crackling of shattering glass sent fear and panic filtering on the faces of the attacked.

In a matter of minutes, it was all over. The Turks and Saints catapulted back across the tracks before the shriek of sirens besieged the area. No one got arrested, and they stayed on alert for months. Subsequently, future attacks on Pacoima's people of color ceased, at least for a while.

2 - Peas and Carrots

As Frenchy relished in the victory at James Restaurant, he stepped with extra swagger to Boppie's house a few weeks later after purchasing his new pair of 501 jeans. But, when he arrived, his mood changed instantly. Tipy and Bobo were on the porch, and Frenchy noticed a downpour of tears streaming down Tipy's rosy cheeks.

"Go! Get out of here, you scumbag," Tipy screamed hysterically.

"It was only one time, I swear!" Bobo pleaded.

"You don't get pregnant just doing it one time!"

"Tip, I swear on my mama."

"Just be with Betty. Go, please. Just leave."

Frenchy was suddenly face-to-face with Bobo, who shot him a sour look before departing. Tipy was sitting with her face buried in her palms, expressively sobbing.

"What happened, Tipy?" Frenchy asked when he approached her.

She slowly looked up at him, pulled a handkerchief from her pocket, and blew her nose.

"Did you know?" She asked.

"Know what?"

"About Bobo and Betty?"

"I don't talk much with Bobo. He's a bit of a jerk and loudmouth. He's a Turk, but that's about it. What about him and Betty?"

"Betty is pregnant. And it's his!"

"What?"

"My best friend and my boyfriend."

"Tipy, you are too good for either of them. I never thought you should be with someone like Bobo. You deserve so much better."

"Is she prettier than me? What does Betty have that I don't?"

"You're not like her. Betty has been with lots of guys."

"What?"

"I hate to say it, but yes."

"Have you slept with her?"

"Hell naw," Frenchy frowned. "That's not me, but I hear things."

"I thought she was a virgin like me. How could I not know?"

"Tipy, it only takes a few minutes to do what they do. It's not like any of the guys take her on dates."

"My mother always says there is a day girl and a night one. She told me to be the day girl."

"And you need to stay that way."

"How can I face anyone?"

"Stand up."

"Huh?"

"Stand up," motioning his hands.

Tipy reluctantly stood up.

"Now, look at me."

She looked into his eyes, and he gently wiped her tears away.

"I'll help you. We will be like peanut butter and jelly. Like peas and carrots."

"What do you mean?" Tipy asked.

"No one will know how hurt you are because you've moved on right away. Let them think you left him for me."

"Really? You would do that?"

"I'd do anything for you. Just stick with me, and Bobo will be Bobo who?"

Just then, they looked over at Betty's yard. Her mother came out with pink rollers in her hair and a suitcase she threw in the trunk. Her father had another bag and scowled, placing it there too. The tension was so thick you could cut it with a knife. Betty ambled behind them and shamefully sat in the back seat; her head hung low. She never looked in Tipy's direction as the car aggressively pulled out of the driveway. Betty's mother glanced over before going back inside the house.

"You won't have to worry about seeing Betty for a while," Frenchy whispered.

"I wonder where he's taking her?"

"Aunt Maggie's, no doubt."

"She doesn't have an Aunt Maggie."

"That's just a phrase for where they take unmarried girls when the rabbit dies. You won't see her for seven months or so."

"Rabbit?"

"You never heard of that?"

"No. My family doesn't talk about things like that. I just know not to have sex. But why only seven months? I thought it took nine?"

"My guess is she's two or three months pregnant."

"Ohhhh. I didn't think of that. Makes sense."

The facial expression on Tipy's face quickly changed.

"They've been having sex for a while. I can't believe this," Tipy said. "That lousy creep. Yeah. Okay. Peas and carrots it is."

Frenchy's lip curled when they hugged as she gently laid her head on his shoulder. He felt like a vulture circling his prey but holding her felt good. It seemed an eternity, waiting for this moment to arrive.

The weeks ahead were magical for them. The conversation was always entertaining as she relished in his knowledge. His worldly outlook helped her forget the humiliating cloud of Bobo and Betty that once lingered relentlessly like a bad cough. When walking to school, they were now always together. He escorted her to class and opened doors like a true gentleman, something brand new to her.

"Thank you for being there for me, Frenchy," Tipy said while they strolled home from school.

"It's been fun. I enjoy you."

"I have one question. How did you know about rabbits?"

"You mean to determine if you're pregnant?"

"Yes."

"Well, I like reading a lot, but that's our secret."

"Okay."

"When a woman is pregnant, she releases a hormone found in blood and urine. They inject it into a rabbit, then dissect the animal to examine the ovaries. Most people think when you inject the rabbit, it only dies if it's positive. But in reality, they all die. Then they look for the hormone. South Africa does it with frogs, but it's the same concept."

"Oh my, you sound like a scientist."

"Naw, medical mysteries are just interesting. That's why I'm getting a job at LA County Hospital this summer to see if that's for me. I plan to buy some wheels with the money."

"That's great. You should be a doctor or something."

"I don't see myself in medical school, but I like doing research and stuff like that. So, I'll see how it goes at the hospital."

"The more I learn about you, the more I'm impressed. You're nothing like the other guys. You're smarter and way more intellectual."

"Thanks, I guess."

"I don't know what I'm doing this summer," Tipy thought aloud. "Probably summer camp again. Boppie and I usually do that, but he won't be with me this year."

"You guys are preppy kids."

"What's a preppy?"

"Well, I have never seen a Black preppy, but if I did, it would be you. Kinda like high society."

"The girls on the other side of Glenoaks say the Joe Louis girls think they are better than them. I guess that's why they call us stuck up."

"Aren't you?" Frenchy asked, laughing.

"Maybe," Tipy replied, tilting her head to the side"

"You know you guys are picky about your friends, clothes, and shoes."

"Not picky enough. Look what happened to me. Bobo, aka Joey Dibbs, did me dirty. It has scarred me for life."

"Uh, I hate to tell you, but you bounced back fast. This is the first time you said his name in weeks."

"That's cause you have been keeping me entertained."

"How about the drive-in on Friday? We can double date with Skip and Carmen."

"I'd love to. What's playing?" Tipy asked.

"Bus Stop."

"Isn't that the one with Marilyn Monroe? I love her. She's got fashion and style."

"I've never been a fan, but I heard this flick is good. She's just another Hollywood showpiece."

"Never underestimate the power of a blonde."

The Laurel Drive-In Theatre had a towering red marquee banner that illuminated excitement upon entry. Frenchy and Tipy cozily sat in the back seat, energized by seeing other San Fernando High kids while they waited in line. Frenchy looked over to the outlying street and saw Boppie and some of the Turks climbing into a car's trunk.

"Check that out, Skip."

"What's that?"

"Eight o'clock, Turks."

Skip looked over, placed his hand over his mouth, and burst out in laughter.

"Those fools trying to sneak in."

Frenchy joined in, shaking his head as well. When they reached the booth, a red-headed clerk glanced inside the car.

"One dollar."

With two quarters already in his hand, Frenchy reached over and paid the fare for Tipy and him.

"Next time we're getting in the trunk," Frenchy chuckled.

"Are you trying to be funny?"

"Me? Never. Skip would do that, though," he said, patting Skip on the back.

After placing the heavy metal speaker in the window, everyone stared at the large white screen in front, waiting for the movie to begin. With his legs touching hers and arm around her shoulder, a warm and pleasant hum warmed Frenchy's blood. He could smell her perfume which made him rub her arm with his index finger. They all sat in silence watching the first film until intermission time came.

Once the credits scrolled, Skip and Carmen headed to the concession stand, leaving Frenchy and Tipy alone. He no longer felt like a vulture but a guy in love, and the desire to kiss her was stronger than ever as he shuffled the nervous excess moisture around in his mouth.

Tipy's head turned, and her eyes signaled that the moment was right, and their bond was tighter than ever.

"I have a question for you." Frenchy expressed, breaking the silence.

"What is that?" Tipy asked with a sexy smile.

"Can I kiss you?"

"Can you kiss me?"

"Yes, Tipy. Can I kiss you? I don't want to assume it's okay. I want your permission."

Coyly prolonging the eye contact, Tipy answered softly.

"You officially have my permission."

Gently placing his hands on her face, Frenchy brushed her hair back, unable to pull away his gaze. Her brown eyes and soothing lips he had endlessly longed for were finally there for the tasting. Slowly moving closer to her face, he gently kissed her, unsure if he was doing it correctly. But it felt so good, right, and romantic that he did not want to stop. The emotion exploded, and they locked lips continuing non-stop until Skip and Carmen returned.

Unlike the first movie, conversation flowed when the Marilyn Monroe film came on. It was a drama, something outside of the usual musical or comedy genre for Monroe. Subsequently, the teens were talking more than watching.

After the movie, they returned to Tipy's house to conclude their perfect date. Frenchy grabbed her hand while they sat on the porch, looking into the mysterious stars twinkling in the galaxy.

"You know I'm on target to graduate spring of 57," Frenchy told her.

"You're not graduating with me?"

"No. I took some extra classes and should have enough credits."

"I never knew anyone that graduated early."

"If you follow the school manual, it tells you how to graduate with honors, high honors, or how to get out early. I had to take more classes without extracurricular activities like football or school clubs. Of course, it helps that I'm a good test taker too."

"I'm definitely not a good test taker. I can pass, but it's usually with a "C.""

"I have another question for you."

"What is that?"

"Do you have a formal dress?"

"No. Why?"

"I think you need to get one so we can go to the junior prom."

"Is that how you ask me?" Tipy frowned.

"Tipy, will you go to the junior prom with me?"

"Well, since I let you kiss me, I guess that would be okay."

"Is that a yes?" Frenchy smirked.

"Yes, silly. You are growing on me."

"You know you're my best friend."

"Is that all I am?"

"No, I've been wanting to ask you something else," Frenchy etched out, realizing this was the right time.

"What do you want to ask me, Frenchy?"

"Will you go steady with me?"

"You mean for real, not just play?"

"I hate to tell you; this has always been real for me."

She looked away and focused on the distant constellations above before engaging an enormous beam.

"What took you so long to ask?"

Exhaling, Frenchy felt a warm surge in his stomach as his gut exploded with relief.

"I've been fighting the ghost of Bobo."

"Bobo, who?" Tipy teased, causing a smile to break through his lips.

"I've wanted you for a long time Tipy. You know we belong together."

The two savored the moment of becoming a couple. It felt enchanting while gazing at the shimmering stars in far-off space. Both wished that night would never end.

Junior prom came in the blink of an eye. Tipy wore a cream-colored satin sleeveless dress. Form-fitted, it highlighted her tiny waist and flared downward to her mid-calves. It was sexy and classy at the same time, and she borrowed her mother's string of pearls to top off the outfit. Black pumps with embedded studs and short white gloves completed the ensemble. Frenchy dapperly sported a black tux. They were a striking couple, the Ken and Barbie of Pacoima, standing out like diamonds in the rough.

<center>~~~~~~~~~~</center>

The loud voice of a guard made Frenchy snap out of his lucid trance.

"Hey, Grandison. Here's the pen and notepad you asked for."

"Thanks."

It had been nearly a week since he last spoke with Tipy. After being sentenced, bailiffs took him into custody, and they never had a chance to talk. As he sat down to write her, the paper stared back at him without offering any hint of what to say.

This can't be real, he thought. It must be a dream, and he would wake up any minute. The DA promised only six-month probation if he resigned and remained silent but never held up their end. Nothing made sense in the jail cell, but all roads led to Marilyn. However, that didn't matter at this point because he needed Tipy to know how much he loved her.

December 20, 1962

Dear Tipy,

'This is the hardest thing I ever wrote anyone. Being locked up is certainly not me, but I will make the best use of my time. There is a lot to think about here, and one thing I know is how much I miss your sweet smell and funny jokes. I didn't always know if you were serious or joking, but as I sit here, I realize you joked more than I gave you credit. Man, I would love to have something to laugh at right now.

They have many books here I can read. I picked up one called To Kill a Mockingbird. It looks interesting. I'll be done before the day is over. Not too many look like something I would like to read.

I feel bad I'm going to miss Christmas with everyone. How are the kids doing? Do they miss me? Lance should be walking when I get home. Man, this is hard. Baby, you know I would never steal anything. This mess is bigger than me, and I will figure it out. In the meantime, if you can get some decent books for me, that would be great. I love you with all my heart.'

Love Frenchy

3 - Seasons Change

The summer of 56 was a tremendous learning experience for Frenchy. Working at General Hospital, although challenging, taught him a great deal about his abilities. At only 17, he tended to take charge of things, identify the big picture, and use his exceptionally sharp analytical mind. He was great with numbers, often calculating without paper or a pen. His memory and accuracy impressed his bosses daily.

Frenchy possessed a natural gift for comprehensively articulating his thoughts, something he discovered early on. As a result, he interacted more with management than with entry-level employees. After being placed in the medical records unit, he immediately concluded the filing system was flawed. He suggested a successful color-coding method for files that all but guaranteed him employment after graduation. His bosses gave him a letter of recommendation he proudly took home. Mo gleamed at her brilliant grandson, took the document, placed it in a gold frame, and hung it on the wall.

When September rolled around, the first day of school saw Frenchy driving his recently purchased 1953 Chevy Bel Air with a sense of accomplishment. The three-month summer netted him over $700, and his grandfather chipped in the rest. He also had extra to spend for the school year. Visions of him and Tipy doing things together filled his head, not realizing the Turks would become a significant competitor for his time.

Telling Tipy he had a surprise, she eagerly waited in front of her house on the first day of school. They spoke on the phone often during the summer and had written letters, but this was their first time seeing each other in months. She noticed a shiny black car creeping slowly down the street, and to her surprise, it was

Frenchy. Her eyes gleamed on this black machine with its sparkling chrome grill and humongous white wall tires.

"Wow! Some surprise," Tipy shrieked.

"You like it?"

Tipy gave the car a once over and shrugged her shoulders.

"Eh, I've seen better."

"Well, hop in and see if you still feel that way."

Excitedly jumping in, Tipy scooted next to him, and the two embraced, passionately kissing.

They blissfully drove to San Fernando High, excited to see those they missed over the summer. Like at the prom, they could feel all eyes on them when they arrived. Even the white kids stared at this couple that looked contrary to their perception of Negros.

As they approached the campus, Tipy's admiring girlfriends bombarded her while Frenchy strutted coolly over to the fellas.

"Nice car, my brotha. You could have given us a ride!" Grover greeted him.

"Next time," Frenchy laughed.

"Dude, we barely saw you all summer. The Turks were lost." Love said.

"Man, I needed to work and get these wheels. What did you do all summer?"

"Just hung out. Bobo was talking crap about you."

"Oh yeah. What did he say?"

"Dude, he actin' like he wants to fight you," Love explained. "He was trying to get some of us to turn against you and vote in a new leader."

"No shit?"

"I tried calling you, but you were never home."

"That bus ride was a drag, so I stayed with my mom. She lives in LA, near the hospital."

"Well, we set him straight. Gilk over there on Vaughn Street is beefing with him now."

"Gilk? Why?"

"Man, he was being his usual bully self and bragging about being a Turk. Gilk wasn't havin' it. So, they went to blows."

"Dang, like that?"

"Yep."

"Frenchy, are you gonna walk me to class or talk?" Tipy reeled as she strolled over.

"I'm coming… Man, I'll talk to you later. I'm setting up a Turk meeting at my house."

"Ooh, can I come?" Tipy asked

"Lookin' that good, you always got a pass to our club," Scratch, one of the Turk troublemakers, said with a gritty voice.

Frenchy glared at Scratch momentarily. "Later, guys," he said, grabbing her hand before departing.

The two entered the brick archway onto the campus. Although this school was the San Fernando Valley's oldest, established in 1896, it was relocated and built at this new Pacoima location in 1952. As a result, its aesthetic beauty was second to none, and it was the most modern school facility in Los Angeles.

"You know, I really don't think you should come to any more Turk meetings. Not for a while anyway," Frenchy voiced.

"What? Why not?"

"We're having problems within the club. Until I get it sorted out, I don't think you should be there."

"You know, I'm starting to think the Turks are more important than me. We spent the whole summer apart, and now you kick me to the curb for them?"

"It's not like that."

"You know what? I think it is. You need to figure out who's more important. I can walk myself to class," Tipy touted, then stormed away.

With the new school year underway, old racial tensions still existed at San Fernando High. The white students were getting bolder with their attacks against Blacks and Mexicans. However, Frenchy got along with everyone and even had one white friend,

Benny, whom he met while working at General Hospital, that also attended the school.

Over the summer, Frenchy's grandfather built a patio so the guys could have their gatherings. Mo was leery, but Tom convinced her the kids were better off there than in the streets.

The following day, Frenchy called the first meeting to order. Tom had come through with the patio design and interior furniture. A red leather couch with bar stools scattered around the room created a comfortable setting for all. Frenchy stood at the room's front, where everyone was visible, with the patio door to his right.

"Fellas, I've been gone a while, and a lot has happened over the summer. I heard some of us been beefing," Frenchy began the meeting. "Look, I know that sometimes we have problems with each other, and that's normal. But we are family. That's what makes us strong. So, we must always honor and stick to our code – TURKS ARE ONE."

Frenchy rubbed his chin as emotion flitted over his face.

"Right now, I need each of you to say that out loud to reaffirm your loyalty and commitment to the club."

Looking to the left, where Love was sitting, he waited for a response.

Holding up his fist, Love chanted, "Turks are one!"

"Turks are one," Grover followed.

"Screw it, Turks are one," Scratch added.

Bobo, the only one standing, rubbed the back of his neck, shifting his weight from side to side.

"Man, who you think you is? Martin Luther King coon or something? Y'all actin' like a bunch of punks. I ain't sayin' nothing."

"Bobo, if you're gonna be a Turk, we need you to say it. If not, you know where the door is," Frenchy glared without blinking.

"All y'all feel that way too?" Bobo asked, looking around the room.

"Man, quit actin' like a bitch. Just say it," Pudgy shouted.

Bobo's nostrils flared, and he abruptly hurled around.

"I'm outta here. Keep your girls club," he scowled, darting out in a fury.

You could hear a pin drop as stillness gripped the room.

"I guess he did know where the door was," Pudgy said, breaking the silence.

Scanning around the room, Frenchy looked each Turk in the eyes.

"Does anyone else want to leave?" he asked.

Nobody responded.

"Alright then. Now there's one other thing we must discuss. The white boys are still trippin' at school. We must make sure we stay in pairs. We are safer together, so don't get caught slippin'. Now come on, everybody. Let's put it in the air, and on three, all say it loud! One, two, three,"

They all proudly raised their fist and simultaneously chanted.

"TURKS ARE ONE!"

The weather began to cool off after the brutal summer, and Pacoima transformed into its most beautiful season. Fall weather crept in, trees turned burnt orange, and empty streets filled with a barrage of fallen leaves. In addition, the Santa Ana winds were making their season debut, creating mini tornado-like dust patterns on the ground before disappearing in a puff.

After their minor lover's quarrel, the couple made up, and things were back to normal. Frenchy made a special effort to prioritize her, but it wasn't without challenges. While walking together through the halls of building one to Tipys locker, they enjoyed what seemed to be a typical school day.

"Everyone is saying you kicked Bobo out of the Turks. Was that because of me?" Tipy queried.

"Bobo made his own decision."

"He loved being a Turk. So why would he do that?"

"Being a Turk is more than just wearing a jacket."

The two parted ways after Frenchy gently kissed her, giving a sexy wink, which was becoming his signature gesture. Then, realizing a few extra minutes remained before the bell, he headed to the restroom for a quick smoke. On his way, he noticed three white boys standing near the hallway, not even pretending they were going to class. Frenchy continued to the bathroom, and as he lit his cigarette, the door crashed open with a loud thud.

"Hey, Boy," a voice hissed like an evil serpent.

"Man, I don't want any trouble," Frenchy shot back.

"You ride high now that you got new wheels. What you got in your pockets."

Quickly realizing he would have to get down without his crew, Frenchy prepared himself, balling his fist up for battle. Not waiting for them to throw the first punch, he aimed at the big guy, striking his face and knocking him off his feet. Then a sudden and forceful tremor sent Frenchy sprawling on all fours while the other two began savagely landing blows on Frenchy's body and face.

"Get the money!" one shouted.

"Jackpot. This spook is loaded," the other screamed, holding up five one-dollar bills.

"No lunch for you, spear chucker," the tall guy said, landing his shoe directly in Frenchy's abdomen.

The three teens scurried off, leaving Frenchy feeling humiliated and defeated. With his face plastered on the cement floor, he slowly pulled himself up while holding his stomach. Then, bruised and in pain, he wiped his clothes and rinsed his face while watching blood drip from his nose into the porcelain sink. The mirror reflected a slightly puffy jaw, which was tender to the touch. His face and body hurt, but his pride was far more damaged.

As the bell rang, Frenchy calmly contemplated his next move, despite his trauma. He had violated the club's policy—his policy. He should not have been there alone, which made him internally frustrated. At this point, telling his hot-headed crew was not an option, for they would surely want to retaliate. He didn't want to be responsible for what might follow. Instead, he opted to go home and tend to his wounds. Besides, he didn't have lunch money now anyway.

Managing to keep his mishap a secret, Frenchy and Tipy headed to school the next day. After icing his jaw, nobody could tell. Well, almost nobody.

"You look different, Frenchy."

"What are you talking about?"

"I don't know. Your face, your posture. What's going on with you?"

"You worry too much."

"I was wondering if you were even going to pick me up after ditching me yesterday."

"Of course. You're my girl."

Tipy smiled and scooted closer.

The moment touched Frenchy like nothing before. Tipy was in tune with him mentally and spiritually, which melted his soul. A rush of warmth flushed his heart, tickling the inside of him. No girl had ever made him feel that way, and he couldn't imagine ever being with anyone else.

"I have something to confess to you," Frenchy whispered.

"What's that?"

"I love you, Tipy," he confessed, with a smile breaking through his crumpled frown.

Tipy pursed her lips together, trying to conceal a faint grin.

"You are? Are you sure?"

"I'm sure."

"That's nice," she said nonchalantly.

"THAT'S NICE?" Frenchy bellowed.

"Well, guess what?" Tipy gave a little whisk of a smile.

"What, now that I poured my heart out to you?

Twisting her hair while gazing out the window, Tipy grabbed Frenchy's hand and rubbed it.

"I'm in love with you too."

"You're such a brat."

After school, while reading comic books at Tipy's house, the deafening sound of the ringing house phone interrupted them. She casually answered, expecting to hear her mother's voice.

"Hello… Wait, slowdown! Now, what? …I don't believe you. Somebody is pulling your leg. I will get to the bottom of this," Tipy said, placing the handset on the base.

"What's going on, babe?" Frenchy asked.

"Someone is playing a sick joke. They said Bobo is dead."

"What?"

"That's what Carmen said, but you know how these fake stories get out. I'm going to call his mother."

Tipy quickly began dialing the numbers on the rotary phone.

"Hi, Mrs. Dibbs," she cautiously uttered. "Hello?"

Tipy remained silent for a minute. Then, her facial expression rapidly turned from carefree to distressed in the blink of an eye.

"It's true? …He's gone? …How? Who?"

Silence fell in the house as tears streamed from Tipy's eyes after she hung up the phone. Then, slowly turning to Frenchy, she tried to speak, but the words wouldn't come out.

"Tipy, what happened?" Frenchy asked

"Gilk stabbed Bobo. He's dead."

Frenchy should have been shocked but wasn't. He stood up and pulled Tipy toward him, who began a full onset of bawling. Rubbing her back, he just held her letting it all get out. Frenchy glanced out the living room window and saw people gathering in the front yard. Tipy broke away from him to see what he was looking at and saw their friends all standing on the sidewalk with their heads hung low.

"Stay here, Tipy. I'm going to see if I can get some details."

"Okay," she softly muttered.

Frenchy went to the sidewalk where Love, Grover, and Pudgy were standing.

"What the hell happened?" Frenchy asked.

"Man, Bobo was talking trash to Gilk again. He was belittling him, calling him names, and Gilk pulled out a knife.

He said I warned you. Cut him right in the chest," Grover affirmed.

"Man! Just like that?"

"Just like that. Gilk got arrested. He's going to jail."

"I don't even know what to say. How's Mrs. Dibbs doing?"

"That's her only child. She's a mess."

"She raised a bully who thought his shit didn't stink," Pudgy touted.

"Man, he still was a Turk. He was one of us." Frenchy reflected.

"Bobo bailed on us. He was a dick. Yeah, I said it," Pudgy added.

"Well, he's gone now. We should see what we can do for his mom," Frenchy suggested.

"What can we do for her? He's dead!"

"Pudgy, you need to grow a heart. You sound like Scratch now."

"I just call it like it is."

"I'm going back to Tipy. Catch you guys later."

When he walked in the door, Frenchy saw her face, and unexpected emotion overcame him. She looked heartbroken, with mucous running out of her nose and face flushed. Their ache felt mutual, generating a quiet, distant stare of disbelief. Although his sorrow was more for Tipy's grief, the moment was painfully somber.

"I know you don't want to hear this, but Bobo was always going to be Bobo, and it caught up with him. They've had beef for a while. Everyone has their limits. Gilk just snapped."

With a blank look, she placed her face in her palms, curling up her knees to her chest. Many thoughts ran through Frenchy's mind about easing her pain. He sat beside her, wrapping his arms tightly around her balled-up body, knowing he would always be there to comfort her.

The funeral was held at Eternal Valley in Newhall because cemeteries did not accept Black and Brown burials in the San Fernando Valley. It was somber and surreal. Frenchy and Tipy went to Mrs. Dibbs's house for the repast paying their final respect to this complex individual.

In a strange twist of fate, Betty asked Mrs. Dibbs if she would adopt their baby. Bobo's mother fell to her knees in joy when her granddaughter arrived. The child was named Jolene, after her father. It was a storybook ending to a tragic tale.

4 – Troubled Turks

The shock and talk of Bobo's death diminished relatively fast, and things returned to normal. Frenchy held no ill will against other white students despite getting assaulted and his money stolen. He spoke regularly with his friend Benny, talking intellectually about math, statistics, and theories, which fascinated him. When playing dominoes with the crew, he thought in numbers to assess what was needed to block or score.

The fellas were shooting dice for nickels at lunch when a white kid brushed up on Scratch. Everyone knew they were trying to provoke a fight, and in the school's eyes, the Blacks would always be at fault. Scratch was pissed but held back from retaliating. He was dark-skinned and wore a covadis haircut. His eyes had a slight slant that meshed well with his crooked smile.

"Let's go take a smoke before I beat someone's ass," Scratch touted.

"Yeah, you look like you need to chill, homeboy," Pudgy uttered. "But I'm with you on kickin' some ass."

"Let's go."

Love, Grover, Pudgy, Scratch, Skip, and Frenchy all headed for the restroom, hoping to find it empty. Most of the guys preferred to stay out of trouble, but Scratch and Pudgy were rebels who often attracted chaos.

The guys were joking around, standing against the wall, when Frenchy's friend Benny entered the smoke-filled room. Pudgy and Scratch eyed each other like predators that had just found their prey. They ruthlessly watched Benny go to the urinal. Scratch put his hand in his pocket and rubbed his knife, feeling a sense of power. Pudgy began shaking as the opportunity to release his anger had arrived. Unfortunately, the other fellows were clowning around and didn't pick up on the negative vibes.

Suddenly Scratch stepped in front of Benny, prohibiting him from passing, leveling an unrelenting sinister stare.

"Hey, honkey. What you got?"

Not understanding what he meant, Benny looked over at Frenchy and shrugged his shoulder.

"He's cool Scratch, leave him alone," Frenchy ordered.

"Ain't none of them cool. They all hate us. I need some lunch money, boy. Hand it over."

Pulling out his knife, Scratch got in his face.

"Give it up."

Benny was petrified. Before Frenchy could stop what was happening, the boys began scuffling. Everything seemed to unfold in slow motion as he watched his crew and a white friend engaged in conflict. Scratch shot forward, and his eyes began to twitch when he put the knife against Benny's throat, aching to do damage. Pudgy snatched the pant pocket, grabbed the wallet, and shoved him, causing the blade to skim the skin. Blood sprinkled from the wound, terrifying Benny, who broke loose and jetted out in a frenzy. Pudgy and Scratch instantly began laughing hysterically.

"You see his face? That was classic," Pudgy boasted.

"That white boy was scared as shit," Scratch added.

Furious with the two out-of-control idiots, Frenchy was at a loss for words.

"What are you guys thinking?" Frenchy yelled. "This ain't no game. All of us will go down for what you fools just did!"

"Wait a minute. We didn't do anything." Love defended. "They did!"

"It doesn't matter. They'll blame us all. This was not cool. NOT COOL!!"

"What? Now y'all are some scary cats. We the Turks," Pudgy countered.

"Turks don't do shit like this. This is not who we are! Let's get out of here."

All of them ran off the campus and headed for Frenchy's car.

"You two can't go with me. Skip brought his ride. Ask him. I can't roll with you guys right now."

Driving off, Frenchy cringed, thinking about what lay ahead. This was bad. The school would punish all of them for sure. Poor Benny was a nice guy, who had nothing against people of color and did not deserve this. *How could he make things right?*

The neighborhood was quiet as they passed San Fernando Park, with only two people walking dogs in the distance. Finally, he parked the car in a gravel patch, and they all sat enveloped in silence.

"Should we go back and explain, Frenchy?" Love asked.

"If we told them we had nothing to do with it, maybe they'd go easy," Grover added.

"Maybe. But unlikely because a weapon was involved."

"We gotta try something," Love said. "My parents will kill me, especially after what happened to Bobo."

"I don't know what those fools were thinking. We should have stopped them," Frenchy reflected. "You can't stand by and do nothing."

"You did do something, Frenchy. You told them Benny was cool. But, man, that shit happened so fast, we didn't have time to do anything."

"We should have done more. I needed to do more," Frenchy echoed.

"What? Scratch was out of control. He might have stabbed us too."

"Right is right, and wrong is wrong. The Turks are a club, not a street gang."

"Somebody needs to tell Scratch and Pudgy that," Grover half chuckled.

"We gotta make some changes. The Turks won't last much longer like this. We gotta be tougher on who stays in."

"Yeah, if we can stay out of jail," Grover said, flicking his cigarette on the ground.

Shapes of kids heading in their direction came into focus.

"I guess schools out," Love blurted.

Frenchy watched as groups passed by, looking for Tipy, hoping his explanation for leaving was understandable. But, since this was his second time abandoning her, more pushback was inevitable.

"I gotta talk to Tipy. She's not going to be happy. So you guys gotta bounce."

"You gonna leave us?"

"It's just a few blocks. You cats can handle it. We'll catch up later."

Tipy was strolling by herself with sadness on her face, which quickly turned to anger once their eyes met. Headed directly towards him, Frenchy saw the wrath of fury in her like never before.

"What the hell, Frenchy? You could have given me a heads-up. I was looking everywhere for you. They came and got me out of class."

"Who came?" Frenchy asked.

"The school. They wanted to know where you were."

"What did you say?"

"Heck, I didn't know where you were. I thought you were in class."

"Something happened."

"You think?"

"Naw, Tip, something bad happened, and you gotta believe it wasn't me."

"Why do they think you had something to do with it?"

"Because I was there–but I didn't do anything. You know I'm not violent. Have you ever seen me out of control?"

"No."

"The problem is a knife was involved. That means I'm probably in serious trouble."

"Why not just tell them who did it."

"I'm not a snitch, and besides, that wouldn't change anything. Either way, hard times are coming. I need you with me."

"Of course, I'm with you. I'll always be with you."

"Can I give you a ride home?"

"I guess."

Having never been in trouble before, Frenchy was unsure of the potential consequences but knew they were always tougher on non-whites. He hoped Benny would tell them what actually happened. *But would that help?* However, he couldn't shake that sinking feeling of impending doom.

"Tipy, my gut tells me this is bad. If they were looking for me at school, it is only a matter of time until they come to my house."

"Oh my God!"

"I must plan for the worst. If I have to go away, I want you to take care of my car."

"Go away?"

"Yes, but I don't know."

They sat parked in front of Tipy's house, talking till the sun went down, and only tree silhouettes were visible. Realizing the time was nearing to part ways, they engaged in heavy kissing and hugging until Veda pulled into the driveway.

"I guess this is my cue," Tipy sadly expressed.

"No matter what happens we'll get through this, as long as you remember the strength of our love."

"How can I forget? Peas and carrots, right?" she said, breathing off an easy smile

Driving off, he knew his life was about to change, but having Tipy by his side made him feel secure and optimistic. He walked into his house and kissed Mo on the forehead, then swatted Dennis on the shoulder, who was at the dinner table. Tom wasn't in view, so he just headed to his room. Barely five minutes later, there was a knock on the door. Frenchy stashed his keys under the mattress, took off his watch, and could hear Mo calling out.

"Lionel."

"Coming."

After entering the living room, he could see two police officers at the door and Mo getting upset.

"Are you Lionel Grandison?"

"Yes, I am," he said calmly.

"You're under arrest."

With those words, a sharp screech came from Mo's mouth.

"Lord have mercy! Don't take my baby!" Mo pleaded. "No, no!"

"It's okay, Mo-Mo. It's okay. Everything's gonna be alright."

"Put your hands behind your back," one of the officers said as they placed the handcuffs tightly on.

Mo continued to scream, "Lord have mercy. No. Jesus, please!"

Frenchy left with the officers regretting the stress this placed on his grandmother. After what happened to her first husband, she was always nervous and didn't trust the police or whites in general. Traumatized by the Klan in Louisiana, she knew their capacity for great evil. In 1932, her husband taught young Black children elevated academics at the local school, and the Klan had been terrorizing him for months. When they torched the building, Mo knew he was dead before news of the fire was even out. She sat in a trance, saying, "Anse is dead. Anse is dead." Nobody paid any attention until one of her nephews came running down the dirt road, saying the schoolhouse was ablaze. Somehow her clairvoyance picked up on that horrible event.

Luckily for Frenchy, Veda spoke with the district attorney and got charges reduced to malicious mischief for him, Grover, and Love. Pudgy and Scratch were tried as adults and ultimately convicted of assault with a deadly weapon. Both received prison time.

The trial was tough on Frenchy when he saw Benny sitting in the courtroom. He felt ashamed because of the relationship they had built.

Frenchy, Grover, and Love received six months at a youth camp. After the sentencing, Benny walked up to Frenchy and extended his hand.

"I wanted to thank you for trying to stop them. I told everyone the truth about how it all went down, hoping you wouldn't get in trouble."

"A part of me feels guilty for what I let happen to you. Besides, it's only camp. I think I can handle that."

"I heard what happened to you at the beginning of the school year. Some kids were bragging about it. You never told on them. How come?"

"Honestly, I saw it being more trouble than not. I believe in karma."

"But you are going to a camp instead of finishing school."

"Well, that's when planning ahead comes through. While I was waiting for this trial, I finished all my tests. I have enough credits to graduate, so I'll be okay. No walking at graduation, but I'm not into that stuff anyway."

"I knew there was something about you. You come off as knowing more than you let on."

"I don't know about that, but life has a way of working itself out the way it's supposed to. So, I try not to question what I can't control."

"Stay cool, Frenchy."

"You stay cool too, Benny. I'm sorry for what they did to you. But don't hate all Black people."

"I won't, as long as you don't hate all whites."

* * *

Camp, as it turned out, was a blessing for Frenchy. While Grover and Love took classes to fulfill graduation requirements, Frenchy intellectually expanded his knowledge. Fascinated by how the world operated and finding a deeper meaning in his existence, books and newspapers helped make time fly. He wrote Tipy every day, and fluttering butterflies filled his stomach whenever a letter from her arrived.

Grateful the weather was not scorching, the green grass with the smell of pine trees and occasional yellowjackets buzzing made for optimal reflection time, something Frenchy rarely did. The book "Catcher in the Rye" forced his inquisitive mind into assessing the challenges of evolving from adolescence to adulthood. So often, he felt isolated and different from everyone else, only to read it wasn't only he who entertained lonely thoughts, and there was a golden ring everyone must grab. After that, he recognized the need to outline his life.

Because Frenchy's home life never aligned with his friends, who all lived with both parents, there were moments he felt alone on a secluded island. He often thought about his father, whose absence never went away. *How could he ignore his own son's existence?*

After his release in June, he would be ready to take on the world, and there was only one person he needed by his side. Tipy still had another year of high school left, but he was determined to make her his wife. They could start a family and give their kids what was missing in his life. He would talk openly, make sure they did well in school, and help them understand the value of family. They would be proud of the Grandison name.

5 - Only You

Jailhouse life had many components, but none were more depressing than chow time. Standing in long lines, waiting for a tray of food that tasted like straw, irked Frenchy. But hunger will make you eat almost anything—man, how he missed Tipy's cooking.

After he picked up his meal from the tiny window, Frenchy headed toward the tables in the dining room. Two familiar faces stunned him when one deliberately brushed against his arm, knocking his food to the ground.

"It's sad how many accidents happen in small quarters," the bullish guard said.

"A lot of shit happens in jail. It's a dam shame," the other one echoed.

The splattered food looked like a poorly painted piece of artwork with colors of yellow corn, crumbly brown mush, and a splat of white mashed potatoes shaped like poop. Frenchy's expressionless eyes slowly looked up and faced them.

"Excuse me, gentlemen," he said, trying to walk past them.

"Where you going? We ain't done with you."

Frenchy could feel the eyes of all the other inmates gazing at this tense situation. The room quieted to a low whisper, with only pots and pans banging in the distance, breaking the silence.

The bullish guard leaned over and whispered in Frenchy's ear with a breath stench that made him nauseous.

"Look here. Your mouth needs to stay shut about the coroner's office. You are never to mention Marilyn Monroe's name ever again."

Remaining quiet, Frenchy stood still, not even blinking.

"Oh, that pretty little wife of yours over there on Montford Street, well, that can be a dangerous part of town. You don't want nothin' to happen to her or your kids," the other guard threatened before they both walked away.

Returning to his cell, disturbed by what he had just heard, Frenchy thought about his agreement with the District Attorney to keep the Marilyn Monroe case quiet. Although their office had not held up their end, the guards made it blatantly clear where that deal stood.

Dispirited, Frenchy sat on his bunk and decided to write Tipy a letter. Today was her birthday, and at that moment, he missed her more than ever.

January 10, 1963

Dear Tipy,

Today is your 23rd birthday and our fourth anniversary. It seems unreal. I wanted to save money and take you to a nice restaurant where we dress up and show everyone that we have class. You are my queen, and deserve the best of everything. My next job must have a top salary. I was thinking about boxing, since I have a pretty good left jab. It can net good money like Joe Louis. Some of the guys are doing that here, but I'm not sure if that's for me. Tough decisions, huh?

Please tell the kids Daddy loves them. I'm counting the days until I get out.

Happy Birthday and Happy Anniversary

Love, Frenchy

He put down the pen and thought about the happiest day of his life and what led up to it, which made him smile and cast off the anxiety of those menacing guards.

After Tipy's graduation ceremony, they held a gathering in the garage. She was in the spring class of 1958, and all her friends and family were at the celebration. Boppie was the DJ setting the festive mood for all the teens to get their party on. But Frenchy wasn't concerned with that, having other things on his mind. He had spent the past few months developing a plan for his life, which featured Tipy at its center.

Boppie loaded several 45 records on the player, and Frenchy's favorite song, "Only You," by the Platters, sounded off.

"Tipy, will you dance with me?"

"Of course."

Holding her tightly in his arms, Frenchy sang the words in her ear.

When the song ended, the two kissed passionately, and Frenchy whispered in her ear.

"I'm going to ask Veda if I can marry you. Will you have me?"

"You know I will."

The kiss resumed as Frenchy, who rarely got nervous, felt tense.

"Okay, here goes nothing."

Ambling up the porch steps, he opened the front door and entered. The noise outside became a blur, as were the faces of every adult in the room, until he saw Veda. She was a beautiful woman who was barely 40 and always dressed stylishly. Her no-nonsense personality was very intimidating, but he grabbed her hand just the same.

"Veda, can I talk to you for a minute?"

"Of course, sweetie."

They went into Tipy's bedroom, and he closed the door.

"What's going on?" she asked.

"Veda, I want your permission to marry Tipy."

It was silent for what seemed like an eternity to Frenchy. Caught off guard, she obviously wasn't someone to make a rash decision. He felt her demeanor change, turning her back to him while you could hear a pin drop. Never thinking of himself as insecure, his mind circled, wondering what his reaction would be if she said no. *Would they still go through with it, or are his dreams crushed?*

"Frenchy, you have made a few poor choices in your life, which concerns me. Some of your friends are questionable, to say the least," she said with a stern look before pausing. "Give me a moment, I need a cigarette."

Veda walked out of the room, leaving Frenchy to ponder her answer. She returned and stared expressionlessly at him as smoke billowed in the air.

"My instincts tell me this is a mistake, but I believe you're a good kid. That's why I helped you."

Veda took another puff.

"My daughter needs security. You can only have my permission if you promise to get and keep a job," Veda articulated. "No more trouble!"

Frenchy exhaled with relief, gratitude, and excitement all rolled into one.

"Yes, yes, yes," he said in a calm but excited voice. "Thank you so much! I won't disappoint you."

Frenchy quickly left the room, then bolted out the front door. He paused to get a grip on himself before telling Tipy and everyone else. Suddenly moans and groans erupted after he stopped the music midstream. About 15 teens stood in the garage and driveway, perplexed by the abrupt ending to their groove.

"Listen up," Frenchy announced, grabbing Tipy's hand. "You all are the first to know. Tipy and I are engaged!"

Reaching for his pocket, Frenchy pulled out a box and placed a ring on Tipy's finger, kissed her tenderly, and everyone cheered as these two 18-year-old youngsters entered the world of adulthood.

Frenchy gazed into her eyes, helplessly in love, pleased his dream was finally coming true as he picked her up and twirled her around in circles to the roaring applause of their friends.

* * *

With high vaulted ceilings, stained tempered glass arches, and menorah candles flickering, the wedding at the First Methodist

Church of San Fernando was spectacular. Frenchy's heart melted when his eyes fixated on an angel gliding gracefully down the aisle.

Tipy's dress was elegant as a silky swan with an A-line pattern gown made impeccably of white lace. It had a tea-length iconic boat neckline topped with a triple-strand pearl necklace.

Frenchy's white tux jacket matched her dress and the black slacks with a black bow tie made for an equally stunning ensemble. However, his focus stayed locked on the most beautiful bride ever.

As they faced each other, preparing to exchange vows, Frenchy felt on top of the world, his pulse racing at light speed. Their eyes caressed in bliss as the minister's voice made this perfect moment real. Extinguished was any nervousness as they repeated each word flawlessly, never once looking away.

"I now pronounce you man and wife. You may kiss your bride."

Lifting the veil, their lips met, and Frenchy could feel the universe clicking into place while everyone watched two souls finally finding their home together. The applause sent chills down both youngster's spines as they faced the guests and walked from the alter, hand in hand. An air of confidence and euphoria made it difficult for Frenchy not to look smug. This was the happiest moment of his life, and internally he felt invincible.

After they were married, Tom used his VA benefits to help them buy a house in Pacoima. It was a lovely home, and relatives from both sides helped with the furnishings and household items. The mortgage was $89 per month. It was a three-bedroom, one-bath place on Montford Street, and Frenchy, soon to be 19, had everything he wanted. Although it was much to absorb at this young age, his life stood just where he planned.

Boppie and his wife Joyce moved in with them to offset living expenses. He had quietly married the year before, and they had a son, Tony. Boppie had a job with Western Carloading driving a big rig truck. It was fun having them around to enjoy some laughs.

Although Frenchy felt blessed to work at General Hospital, a county facility, it was a bit monotonous for an analytical person like him. Knowing how upward mobility worked, he took promotional tests at every opportunity.

In the meantime, Tipy blessed him with his first child eleven months after the wedding. The birth of his son Lionel Grandison Jr. netted him emotions he never knew existed. Holding the newborn baby left him breathless, and he knew nothing could ever make him abandon this blessing from God. His blood ran through these tiny veins, and baby Lonnie, which is what Tipy called him, would never question who he was or being loved.

Frenchy landed a position at the county coroner's office in 1960 as supervising clerk, which gave him a feeling of accomplishment. His success at General Hospital and solid recommendations earned him this highly coveted job. The new workplace had energy and activity, exactly what he wanted.

The Los Angeles County Coroner's Office was located downtown inside the Hall of Justice. The structure, built in 1925, occupied two-thirds of the block between Temple and First and Broadway and Spring streets. The boxy tan multilevel building also housed County courts, the Sheriff's office, and the District Attorney.

Heading the coroner's unit was chief medical examiner Dr. Theodore Curphey, the highest appointed official in the County of Los Angeles. He got that position in 1957, a few years before Frenchy arrived.

The first person he met was Paul Schwartz, the supervising deputy for the investigation unit, who greeted him with a stoic welcome. He was a white man in his 40s wearing the typical grey suit with a white shirt and tie. He had dark hair with a receding hairline that extended to the middle of his scalp.

"Good morning, Lionel. Welcome to the team," Schwartz greeted him.

"Good morning, sir."

"Let me introduce you to your coworkers and show you to your desk."

They began purposefully walking, and as they passed an office on the right, Schwartz pointed to the door with a sign that read "Robert Rayban." He drew Frenchy's attention to the name with a scrunched face as if to be afraid.

"Rayban is our boss. As long as you do your job right, you'll be fine, Lionel," Schwartz informed.

Frenchy realized he had to get used to being called by his real name, which had been rare. Even at San Fernando High, his teachers called him Frenchy, as did his General Hospital co-workers. However, in his new position, he decided not to correct anyone, feeling older and more responsible now.

"Lionel, we must ensure the death certificates get done promptly. Cause of death, date, time, and place are all important. That's officially the deputy coroner's aides' job. However, you must be mindful of that. As you know, our filing system is virtually identical to GH. We're looking for you to do for us, what you did for them. The file clerks will help you with that. Make sure they keep up-to-date logs on the status of open investigations. We're short-staffed, so your job duties also include public inquiries."

"I can handle that."

"Believe me. It's not easy as it sounds. Come on, let me introduce you to Deputy Lenny Goldstein."

Schwartz stopped at a well-dressed man sitting at an immaculately organized desk, blowing streams of smoke from his nose.

"Lenny Goldstein, this is Lionel Grandison, your new right-hand man."

"Welcome, Grandison. This is where all the action happens unless you're looking for ghosts. That's down in the basement. They don't get out of hand too much unless their murder goes unsolved, which isn't on us," Goldstein snickered.

"I don't blame them. I'd haunt the halls too," Frenchy joked. "Nice meeting you."

The two men continued walking until they reached a messy counter where Alvaro Diego, a Mexican man in his late 20s, was attentively placing files in large metal drawers.

"Alvaro, I want you to meet your new supervisor, Lionel Grandison."

"Nice to meet you, Mr. Grandison," Alvaro cheerfully uttered.

"Alvaro will help you keep the files current for the investigation department," Schwartz added.

Frenchy gracefully extended his hand, knowing the importance of having good staff.

"Nice to meet you," Frenchy said.

"Alvaro is also your liaison with the medical department," Schwartz added.

"I'm your man," Alvaro confirmed. "I can slide through and introduce you to all our clerks later if you like."

Alvaro was a little flamboyant with an air of confidence that Frenchy liked. He was short with a grainy voice that sounded like he hung around Blacks and smoked one too many cigarettes. Frenchy liked him instantly.

"That would be excellent. I look forward to meeting everyone."

The office atmosphere, although busy, seemed to have a good vibe. As Schwartz led Frenchy away, they approached an oak desk with stacks of papers piled sloppily on each other. This was his desk, and the work appeared to be waiting for him.

"You're on your own now. You know where to find me if you have questions."

"Thank you, sir. I think I'll be fine," Frenchy said, as Schwartz walked away.

Looking around, Frenchy noticed the only two people of color were himself and Alvaro. The demographics were quite different than the hospital which employed many more minorities. The coroner's office consisted entirely of white males. Exploring his desk, he opened the drawers, and it looked like the previous person had left abruptly. Nothing was in order nor cleaned up for a new hire. Having no idea what all the documents on his desk were, he slowly looked at them one by one. Most of them were reports from different investigations that likely needed filing.

Popping his head in front of Frenchy, Alvaro suddenly appeared.

"Hey, Mr. Grandison, are you ready for the tour? There's a lot to see. Especially the morgue."

Anxious to explore the rest of the building, Frenchy placed the file back on his desk, ready to walk around.

"Sure, let's go. You can call me Lionel."

As they went downstairs, the ominous ambiance of the morgue was intriguing yet spooky. The cold stainless steel-based gurneys were in the room, with bodies everywhere in no particular order. Some corpses were wrapped in see-through cellophane, while others had white sheets. You could see documents in clear plastic sleeves to identify the deceased on some but not all. The toe tags stood out only on a few. It smelled like formaldehyde coupled with other embalming agents, which Frenchy found unsettling.

"This is where the bodies first come. Initially, they need to be weighed, measured, and, most importantly, tagged. Then they are cleaned, photographed, and put aside until the autopsy is complete."

"Wow. That's a lot of bodies."

"We stay busy here. Then they are placed in crypts," Alvaro said casually. "It has to stay 45 degrees because of decomposition."

"That explains why I'm shivering," Frenchy laughed.

It seemed unnatural inside a room with so many dead bodies, all with a story of an untimely death. Frenchy walked past a gurney where a hand was lying colorless off the side. The head, enshrined in a clear plastic bag, was ghastly, with hollow, open eyes looking at the ceiling.

"They should have closed his eyes," Alvaro explained, as they continued walking. "We are mandated by law to investigate and determine the circumstances, manner, and cause of all violent, sudden, or unusual deaths within LA county. That includes homicides, suicides, accidental deaths, and natural deaths where the deceased has not seen a doctor within 20 days."

"Sounds like you've been around a while. You know a lot," Frenchy commented, extremely impressed.

"The more you know, the more valuable you are. But you gotta watch out. Things can turn good or bad quickly."

"That's good to know," Frenchy said, not sure exactly what Alvaro meant.

After organizing his paperwork, familiarizing himself with the filing system, and getting to know his staff, it was time to clock out. With the first day under his belt, Frenchy felt surprisingly confident he would handle his position well.

When he arrived home, his son Lonnie, barely three months old, slept quietly in his crib. Tipy was in the bathroom making gagging noises followed by a splashing sound. He heard the toilet flush before Tipy appeared, wiping her mouth with a towel. Her first words were, "Guess what?"

"I don't need to guess. You got the flu."

"Something like that. It's called the nine-month flu," Tipy said humorously.

"So, we're having another child? That's great! Can I get you something? You look pale."

"A new stomach would be great. I wonder why it's named morning sickness when it's 6 in the evening?" Tipy joked. "How was work, sweetie?"

"The job is good, but the odor in the morgue will take some getting used to."

"Did you see any bodies?"

"Yes."

"Really?"

"Yes, Tipy. It's the coroner's office. They do dead bodies."

"Did it trip you out?"

"No. Not really. It just stinks."

"Eww! I guess I won't be visiting any time soon. Dinner will be ready in a few."

Boppie was watching television, looking bored, while Joyce was in the kitchen with the sizzling sound of grease splattering and a spoon clanking on a pot. The scent of fried chicken greeted him, causing his stomach to growl, but Frenchy was mentally exhausted and needed to unwind.

"Hey! Wanna slap some bones?"

Boppie's face lit up, and he quickly came to life.

"Sure, but we need some drink. Let's go to the Hub."

Opening his eyes the next morning, Frenchy was appreciative of sacrificing his summer at General Hospital while in high school. It put him on a path none of his friends have experienced. Eager to start the day, he jumped in the shower, grabbed some toast, and was out the door.

Driving to downtown LA from the San Fernando Valley was challenging. With no freeways, street traffic could be stressful. Still, Frenchy never got upset with other motorists. He was even-tempered even when aggressive drivers were enraged.

When he arrived to work, after barely sitting down, a sharply dressed Goldstein asked him to pick up line two. Goldstein was in his late 30s, with dark curly hair, and wore Stacy Adams shoes to work, which Frenchy immediately noticed.

"What's it regarding?" Frenchy asked.

"The George Reeves case. It's his mother, Mrs. Besselo. She's trying to get Curphey to open an inquest into her son's death."

"George Reeves? Superman?"

"Yes, Superman."

Frenchy slowly picked up the phone with adrenaline running a bit high. He was familiar with the story from the newspapers. Reeves died from a gunshot wound last June that Dr. Curphey ruled a suicide. Frenchy's curiosity peeked.

"Coroner's office, Grandison speaking. May I help you?"

"I'd like to speak with someone regarding the inquest for my son George Reeves," Mrs. Besselo requested.

"Sure, let me get the file. Give me your name and the spelling?"

"I'm Helen Besselo. B-E-S-S-E-L-O. I'm next of kin to my son George Reeves R-E-E-V-E-S."

"One minute."

After grabbing the file, Frenchy was puzzled, seeing it had been closed. He had no idea what to tell this lady, so he went to Goldstein, who had a peculiar grin as if he knew what Frenchy was about to ask.

"Goldstein, this file was closed. How do I handle it?"

"She calls all the time. Grieving relatives are one of our biggest problems. She's a pill. You may want to ask the big man, Curphey."

Having not yet interacted with the Chief Medical Examiner and being the new kid on the block, Frenchy felt thrown into the fire. *But there's a first time for everything, right?* Strangely, he felt everyone's eyes watching, making him self-conscious about handling things perfectly, being only 20 years old.

"Mrs. Besselo, can you give me an hour? I need to talk to the chief examiner, and I'll give you a callback."

'The Adventures of Superman' was a favorite show, and Frenchy remembered watching it when his grandmother got her first console television in 1955. It was an intimidating box with a giant glass screen surrounded by paneling with two knobs on either side and a volume switch. Whereas theater movies fascinated

Frenchy, the television set took it to another level. He wanted more than anything to understand how it worked. Still, in the meantime, he and Dennis enjoyed watching the series. Superman was a hero.

Sitting at his desk, he toyed with going to Curphey's office or calling him on the phone. Slightly intimidated, he chose the latter.

"Yes, Dr. Curphey, this is Lionel Grandison. I'm the new supervising clerk in the office. We've got a woman on the phone asking about an inquest for the George Reeves case."

"So, they gave Besselo to you?" he asked with a nasally Canadian accent.

"Yes, sir."

"Well, this is an unusual case, Grandison. Mrs. Besselo commissioned an independent investigation outside of our office."

"What does that mean, sir?"

"Just listen, and I'll tell you. She received a court order to have the body exhumed and paid for a second autopsy. That means Mrs. Besselo is on her own. Based on our autopsy findings and the LAPD investigation, Mr. Reeves committed suicide. No inquest will be scheduled."

"Excuse me, Dr. Curphey, but what if her investigation turns up something?"

"Young man, you are new here and have much to learn. Unfortunately, there is nothing we can do, and that's what you tell Mrs. Besselo. No inquest!" Curphey adamantly shrieked, hanging up the phone abruptly.

"Thank you, sir," Frenchy muttered, hoping no one heard Curphey's reaction. Then, after scanning the room, he placed the receiver down.

Bewildered, he had to give this serious thought because common sense tells you accuracy is more important than anything. At least in Frenchy's mind.

Goldstein smirked, peering over at Frenchy, who was deep in thought.

"How did your first Curphey experience go?" he asked.

"Warm guy," Frenchy sarcastically replied.

"Curphey is under a lot of pressure. He must determine the cause of death for any person with a traumatic injury, whether self-inflicted, by accident, or at the hands of another. It's a tough gig."

"Apparently."

Frenchy realized some aspects of his new job would be challenging. Despite many calls coming in, he still deliberated on how to handle Mrs. Besselo. He knew he had to call her back, and just then, his phone rang.

"Coroner's office. Grandison speaking."

"Mr. Grandison, it's Helen Besselo. I'm just calling back to see if you have any additional information about my son?"

"Hi, Mrs. Besselo. I have some bad news for you. Our Chief Medical Examiner, Dr. Curphey, said there's not enough new evidence for an Inquest."

"Well, Curphey's an ass. My detective has uncovered facts that did not match up with the Police investigation. George's fingerprints were not on the gun that killed him, and the spent shell casing was found underneath his body. Also, the wounds did not line up with the path of the bullet."

"Have you taken that information to the police?"

"Of course I have, but they refuse to listen. This does not support the ruling of suicide."

"I'm sorry, Mrs. Besselo. I wish I could help. But there's nothing I can do at this time," he sympathetically conveyed.

"Mr. Grandison, please, I need someone to help me," she desperately pleaded.

"Mrs. Besselo – I don't know what more I can do, but if you get any additional information, let me know. In the meantime, I will keep an eye out for any LAPD updates."

"Thank you, Mr. Grandison."

Frenchy found himself a bit concerned with the callous attitude of Dr. Curphey. Mrs. Besselo had uncovered significant evidence about her son's death. *Why wouldn't Curphey launch an inquest?* An inquest is a formal proceeding conducted when a death is sudden or unexplained. A judge or jury determines the outcome after hearing testimony and evidence. However, it was an irrelevant point because Dr. Curphey had already made up his mind. Nevertheless, Frenchy wanted to know more about the man who hung up on him. He knew Alvaro would enlighten him.

"What can you tell me about Dr. Curphey?" Frenchy snuck in, while they were alone working.

"Man, that cat? I stay away from him. You guys get to deal with that attitude."

"What's his story?"

"When that dude got here, he was in trouble by the end of his first year. He couldn't run this place for nothing. Morticians complained like crazy about not getting death certificates on time and messed up autopsies. The dude also got investigated for misconduct. He's a hot mess."

"Why is he still here?"

"Got me! I'm just a clerk. I know he ain't supposed to get any more complaints."

"I see. Thanks, Alvaro."

Being so young, Frenchy didn't have much experience in political correctness, but realized quickly, learning was imperative if he wanted to succeed at this job. Mrs. Besselo continued to call, and he was always as helpful and compassionate as possible until he was summoned to Curphey's office a month later.

Walking down the long hallway, he could hear his footsteps echo off the wall. It was his first time going to Curphey's office, and he was curious about what the big man wanted, wondering if he had done something wrong. On the other hand, no one was upset with him, and he had handled Mrs. Besselo with kid gloves, so this request seemed odd.

Entering the stale smoke-filled office, Frenchy greeted Curphey. He had a long narrow face with oval-shaped glasses. His thick eyebrows and elongated nose were reminiscent of Groucho Marx down to the oddly trimmed mustache. The only difference was his balding head. He didn't smile or act cordial, so Frenchy patiently waited to see what he wanted.

"Lionel, I appreciate how you've handled Mrs. Besselo. I haven't had to deal with her in quite a while."

"Thank you, sir."

"You must do one more thing before we can put this to rest."

"What is that?"

"We exhumed Reeve's body and had it cremated. I want you to inform her that she can come and pick up the ashes."

Standing there in pure shock and disbelief, Frenchy was flabbergasted. The office walls began slowly closing in on him like a slow-motion film. His shallow breathing made him take a seat to gather his spiraling senses.

"When did she request cremation?"

"She didn't. You need to inform her," Curphey said coldly.

"You mean we didn't have her consent?"

"Grandison, are you questioning me?"

"No sir."

"Tell her to pick them up asap," Curphey scowled. "That's all."

Finding it difficult to swallow, Frenchy looked intently at this cold-hearted man, feeling helpless and betrayed. He worked hard to establish a relationship with this woman, and now he must cut out her heart like Jack the Ripper. Curphey knows she will be devastated but does not care. It was low as one could go.

"Yes sir," Frenchy said, retreating to his desk.

This man was the most powerful in the county and Frenchy wondered about his motives. *Could he fall prey to big business like Hollywood movie studios?* Suicide is one-and-done versus a murder investigation and money talks, Frenchy thought. Somebody just wanted Superman to go away. He didn't know any of that for certain, but it sure seemed possible.

"Mrs. Besselo, this is Mr. Grandison from the coroner's office. I'm calling with some news for you."

"Please tell me they're going to have an inquest."

"I wish that was the case. But, unfortunately, I just got word the coroner's office has cremated your son's body and is requesting you come to pick up the remains."

"I don't believe I heard you correctly."

"Your son's body has been cremated."

"No! He was buried!"

"The office wanted to take another look based on your private investigation. After the examination, the body was cremated."

"Who gave anyone the right to do that? What kind of barbarians are you people? You exhume his body without my permission and burn it? You guys will pay for this!"

The line went dead with a loud thud, and the hum of a busy signal pounded Frenchy's ear.

A few days later, Curphey called him back to his office.

"Lionel, I just got word from the mayor's office that one of his representatives is coming to discuss the Reeves case. I want you to meet with him and explain how we conducted ourselves throughout the process. I told him you were handling this investigation and the excellent job you've done."

"What do you want me to tell him?"

"That Mrs. Besselo's claims have no merit, and the coroner's office has followed all the guidelines in addressing her concerns. Grandison, this is very important to this office. Make us look good."

"Yes sir. I'll do my best."

Curphey's office was not a place he liked to be.

After Frenchy returned to his desk, Rayban arrived with a tall, dark-haired man in a suit.

"Lionel, this is special deputy Boozer from Mayor Poulson's office. He wants to speak with you. You two can use my office."

"Pleased to meet you," Boozer said.

"My pleasure."

They followed Rayban, and both took seats. Understanding Curphey's wishes, Frenchy observed Mr. Boozer and assessed his demeanor to determine if he was reasonable.

"Mrs. Helen Besselo has made some unusual claims about how this office handled her son's case. Can you brief me on that?"

"What kind of claims has she made?"

"She said the coroner's office has refused to investigate new evidence regarding her son's death and exhumed and cremated his body without her knowledge."

"Mrs. Besselo is a sweet woman, but she's also a mother grieving her son's death. Her private investigation revealed some circumstantial evidence, but not enough to reopen the case. However, Dr. Curphey, at his discretion, decided to exhume the body, which I assume was to take another look. She had called hundreds of times and, like most of us, wanted closure once and for all."

"So why was the body cremated?"

"Once again, that was a decision made by Dr. Curphey. However, I will say he handled this difficult case the best he could and followed all LA County rules and regulations. Mr. Boozer, we deal with grieving families often, and it's never easy, especially when they are celebrities."

"You've answered all my questions. I think I have enough to report back to the mayor. So I'll let you get back to work."

After Boozer left, Rayban extended his hand to Frenchy with a subtle smile.

"Nice job. You handled that well."

The following day, Mrs. Besselo arrived despondently to retrieve the ashes. Her face was flushed, and gigantic tears streamed uncontrollably. She quietly took the urn, barely saying anything, kissed it, and left.

Frenchy felt a sense of conflict surging through his body. Grappling with these opposing emotions was a challenge. On the one hand, he had a job to do; on the other, seeing the unrelenting pain streaming from Mrs. Besselo's eyes made it difficult to rationalize how they handled her case. Unbeknownst to Frenchy, Mrs. Besselo died a few months after that.

Frenchy went home that day to Tipy and little Lonnie and relished his family. The day was emotional and overwhelming, with a lot to process. He gave Tipy an extra-long hug, grateful for what easily could get taken for granted.

With Tipy expecting in November, he realized home life would be just as chaotic as work. So, Frenchy decided to get away for the weekend to help clear his mind. Mo watched Lonnie while Tipy, him and his mother went to Yosemite to bathe in the serenity of nature. The tall redwoods and blue, crisp waterfalls relaxed his soul, if only for a weekend.

7 - Ramping Up

The months flew by like lightning bolts in a tropical storm, with days rapidly merging as Frenchy tackled back-to-back cases like a pro. Finally, nine short months after working in the coroner's office, his supervisor Robert Rayban called him into the office. Things had been going exceptionally well. He had mastered the procedures and was very personable with the public. Everyone seemed to like his work skills, so he could not imagine why Rayban wanted him.

Sitting in the office was Paul Schwartz, which sent a sliver of concern. He remembered the initial warning to do his job correctly. However, every interaction with Rayban had been positive.

"Have a seat, Lionel," Schwartz said.

This could not be good, Frenchy thought, plucking at the cuff of his shirt. He scanned their mannerisms, trying to pick up a clue as to the nature of this meeting. Cautiously sitting down, he focused on their unreadable facial expressions.

"Sure. Is everything alright?" Frenchy asked.

"That depends. We just had a situation come up that we wanted to discuss with you."

"Okay," Frenchy said, feeling uneasy.

"The Board of Supervisors is giving us another deputy coroner's aide position. What would you think about filling it?"

"Are you serious? I've only been here for nine months. Do I qualify?"

"We're pleased with your work, and more importantly, Dr. Curphey is satisfied with how you handle yourself. We wanted to fill this position from within, and you have demonstrated excellent knowledge of procedures and great customer relations, so we believe you're the right man for the job."

"Well, what can I say but thanks, gentlemen," Frenchy said ecstatically.

"Well, don't thank me yet. Let me tell you exactly what this position entails. As coroner's aide, you will assist in establishing the cause, manner, and circumstances of death, which includes conferring with all law enforcement agencies to coordinate investigations of deaths resulting from possible criminal acts. You are also responsible for the bodies, evidence, and property related to the deceased at the death scene. These positions do not become available often and require a personal commitment to this office, Los Angeles County, and the public."

Frenchy snapped to attention, raising his chin, with a look of pride.

"I'm honored that you and Dr. Curphey are willing to entrust me with this incredible responsibility. I promise to do my absolute best."

"We need to get you sworn in, give you your badge, along with a few other formalities, and you're all set."

"I'm speechless, gentleman."

"Don't get speechless now. Talking is a prerequisite for this position." Rayban said, laughing.

When Frenchy left work, he felt a strange, elevated sense of worth and achievement. Thoughts of being equivalent to Schwartz and higher up on the food chain made his head spin with triumph. After all, this was 1961. He was Black and only 21 years old. He wanted to celebrate and shout it out to the world and knew Tipy would be excited too.

Nine months had netted new additions on the home front. His daughter Crystal was born in November, and thoughts of having two children, a beautiful wife, a house, and a respectable job were numbing. Waves of anxiety briefly engulfed him, but Frenchy knew he worked well under pressure, so luckily, that was short-lived.

When Frenchy turned on Montford Street, he saw an orange glow of clouds illuminating a beautiful sky above the San Gabriel Mountains. He turned up the volume, bouncing to The Miracles'

"Shop Around" on the radio, mimicking their lead singer Smokey Robinson. The moment compelled him to sing out.

Pulling into the driveway, excitement rushed through Frenchy in anticipation of Tipy's response. He sang until the song ended before turning off the engine.

As soon as Frenchy walked in the door, madness, chaos, and mayhem lunged out at him. Three-year-old Tony was pushing Lonnie down, who had just learned to walk and was now screaming. Joyce was attempting to calm her baby Danny, who was hollering like someone pinched him and ran. Crystal was whaling bloody murder while Tipy bathed her in the kitchen sink and wiped soap from her eyes. Boppie was out of view, and all Frenchy saw was pandemonium. With the wind taken out of his sails, he decided to hold off on sharing the good news until a better time. He retreated to the bedroom, closed the door, then flopped on his bed. Shortly after that, Tipy entered with a colorless face and a look of exhaustion.

"Hi, baby. You're home kind of late. I put your plate in the oven."

"Oh, okay. I'll eat in a minute. I have some good news."

Suddenly, a forceful hyperventilating cry came from the kid's room, accelerating by the second. Instinctively Tipy whirled around to address the problem.

"Hold on. It's been like this all day. Let me see who's crying."

All four kids slept in the same room. Frenchy exhaled at the frustration of trying to share his news with her but remained patient when Tipy left.

"I'm going to go eat," Frenchy said, getting up from his prone position.

The kitchen was small but clean and orderly, with a clay cookie jar, lace curtains with ties, and sparkling countertops that smelled like Ajax cleanser. Frenchy opened the oven and saw a porcelain plate with aluminum foil neatly tucked around it. Still warm to the touch, he took it to the kitchen nook and slowly sat down. There were slices of meatloaf, fresh green beans, and mashed potatoes carefully placed with the exact amount of gravy

Frenchy liked. He was about to take his first bite when Tipy reappeared.

"Sorry about that. Crystal is teething, so she has a few tough months ahead. Lonnie is into everything since he started walking, and it's the funniest thing. Tony hears me always telling Lonnie 'no' and thinks he shouldn't be walking. That's why he keeps pushing him…." Tipy abruptly stopped telling her story and saw Frenchy staring at his plate, disinterested.

"You had something to tell me?" she continued.

He took another bite and shuffled his food with his fork, less enthusiastic about sharing his news.

"Frenchy, it's just so hectic here. I don't mean to ignore you. What were you going to tell me?"

"Well… Today I got a promotion. I'm a Deputy Coroner's Aide!"

"OH MY GOSH! That's out of sight! I knew you were going to be successful at that job. This is so exciting. I can't wait to tell Veda. We gotta have a celebration dinner!"

"Slow down, Tipy. Slow down. Yes, it's a big deal but let's enjoy the glory before we get ahead of ourselves."

"How much is your raise?"

"Funny you ask. I was so stunned by getting offered the position that I didn't ask."

"It doesn't matter. I'm so proud of you."

Unable to keep a secret, Tipy blasted the news to both Veda and Mo with the energy and enthusiasm of a sports announcer. After being sworn in a week later, Veda hosted a celebration dinner at her house.

* * *

Having a badge was a big deal, and the next eight months accelerated Frenchy's knowledge, leadership, and position. Although not part of the good ole boys club per se, his race was never an issue until April 27, 1962, when a Black Muslim, Ronald T Stokes, was shot by LAPD. But another prominent case preceded that to set the stage for him to discover the dark side of the Los Angeles Coroners' office.

The year 1962 was plagued with scandal and high-profile cases. It was on January 13 that a now-forgotten but once-famous comedian Ernie Kovacs, some categorized as a genius in his field, died in a car crash. Kovacs appeared on television, starring in "The Ernie Kovacs Show," and did multiple specials for the major networks. He hob-knobbed with Hollywood's A-list. Frenchy immediately knew who he was after receiving the phone call from California Highway Patrol while working the graveyard shift.

"We have a vehicle casualty on the corner of Beverly Glen and Santa Monica Blvd. It's Ernie Kovacs," the officer stated.

"The comedian?" Frenchy asked.

"Yes."

"What time was the accident?"

"Around 1:30 am."

"I will dispatch a unit to pick up the body."

"There's no need. No one else was involved, and no alcohol was detected. Pierce Brothers are on the way. The family wants this mortuary to be in charge. I need you to approve this."

"Under the circumstances you described, that would violate the law, and I'm sure the mortuary is aware of that. So they can contact us to get the body."

"You are making a mistake. What is your name?"

"This is Deputy Lionel Grandison, and I'm following protocol."

"This is high profile, and the family wants no leeks or unauthorized photographs. It's not a standard accident."

"We will handle this with care."

"Be sure to note there was no one else involved and no alcohol! Do you get that?"

"Thank you, officer."

Frenchy found that conversation odd. A police agency has control regarding natural deaths within its jurisdiction, but the LA County Coroner has absolute authority in all accident cases. Moreover, there was no scientific way to assess alcohol on a Beverly Hills street pavement, and drawing that conclusion would not be responsible. The situation felt off balance, which left Frenchy befuddled.

The following day Kovacs' wife, singer Edie Adams, and actor Jack Lemmon were awaiting Dr. Curphey when he entered the office. Frenchy assumed it was about releasing the body but wasn't sure because they were adamant about who they wanted to see. Curphey arrived a little earlier than usual and looked at Frenchy with an icy-cold stare.

"Don't go home yet. We need to talk," Curphey sharply said.

Sticking around, he finished up some work, then Curphey appeared, motioning to be followed. Frenchy knew this was serious.

"I have to say your judgment in this Kovacs case is poor. Why did you order those toxicology reports?"

"The officer wanted a waiver on us bringing the body here and was acting strange."

"Listen, Grandison, when law enforcement tells you everything is alright, consider it fact and follow their advice."

"Yes sir," Frenchy replied, confused about why Curphey was upset.

A day later, Frenchy was catching up on his caseload, still stumped about Curphey. Alvaro appeared with a file and placed it on the desk.

"Que Paso, amigo. You're quiet today. What's wrong? You didn't get none last night?"

Amused by Alvaro's words, Frenchy chuckled.

"Naw, I'm good. What you got there?"

"The Kovacs file. This is going to trip you out."

Frenchy opened the folder and picked up a photo. It showed a white Corvair station wagon wrapped in a "U" shape around a utility pole, mangled in shreds. The force appeared to wedge Kovacs' body on the passenger side while pinning his leg under the seat. The door was open with Kovacs head hanging down, inches from the wet ground.

"They said emergency rescue teams had to pry him out," Alvaro commented, still stunned by the gross images. "The word is he had just left a party at director Billy Wilder's house in Beverly Hills. Dean Martin, Lucille Ball, and all the big stars were there. It was a baby shower for Milton Berle's wife. Poor dude's cigar was lying by his head on the wet ground."

"Man, what a drag. I liked his show."

"I never saw it."

"You always impress me, Alvaro. One of my high school homies, Love, used to be like you. He always had the scoop."

"The key to survival is information."

"Looks like you're gonna live a long time, ese."

Buried beneath the photos was the toxicology report. Frenchy's eyes widened when it revealed an excessive level of alcohol in the bloodstream. He was right to order the test! This was redeeming. Expecting praise, Frenchy brought the news to Curphey.

"Sir, here is the toxicology report for Kovacs. There was alcohol in his system, nearly twice the legal limit. The CHP was wrong."

"Grandison, let me make this perfectly clear. Do not ever, ever question my authority again."

Frenchy's posture suddenly stiffened.

"I wasn't questioning your…."

"That's all, Grandison!"

The building felt cold at that very moment. Frenchy's head began to pound, trying to make sense of this illogical reprimand. He never defied or questioned Curphey, only presented him with information while doing his job. Dumbfounded and confused, he exited his boss's office.

When he returned to his desk, Alvaro was waiting, a friendly face he welcomed.

"What's going on, Al?"

"I got a little bit of information for you."

"What's that?" he said, still bothered by Curphey.

"There's a reason they didn't want Kovacs' body here."

"Why?"

"Insurance. Because of a clause, his wife, Edie Adams, can't collect if his death is alcohol-related. Everyone knew this could be a problem way before the accident. They made sure the mortuary was prepared. Get this, and his wife wouldn't even go to the party with him. They drove separate cars."

Frenchy's eyes scanned down the hallway toward Curphey's office. He slightly squinted, trying to put things in perspective.

"That means Curphey has an agenda. He was trying to help the family," Frenchy deducted. "How do you know this?"

"No one pays attention to a Mexican. We are invisible, so they just talk. Mi esposa is a maid, and they think she don't speak English. Those Hollywood walls have crazy secrets."

"Well, I appreciate the info even though I don't know what exactly to do with it. That's a lot of sand on the beach."

"Shoot, all I know is personas with power are shady. Just watch out for Curphey. That's the main thing."

"Thanks, Alvaro."

Getting another dose of how easily facts can be hidden and manipulated plagued Frenchy's mind. Curphey was trying to hinder the truth with external pressure from those in powerful places. Based on Alvaro's information, millions of dollars can be at stake in these investigations. Just like in Superman's case, there's always more going on than what's on the surface. One thing's for sure, because of this, Kovacs' wife and a few others will hate him for the rest of their lives.

Living in Pacoima was, in many ways, a haven for Blacks. Being a working-class, ambitious community, they knew their neighbors, store owners, barbers, and teachers. As a result, crime rates were meager to the point where many didn't even lock their doors. Still, the city built a new police station there in 1961, which patrolled the north San Fernando Valley.

It was Saturday morning, April 27, 1962, and Frenchy was relishing his day off, taking in the warm spring morning and getting to know his newborn son, Lance, who was born on March 6. Tipy was frantic because of the unrelenting demands of three children, one being a newborn. Unlike the other two, Lance commanded attention and seemed to cry non-stop. Frenchy decided he would help with the baby after reading the morning paper.

The first story jumped out to him like a blinding light. The newspaper headline read:

Los Angeles Times – April 28, 1962
'MUSLIMS' RIOT
Cultist Killed, Policeman Shot
Four Wounded, 26 Taken Into Custody

One policeman was shot and two savagely beaten in a blazing gunfight during a riot at the anti-white Muslim headquarters early today.

One black-suited cultist, Ronald T. Stokes, was slain and six others felled by police bullets before 13 officers quailed the riot at 5606 S. Broadway.

Unfamiliar with the Muslim religion, Frenchy didn't know what to think of this story. His family was Baptist but he never attended church regularly. Mo and Tom attended Greater Missionary, a few blocks away, when they first moved to Pacoima. Their minister, Reverend TG Pledger, was a compelling preacher whose services attracted most Blacks until other churches emerged. However, Frenchy was with his mother during his early years, who rarely went to church. It wasn't until he and Dennis moved away they would occasionally go. Unfortunately, that was short-lived because Mo became increasingly fearful of large crowds.

Therefore, Frenchy was never thoroughly indoctrinated into Christianity and only vaguely familiar with details about other faiths. His only reference point for Muslims was a CBS News report he watched, "The Hate that Hate Produced," which depicted them as hostile and violent militants. He had no idea this would be a mind-changing, enlightening moment that would profoundly affect him for the rest of his life.

When he went to work that Monday, it was clear this was anything but the typical environment. Instead, the office seemed edgy as his co-workers Schwartz and Goldstein were uncharacteristically quiet.

"Hey, Goldstein. What's going on? Why's everyone so quiet? It's like a morgue in here," Frenchy snickered.

An echoing silence bounced off the office walls.

"We've got a hot new case," Goldstein finally replied. "But I'm out of here."

"Lucky you. Have a good one."

While diligently sorting through the mounds of papers on his desk, Frenchy saw several autopsy reports ready to be dispensed. Scanning the room for Alvaro, he purposefully waved for his attention. The name on the first report immediately stood out, Ronald T. Stokes. Remembering it from the newspaper, he looked more closely.

Death due to: *Gunshot wounds*

Manner of Death: *Homicide*

How Injury Occurred: *By on-duty law enforcement officer*

Antonic Summary:

Gunshot wound #1 Left upper chest:

> *Entrance Upper left chest*
>
> *Exit Upper left-back*
>
>> Associated injuries:
>>
>>> *Perforated left-lower lung lobe. Left hemothorax 150 grams*

Gunshot Wound #2, Left pectoral chest, perforation heart:

> *Entrance wound left nipple*
>
> *Exit upper left back*
>
>> Associated injuries:
>>
>>> *Pericardial and pleural hemorrhage left coronary artery*

Gunshot Wound #3, Right hand:

> *Entrance right hand*
>
> *Exit: right hand*
>
>> Associated injuries:
>>
>>> *Right first digit proximal phalange fractures*

Additional Injuries

> *Blunt Trauma, head*
>
> *Right eye Abrasion*
>
> *Frontal subgaleal hemorrhage*
>
> *Rear skull hemorrhage.*
>
> *No powder burns*

The autopsy report revealed three bullet entry points: the heart, left lung, and right hand. It also noted abrasions above the right eye and rear of the skull and indicated no powder burns. Dr. Melvin Shatavsky signed it.

Struck immediately by the inconsistency of the autopsy report and what he read in the newspaper, Frenchy's internal radar peaked. He wondered if this was the reason for the change in everyone's demeanor. Alvaro then appeared seemingly unaffected by the office melancholy, behaving like his usual cheery self.

"Good morning, Alvaro."

"And hola to you Señor Leonel. Did you have a good weekend?"

"It was filled with the energy of two kids and an infant, but it was good, thanks. You?"

"Heck, trabajando, I was here working."

"You really need to take some time off, my friend. Look here, I need this to go to Curphey and this goes to Goldberg. When you're done, we have stuff to be logged in."

"Got it, boss."

Looking to see his priorities for the day, Frenchy discovered one case that had officially closed and completed the final paperwork. As he was finishing up, the 'Jeeeeeeeng, jeeeeeeeng' sound of his phone startled him. Surprised by his jumpiness, he picked up the receiver to hear Curphey's gritty voice.

"Grandison, I need everything for the Stokes case."

"Alvaro is on his way now with the autopsy report."

"I need his belongings too."

"They're locked up."

"I don't need them locked up. I need everything in my office. NOW!!"

"Yes, sir."

Perplexed by the sudden change of procedures, Frenchy grabbed the property room keys from his drawer and found Alvaro, who was working alone in the small stuffy file room. He entered and slowly closed the door.

"What is going on with the Stokes case?"

"Amigo, can't you feel the tension here?"

"Yes, I do, but no one is talking."

"Let me tell you, the Muslims are hot as a dash of chili pepper and are accusing the police of lying. Our boys hate that. Now I'm hearing that Malcolm X himself is coming to town. The bigwigs are trying to figure things out. Everyone is in on this."

"Who's everyone?"

"Man…Mayor Yorty, Police Chief Parker, Curphey, and the press. They had their heads together yesterday."

"Alright, thanks. Can you take the property bag with Stokes items to Curphey?"

"Ay caramba. He just snapped at me when I gave him the autopsy report. I hate dealing with him."

"You can do this, hermano. Thanks," Frenchy said, reaching into his pocket and getting the keys. "Make sure you return these immediately."

"I take back all the nice things I said about you," Alvaro said with a friendly smirk.

When Frenchy returned to his desk, the metallic ringing of his phone was at it again.

"Coroner's office, Grandison here."

"Yes, I'm calling about the Ronald Stokes case. This is Malcolm."

Frenchy paused curiously.

"X?"

"Yes. I'm looking for information about the date and time of the inquest.

Frenchy hesitated, wondering if this was a joke. He scanned the room, but no one seemed to be paying attention. Finally, with a crinkled frown, he proceeded to answer.

"I don't believe we've scheduled one."

"I was transferred to you for that information."

Frenchy cleared his throat, tapping his pencil on the desk.

"I understand. To be honest, things are a little crazy around here. Let me get your number, and I promise to get back to you as soon as I know something."

"I'm in New York now, but I plan to be in LA for the funeral on Saturday."

"If you haven't heard from me before you leave, call me when you get in town," Frenchy advised, then wrote down the number.

"Thank you, brother. What was your name again?"

"Deputy Lionel Grandison."

"Thank you, Brother Lionel. I appreciate your help. You know, they can't keep killing Negro people," Malcolm voiced with passion.

Frenchy let out a breath he didn't even realize he was holding before carefully choosing his words.

"You're right. I'll do the best I can."

"As salaam alaikum," Malcolm responded before the line went dead.

A little star-struck, Frenchy hung up, more confused than ever. *Why did they transfer that call to him, knowing he had no information on the case?* Malcolm X was an outspoken member of the Black community and Frenchy was the only Black in the office. Perhaps that explained it. He pinched his chin, looking at the notepad on his desk.

"You handle your people well, Grandison," Schwartz bellowed from his desk.

"I thought I was past getting punked."

"Quit acting like a rookie. You know how this game works."

"Yes, I know. The office comes first."

Things felt strangely different like dark eyes were plotting against him, but perhaps he was reading too much into this. He had never felt different in the workplace, even though he knew he and Alvaro were. Yet, it still seemed like cock roaches were hiding in the walls waiting to come out when the lights went off. Being pragmatic, this couldn't be true.

On Tuesday, Frenchy learned the Muslims were holding a press conference on Friday regarding the Stokes killing. Only he, Schwartz, and Alvaro were in the work area when finally, the topic of the Muslim case came up.

"Those Moslems are organizing one of those protests," Schwartz belted.

"I hadn't heard," Frenchy responded.

"Yeah, it's supposed to be at that Hilton on South Grand where the coloreds like to hang out."

"The Statler Hilton?"

"Our police suspected that the cult was stockpiling weapons. A bunch of fine officers got attacked and had to get medical treatment. They're lucky only one of those savages got killed. They have no right to protest anything."

"The police didn't find any guns," Frenchy defended.

"Well, everyone knows how they feel about whites. I'm sure they were planning something."

"That sounds presumptuous," Frenchy said, trying not to be rude.

Grabbing his items from the desk, Schwartz unapologetically stood up with a callous grin.

"Well, it's time for me to go," he said. "But for the record, I'm always on the side of law enforcement."

When Schwartz left, both Alvaro and Frenchy's eyes connected in unison.

"It would have been better if that gringo kept his opinion to himself. He doesn't know what we see out there on them streets," Alvaro blasted.

"We both know how privilege works. It's sad some of them just don't get it."

"It's worse than that. The press is calling Muslims a cult on purpose. That even makes a Chicano, like me, mad. But Muslims are some cool cats. And their bean pies are muy bueno."

"I'm getting a crash course on how things are, that's for sure. They are afraid of something. That's why they quickly decided to hold an inquest."

"Word is, Mayor Yorty told Curphey to hold it because of pressure. But you didn't hear that from me." Alvaro winked.

After learning they scheduled the inquest for Monday, May 14, Frenchy tried contacting Malcolm, but his wife said he had already left for Los Angeles. Then, to his surprise, Curphey called him to meet and discuss details.

"Grandison, we need you on our team for this."

"What do you mean, sir?"

"We have the Stokes inquest coming up. Those Moslems are going to start some trouble. We need you to handle them and keep things calm."

"I'll do my best."

"You must do better than that. We can't have them starting a riot here, and that's what those people do. They are violent, hate whites, and that will not be tolerated here. They are a terrorist cult, and that's unacceptable."

Frenchy got light-headed with a montage of feelings he couldn't even articulate. So he slowly stood up, feeling his heart pounding and eyes drifting to a blurry focus.

"I will handle it," Frenchy said, struggling internally to keep his cool.

Curphey was the worst of the worst in Frenchy's mind. Never had he seen so much deceptive venom embedded in a human being. But clearly, his sheltered suburban world had hidden many elements of sociopathic white behavior. The stuff that happened at school and in the neighborhood seemed petty, compared to the subtle agendas of the real world. Frenchy could see this hateful behavior rearing its ugly face and didn't like the unfolding vision. For the first time, he grappled with his Black identity.

When Friday rolled around, the office climate had not improved. Sitting quietly at his desk, he looked at Schwartz and Goldstein. Schwartz was heavyset with dark hair and wore the same gray suit every day. He was shadowy yet personable. On the other hand, Goldstein wore newly tailored suits and came from a well-to-do Jewish family. As a result, he didn't quite fit in as a deputy. However, he seemed to know everything going on, like an inside mouse was feeding him information. Oddly, scooping him was nearly impossible, which surprised Frenchy on many occasions.

Frenchy's phone was constantly ringing, and pressure inside the office was mounting.

"Coroner's office, Deputy Grandison speaking," he answered, wondering what was next.

"My name is Charles Brody. I'm the attorney for Ronald Stokes' family. Who can I speak to regarding the upcoming inquest?"

"Maybe I can help you, sir. What do you need to know?"

"The family has expressed an interest in attending and submitting some questions. I need some procedural information along with the date and time."

"The date is Monday, May 14, at 10 am. How many seats are you requesting?"

"I'll need at least five. Minister Malcolm X will be attending along with our legal team and Delores Stokes, wife of the deceased."

"The minister called, and I haven't been able to reach him to give him the date."

"I'll handle that. He's holding a press conference today, and I will see him."

"Thanks. I'm going to put you in touch with the inquest deputy for the procedures and list you for five seats. What was your name again?"

"Charles Brody."

"Okay, Mr. Brody. Hold for a moment."

"Thank you."

Frenchy looked around the office for Longhorn, the deputy in charge of inquests. He was in his mid-50s with white hair, oval glasses, and skinny lips but wasn't within immediate view.

"What do you need, Grandison?" Goldstein asked.

"There's a question about the inquest procedures, so I'm looking for Longhorn."

"I can take that," he said, quickly grabbing the phone.

"Yes, this is Deputy Goldstein... Just bring your questions to the inquest. There shouldn't be a problem as long as you're on the guest list… You're welcome."

Goldstein smiled and winked at Frenchy.

"See, that was simple. But, so you know, we will handle this case differently than others."

"Why is that?" Frenchy asked.

"The community pressure is big. Mayor Yorty's involved. We all have to step up our game."

Longhorn then appeared in the office, blowing a string of smoke out of his nose.

"What's going on?"

"The Stokes attorney had a question about the inquest. Goldstein answered it," Frenchy explained.

"We need to meet in my office, so we are ready for this. Goldstein, Grandison, and Schwartz Let's go."

The three men marched to Longhorns' office, stepping purposely down the corridor. Longhorn sat in his high-back desk chair, a hand-me-down from Curphey, and took out his notepad. Frenchy and Schwartz took a seat while Goldstein stood beside them.

"All eyes are on us, and we need everyone on the same page," Longhorn began. "Any troublemakers or police critics need to be weaned out. Does everyone understand?"

"Yes," they all echoed.

"Goldstein, you handle the guestlist for media and observers. As you know, our room seats only 25 people, including the press. Grandison, you validate the credentials. Schwartz, you get the witness questions and give them to me. No surprises while I'm conducting this inquiry."

"Alright," Schwartz replied.

"Did the rules change about the questions?" Frenchy asked.

"Even though this is Curphey's case, it's my inquest. The procedures are the same as always. We may need to make adjustments to avoid problems with the cult, but this will be peaceful and organized."

Frenchy gazed over at Goldstein, touching the base of his neck, a bit baffled. Typically questions had to be submitted three days in advance, and everyone knew that. Then, to top it off, Longhorn referred to the Muslims as a cult, which rubbed Frenchy the wrong way.

"The press release will go out Tuesday next week, so be prepared for this place to become a madhouse," Longhorn stated.

Frenchy opened his mouth and began to say something but quickly decided against it. Things were feeling out of sorts, but riding this wave was his best option as the meeting concluded.

When he went home that day, he couldn't help but think of the unusual atmosphere within the office. Curphey was downright vicious, and the other deputies were acting similarly. The whole week made him uncomfortable, and when it came to racial acuities, he was treading on unchartered territory, making him feel unsure of everything.

On Sunday, Lance was turning two months old, and family time was a welcome change from the drama at the office. But unfortunately, picking up the newspaper took him right back to the social theatre he thought he had left behind.

Los Angeles Times – May 5, 1962
Muslim Leader Accuses Police of Murder

Malcolm X, New York leader of the Black Muslim sect, Friday accused police of shooting down "seven innocent unarmed black men" in cold blood in a melee near Muslim headquarters the night of April 27, 1962.

Citizens News – May 5, 1962
Gestapo Tactics Charged

A top Black Muslim leader today compared Los Angeles Police Chief William Parker with Hitler and charged that "Gestapo" police were guilty of "Cold-blooded murder" in the battle last Friday near a Muslim Mosque on South Broadway.

Malcolm X, minister of Mosque No 7 in New York City and national representative of Black Muslim leader Elijah Mohammed lashed out at Parker, Los Angeles Police, and the "White Press" at a news conference at the Statler Hilton Hotel.

He accused the police chief of misleading the press to spread false propaganda about the Negro community.

While reading the papers, Frenchy's mind drifted to thinking about truth. Either the police shot Stokes in cold blood, or he attacked them. One thing he knew was truth is universal. It's one of the most vital forces in the cosmos, binding everyone, and once subverted, chaos ensues. One side of this drama was being deceptive, and that, he knew for sure.

As he continued reading the LA Times, a curious story that seemed unworthy of the front page stood out.

Los Angeles Times – May 5, 1962
Negro Deputy of Yorty Gets Phone Threat

Police protection was ordered for Mrs. Ethel Bryant, 44, a field deputy to Mayor Yorty, after she received an anonymous "Muslim threat" by telephone late Friday.

Mrs. Bryant, the first Negro field aide ever appointed by a Los Angeles mayor, received the call in her office at the City Hall shortly before 5 pm. She said a voice told her:

"I'm calling for the Muslim. We're going to get you over the weekend."

Mayor Yorty stated, "If this (threat) is authentic, it is proof that the Muslims are not only an anti-white organization but anti-democratic as well."

After reading the story repeatedly, Frenchy concluded it didn't make sense. Allegedly, the Muslims called a Black woman, told her who they were, and threatened her without explanation. You don't threaten a Black woman to rebuke democracy or promote anti-white sentiment. The caller said nothing about hating white people. The absurdity was astounding.

Once again, Alvaro was correct about the press, specifically the LA Times. *Why is this front-page news unless it was a predicate for something more ominous?* Frenchy's curiosity got the best of him. Ethel Bryant was a prominent woman in the Pacoima community. So, he reached out to Veda, knowing she would have her home phone number.

"Hello, Mrs. Bryant. This is deputy Lionel Grandison from the LA Coroner's office. How are you today?"

"Oh my God. Who's dead?" Mrs. Bryant panicked.

"Oh no, I apologize. This is NOT a next-of-kin call. I wanted to ask you about the death threat you received."

"Oh, thank Goodness. You scared me," she said, exhaling.

"First, let me tell you this is not an official call. I got your number from my mother-in-law, Veda James."

"Oh, Veda! LAPD's finest. How is she doing?"

"She's great. She just transferred from Newton to Foothill Division here in Pacoima. But I wanted to ask you about that call."

"Oh," she said, exasperated. "That. Lord have mercy."

"Why do you say it like that?"

"I'm sorry, no reason. What do you want to know?"

"You told the authorities the caller said, 'I'm calling for the Muslim. We're going to get you over the weekend.' I just want to know how the voice sounded?"

"I'm not sure I understand."

"Did the voice sound Negro?"

"I couldn't tell. It was muffled."

"How was the pronunciation?"

"What do you mean?"

Thinking for a moment, he remembered how Malcolm X enunciated his words.

"Well, did they say Muslim or Moslem?"

"Definitely Moslem. Why do you ask?"

"Non-Muslims say it differently than real Muslims."

"Which is which?"

"Just listen to your boss Yorty say it, then listen to Malcolm X."

"Interesting. I never thought of that."

"Well, thank you, Mrs. Bryant, for your help. Have a good day."

"No problem. Tell Veda I said hello."

That knot in his stomach was returning while the hair on his arms stood up. More questions than answers were brewing through Frenchy's mind. There was a rally coming up next week at Second Baptist Church and then their inquest on Monday the 14th. He felt he needed to slow down his thought process and let things digest while staying level-headed. After all, he had a family to feed. Still, his curiosity to hear Malcolm X speak was growing strong.

His scheduled work hours changed regularly, with the latest netting him the swing shift, which was 4pm until midnight. Two deputies were assigned together, and in a frustrating twist of fate, his partner for the cycle was Goldstein.

Monday started relatively slow, so after going through his current cases, Frenchy began reading the California Eagle, particularly interested in their coverage of Stokes.

The Los Angeles Times and The Valley Times were the leading publications in the area. However, the California Eagle focused more on Negroes and provided a different viewpoint. Their mission statement said:

'The California Eagle stands for complete integration of Negroes into every phase of American life through the democratic process.'

The one drawback, it was only published weekly on Thursdays.

> *California Eagle - May 10, 1962*
> **"Muslims Deny Any Threat to Ethel Bryant"**
>
> The Muslims Saturday rejected out of hand an accusation that one of their members, in an anonymous phone call, had threatened they would "get" Ethyl Bryant, field secretary to Mayor Yorty.

"You sure do read a lot, Grandison," Goldstein commented, interrupting his thought-provoking read.

"Yes, I do."

"That California Eagle is garbage. You should stick with the Times."

"I like reading them all to get everyone's perspective."

"Ahh, a worldly kind of guy. You know what they say about too much knowledge and curiosity?"

"Yes, they say you're smart."

"Nope. It killed the cat."

"What? Knowledge?"

"No, curiosity."

"Is there a difference?"

"Not really, but you better be careful, or they will pull you into the cult."

"I don't believe Muslims are a cult, but I'll be watchful."

Minutely shaking his head, Frenchy returned to reading until his phone rang. It was someone inquiring about the inquest. Clearly, this would be the highest-profile proceeding since his employment at the coroner's office, at least up to that point. The biggest issue was the inadequate size of the room, or so he thought.

"We haven't even put out the press release yet, and folks are trying to get on the list," Frenchy said.

"Who was that?

"Independent Sun News."

"They are one of the good ones. I'll put them on. Did you get a name?"

"We need their press credentials first. They need to come in and fill out the media form."

"Grandison… I believe I'm handling the press. Transfer those calls to me."

"Well, here are some names to add to the list," Frenchy said, handing him the Stokes request.

Looking at the paper, Goldstein frowned, twisted his jaw, and put it on his desk.

"You heard Longhorn. We gotta limit the troublemakers."

"Troublemakers? That's the family of the deceased. We don't want bad press for the coroner's office, do we?"

Snapping the pencil in his hand, Goldstein looked away from Frenchy, displaying a rigid posture. They barely spoke the rest of the shift.

For the next few days, the news continued to mount on both sides. Racial tensions in the community were growing like wildfire. Muslims vehemently denied headlines in the Black media about threats to Yorty's staff member Bryant.

But mainstream did not read Negro papers. They read LA Times and the like, which amplified a different story. It was called a "wild riot" and they referred to Muslims as a "semisecret black supremacy cult with hatred that threatens society." Mayor Yorty was calling on Attorney General Robert Kennedy to label them a 'subversive group' so the city could monitor, confiscate, and use otherwise prohibited resources. Frenchy saw no evidence this was true, yet they continued making people believe it.

The attorney, Brody, called Frenchy daily to ensure they were on the list, and he assured him they were. But while leaving additional names at Goldstein's elegant and organized desk, he saw the inquest log. Shockingly, it omitted Malcolm X and the Stokes family.

Surprised at the blatant disregard, Frenchy was determined to make sure he did not get away with this. So, with only a few minutes before Goldstein returned, he quickly grabbed a blue-ink pen matching the log, adding the five Stoke's names.

Frenchy knew this anal-retentive type would notice any disruption to his workspace. He placed pens by color, stacked papers annoyingly in size order, and drew desk calendar lines with a ruler for all entries. This wasn't normal, and everyone knew it, but no one said anything besides a few harmless jokes. Frenchy wondered if Goldstein's quirks were why he was always on dates with different women and never settled down. His parents owned C & R Clothier, a men's suit and furnishing warehouse with multiple stores throughout California, and were quite wealthy. So he was out of place at a county civil service establishment.

Frenchy made it back to his desk just in time. After Goldstein returned, he looked intensely at his work area like a dog sniffing out a strange odor. Suddenly Frenchy noticed he had left his marker.

"Hey Goldstein, can you toss me my pen? I dropped it over there by your desk."

"Sure," he said, throwing it to him, irritated. "What were you doing over here?"

"Working. What are YOU doing over there?"

"You got jokes," Goldstein flatly mumbled.

"We're all on the same team, right?"

Goldstein scrutinized his desk once again.

"Absolutely."

Saturday didn't arrive soon enough for Frenchy. He looked forward to spending time with Tipy and the kids. He watched her cook a breakfast consisting of grits, bacon, scrambled eggs, and biscuits. With the hickory smell of the bacon sizzling on the stove, Tipy mixed Bisquick in a bowl that always netted a fluffy mouth-watering creation after she baked it. Even though Lonnie and Crystal were running around with their cousins and Lance was in his crib crying, Tipy still took her wifely duties seriously.

"What's new in the paper?" Tipy asked, placing his plate on the table.

"Same old bad news," Frenchy complained, placing the newspaper down. "We haven't had a chance to talk much, but things are really strange at the office right now."

"What's going on?"

"Well, you're not going to believe this, but I spoke with Malcolm X."

"What? Why? Why would you ever talk to him?"

"Why wouldn't I? We have a big case that he's involved in. Did you hear about the police shooting at the temple?"

"It's been on the news, but I didn't pay too much attention. I just know it had something to do with those Moslems."

"It's Muslim."

"Frenchy, we are Christian. Not Moslem or Muslim or whatever. Why do you even care about them?"

"Why does anyone care about anything? A lot is going on here. First, I read in the paper that one bullet killed Stokes. The autopsy report said three, so they are lying about it. Second, the press is making all Black Muslims out to be bad people."

"They ARE bad people!"

"How do you know that, Tipy? How? You don't!"

"Everyone knows that. I do read the paper when I can."

"Which paper? I hate to tell you, but some of them lie."

"They can't lie because they can get sued. Plus, Moslems are anti-police, violent, and hate whites. They're making all Negroes look bad."

"I believe the police killed an innocent man."

"So now you believe all police are bad? Frenchy, Veda works for LAPD. Is she bad too?"

"I don't want to fight with you about this. Your mother is not bad. It's just that I'm seeing things that don't add up. So I'm going to a Malcolm X rally tomorrow to see if I can get some answers."

"Why? This is just making it worse for us all. They need to be quiet and stop poking the bear."

"Guess what? The bear was never asleep. It's our choice if we bury our heads or learn the truth. I was not looking for this. I want to get along with everyone, but they are lying. Police put three bullets in an unarmed man. He had unexplained head injuries; witnesses said the police were kicking them after the shooting, and most importantly, they're lying about everything. How can I ignore this, Tipy? How?"

"I'm not going to tell you what to do. Just think about them," Tipy said, pointing at the kids.

Frenchy paused for a moment. "I am thinking about them."

"Well, then are you thinking about me?"

"Tipy, I have proven to you over and over you are important. I don't know how you can even say that."

"I say that because sometimes your actions don't match up with your words. Let me tell you this. I do not want you going to that Malcolm X thing. I don't. I mean it, Frenchy! Promise me."

Making no attempt to give a definitive answer, Frenchy gripped her in his arms feeling her resist and pull away.

"Don't try to soften me I want you to promise me you won't go," Tipy reiterated.

"I thought you weren't going to tell me what to do? You are contradicting yourself, but fine, Tipy, I won't go. Is that what you want to hear?"

"Thank you," Tipy said, extending her arms and embracing Frenchy with a warm hug.

10 – The Awakening

Despite his promise to Tipy, Frenchy could not resist the allure of Malcolm X and made the risky decision to attend the rally. Second Baptist, the oldest Negro church in Los Angeles, was a leading hub for the Black population. Located along 24th street just west of Central Avenue, Frenchy pulled up to the large rustic building that reminded him of churches he saw in European books. It featured an imposing tower capped with a colossal white cross. Large colonial arches loomed over the main entrance, with stairs on both sides. The rails featured a distinct architectural design.

In Pacoima, there was only one place of worship comparable to this, Guardian Angel, which was built in 1929 and had a large Catholic following. It surprised Frenchy when he discovered how many Blacks attended that church, having always regarded them as Baptists.

There were droves of cars searching for street parking, and Frenchy forecasted this would be big. He saw swarms of journalists with cameras. This raised concerns about the coroner's office discovering he attended a Malcolm X protest rally. They would view him as a traitor, so keeping a low profile was an absolute must.

When he entered the building, he could smell clashes of perfume and cologne as he observed the barrage of people. Upfront, there was a row of Muslims dressed in black suits and ties, seated with Malcolm X behind the podium. Most of the women wore church hats or hijabs and nice dresses. White lights were hanging from the ceiling with rows and rows of seats filled by men and women from Baptist and Muslim denominations. There were about 1200 people in attendance.

The first keynote speaker was Wendell Green, chairman of the Negro Committee for Representative Government, who primarily charged that the LAPD acts like a conquering army in an occupied country when dealing with Negros. However, he made it clear the meeting's purpose was not to inspire an emotional binge.

"We must find a positive program to correct these wrongs," Green said, warming up a crowd ready to hear from the Nation of Islam minister.

When Malcolm X took the podium, he was larger than life. Frenchy had never felt such energy, connection, and unity as when X spoke. Then, he began talking powerfully about self-hatred within the Black race.

"Who taught you to hate the color of your skin? Who taught you to hate the texture of your hair? Who taught you to hate the shape of your nose and the shape of your lips? Who taught you to hate yourself from the top of your head to the soles of your feet? Who taught you to hate your own kind? Who taught you to hate the race that you belong to so much that you don't want to be around each other?"

The crowd all belted out wild cheers, captivated by Malcolm's words, unlike anything Frenchy ever saw or heard before.

"They say we hate because we tell the truth. They say we inflame the Negro. The hell they've been catching for 400 years has inflamed them! We were bought here 400 years ago in chains, and it has been 400 years of undiluted hell. If we don't hate the white man…then you don't know what you're talking about."

Showing a picture of Ronald Stokes' bloody body, Malcolm continued.

"Let us remember that we're not brutalized because we are Baptist. We're not brutalized because we're Methodist. We're not brutalized because we're Muslims. We're not brutalized because we're Catholics. We are brutalized because we're Black people in America."

The crowd rose to their feet with thunderous applause while giving a standing ovation. Frenchy was upright with goosebumps twitching like molehills, a new phenomenon for him. Everyone was touched significantly by Malcolm X's profound words. Every single vowel, verb, noun and adjective struck a core of truth and relatability. Frenchy knew he was changed forever.

The Church's Reverend Henderson spoke last before they voted on a resolution charging police brutality. His concern was keeping his church from being associated with violence like the Muslims.

"With the inflammatory speeches made today, we don't want it said the Muslims ran this meeting. We are not in favor of hating anyone," he said before the vote passed unanimously.

Leaving the Second Baptist Church, Frenchy knew there was knowledge out there for people like him. He had this unexplainable urge to read more Black books and understand history better. Malcolm talked about things he never gave much thought about, but were absolutely and undeniably true. His thoughts drifted back to young Emmit Till and how that murder affected him. Life was like a matrix of knowledge. Either you want to know, or you stay in a bubble of ignorant bliss. Frenchy not only wanted but needed true self-awareness at its core. Yes, he wanted to know.

The morning of the inquest arrived, and people were everywhere. The lobby was a madhouse with press and witnesses waiting to enter the room, which resembled a court but was much smaller. It had a jury box, witness chair, inquest deputy desk, and seats for the onlookers.

Frenchy had Alvaro help with the press forms while working through the limited seat availability. With enough room for only ten media outlets, Goldstein, who procured the list, brought it to Frenchy.

"Here's the press list for the media passes," Goldstein said. "We had to cut it back a great deal."

"Thanks," Frenchy replied.

Looking at the list, Frenchy saw no Black media outlets. He knew he had verified credentials for at least three and put them in Goldstein's box, but somehow they were all omitted. It included only white media outlets, and this was a problem.

"Goldstein, why is there no Negro media?"

"That list went through Curphey. It wasn't my call. We had hundreds of requests. Here's some coffee for you. You just might need it."

"Thanks. But we will need at least one Negro outlet, or it will get ugly."

"What do you suggest we do? Defy Curphey?"

"We do the right thing."

"Look, Grandison, don't be naïve. Malcolm X is here and wants to prosecute the LAPD. Do you really think that's going to happen?"

"Suppressing the media and the facts is a disservice to the truth."

"The only truth is what the LAPD and coroner's office say."

"That doesn't bother you?"

"I just do what I'm told," Goldstein said, walking away towards the inquest room.

Thoughts of how to get at least one Negro media outlet included swirled through Frenchy's mind. It was wrong to exclude them from this procedure altogether. But, unfortunately, he knew more potential problems could still arise.

Entering the Hall of Justice, Malcolm X became the center of attention as the crowd began piling into the room. Goldstein told Brody he could present his questions at the inquest, and Frenchy knew this would be an issue. Unfortunately, they were still playing games, and sure enough, Brody found Frenchy and was quite upset.

"Deputy Grandison."

"Mr. Brody, How are you?"

"Not good. I just spoke to Schwartz and Longhorn. They said the questions had to be submitted three days in advance. The deputy on the phone said to bring them today. So what nonsense are they trying to pull?"

Just then, Malcolm walked over to them.

"Who is in charge here? I want to speak with him. We were told to bring the questions in today. Seven innocent unarmed Black men were shot in cold blood. This inquest should hold those policemen accountable. We are not going to let them cover up what these police officers did."

Tensions were getting heated, and Frenchy knew this would work against the Stokes family. This whole situation seemed like an intentional ploy to incite a radical reaction. Frenchy listened as Malcolm continued his rant. Police officers were present to prevent any escalation, and one walked over after noticing the disruption.

"Keep your voice down."

"You don't tell me what to do. This is a cover-up. It is the police who should be on trial here in Los Angeles." Malcolm said.

"We are going to get rid of all you militants," the officer touted.

Frenchy instinctively knew he needed to intervene.

"Gentlemen, Gentlemen, let's get back to business. All witnesses must report to the inquest room. Anyone with a seating credential, please go to your seat," he said, waving his hands like a referee.

However, reporters in the vicinity also noticed the disruption and circled Malcolm with questions.

"Malcolm. Why are you here?" a LA Times reporter shouted.

"I'm here to get justice," he replied.

"Why did you say cover-up? The reporter continued.

"The people who saw what happened aren't being allowed to testify. Our lawyer is prohibited from submitting any questions. Does it sound like they are trying to get to the truth?"

Having articulated the narrative the office was trying to control, Schwartz came over to Frenchy, sweating profusely and a bit jittery.

"See if you can defuse this situation. If I have to call sheriff deputies, this might get ugly," Schwartz pleaded.

"You want me to clean up Goldstein and Longhorn's mess? No problem," Frenchy said, exasperated. "I'll see what I can do."

Realizing this was an opening to turn this injustice around a bit, he motioned the attorney over. Brody seemed like a logical, empathetic guy, similar to his grandfather. He was in his 50s, with short hair, a clean-shaven face, and a nice suit. Frenchy liked how he spoke slowly and pronounced his words carefully.

"Listen, Mr. Brody, this is a setup. LAPD is already here with itchy trigger fingers, and more sheriff deputies are coming. The inquest will never happen if we don't resolve this right now."

"So what are you suggesting, deputy?"

"Simply this. Give me five questions, and if it's at all possible, I'll get them in. I need you to trust me. This is the only way."

Brody reluctantly looked over at Malcolm, who raised an eyebrow and slightly nodded. He then pulled out his notepad with questions and began circling.

"Here are our questions," Brody said.

"Why are you helping us, Deputy Grandison?" Malcolm asked. "You might lose this Uncle Tom job."

"Maybe so. I saw your speech yesterday, and it made me think. We all must do our part to improve this world for our kids. Now go on back to your seats before they find another excuse."

"We must fight with all we have," Malcolm said.

Frenchy finished up in the lobby and headed inside. He stood next to Schwartz and Goldstein, who were waiting for the proceeding to begin. Longhorn was on the bench, shuffling papers. The jury was all white, with four women clutching their purses tight and three men sitting with vacant facial expressions occupying two rows behind a wooden divider.

Frenchy rewrote the questions on the proper forms before he came inside and was grappling with how to sneak them in. Schwartz had placed them in a small box he was holding that he would give to Longhorn once everything began.

Thinking quickly, Frenchy accidentally knocked the box out of Schwartz's hand. Boom! The noise from the metal hitting the floor echoed throughout the room, and suddenly it was quiet. Embarrassed and stunned, Schwartz found himself rattled, with all eyes focused on him. Smoothly, Frenchy bent down and began picking up the forms carefully and placing his five questions with the rest before handing the box back to Schwartz.

After the Miner disruption, Longhorn called Officer Donald Weese, the cop who shot Ronald Stokes, to the stand.

"What information led you to the building at 56th and Broadway?" Longhorn asked.

"We got a tip from one of our informants that guns were at that location," Weese answered.

"What happened when you got there?"

"These men were unloading something out of the trunk of a car. It looked suspicious, so we ordered them on the ground."

"What happened after you ordered them down?"

"Some of them broke and ran toward the building. Believing there were weapons inside, we defended ourselves and called for backup."

"Did you feel this gave you probable cause for entering the property?"

"Yes, we did."

"What was Ronald Stokes doing when you shot him?"

"He came out of the Temple door with about two dozen others chanting in Arabic. I shouted to freeze, but they kept coming and struck my partner in the head with a five-gallon water bottle."

"Then what happened?"

"I felt someone get a chokehold on me from behind, and it was Stokes. My knees buckled, and when I struggled to my feet, I saw Stokes coming at me again with hands stretched out in a choking gesture. It was then I shot him," he said with a tense emotionless tone.

"How far was he from you?"

"Five or six feet."

Feeling a nauseous barrage following a quick flow of blood to the brain, Frenchy was stunned. The story made no sense. If he supposedly had the officer in a chokehold from behind, he would not have been 5 or 6 feet away. They didn't even mention the abrasions from the reported kicking after the shooting. This version of events smelled to high hell. Nothing added up. Frenchy then noticed a change in the tone of the questions.

"Did you find any illegal weapons on the premises or on any of the suspects?"

"No. They probably moved them before we got there."

"Can you explain why the three injured men were… shot?" Longhorn raised his eyebrows while pausing on the last word.

"They were attacking my partner, so I picked them off one by one," he described in a steel monotone demeanor.

"When did you discover these men were unar…." Longhorn paused, shuffling through the cards. "Never mind. I think we're through with the questions."

Longhorn viciously hit the gavel on the table, abruptly ending that portion, clearly frustrated. Eleven other officers testified, and their stories painted an unrealistic picture of what happened that night but were consistent with Weese's version. Longhorn had no intentions of calling the Muslim witnesses to testify, which infuriated Malcolm. All the Negros were in the back of the room when Malcolm and eight others suddenly got up and stormed out as Longhorn sent the jury to deliberate. It took them half an hour to find the murder justified.

After exiting the inquest room, Frenchy noticed Attorney Brody nearby with a sullen face.

"I'm sorry about the way things turned out," Frenchy said.

"Well, we all know how the system works. By the way, Malcolm told me to give you a message."

"What is that?"

"He said to tell you they appreciated all your help. And I do too."

"I was just doing the right thing. Can I ask you a question?"

"Sure."

"What really happened that night at Muhammad's Temple of Islam #27?"

Brody's expression transformed into a frown, as he prepared to answer.

"The police ordered those brothers out of their masjid then shot them in cold blood. Everything you heard in there was a lie except for one thing. They didn't find a single weapon."

That day Frenchy left feeling powerless and somewhat disillusioned. The forces were too big, the lies coordinated, and the target clear. Negroes. *How could this machine of cops, district attorneys, mayor, coroner's office, and media ever be challenged?*

For the first time in his life, Frenchy saw a parallel between the plight of slavery, where many had no place to run, and today, a system of deception with invisible shackles just as perilous. It ties your foot with a chain, expecting you to run a race, and then devilishly moves the finish line. This was too much emotion for one day.

Laying in the jail bunk, Frenchy realized how much the Stokes case had changed him. Despite not fully understanding what had unfolded during that time, the optimism he once had as a hopeful kid of a racially integrated society had vanished. By design, whites never created the system for Black people. Stokes, and now this cell was proof.

As he plucked the dirt from his fingernail, he realized he needed a clipper. It made him think about Tipy, who always groomed him, and the family he missed so much. He wondered if he should have paid closer attention to the signs that landed him here.

The problem at large was his love for the job. The position of Deputy Coroner's Aide was his highest honor. But he had no idea what was buried underneath and that his passion would ultimately lead to his doom.

~~~~~~~~~~

Thoughts of getting fired plagued Frenchy's mind because of adding those questions at the inquest. It was the riskiest thing he had ever done. The way Longhorn slammed down the gavel with immense anger was frightening. The devil's rage plummeted upon him after his charade hit a snag. His eyes echoed hollowness, with Lucifer tucked away somewhere deep inside. It was downright spooky.

Heading home, Frenchy would also have to deal with Tipy, who was furious with him for attending the rally on Sunday. What made perfect sense to Frenchy made him 'hero to zero' overnight. They were on two opposite ends of the spectrum regarding the
~~~~~~~~~~

complexities of race. Veda was in law enforcement, and Tipy grew up going to police picnics and socializing with detectives. He understood the conflict because her family was thoroughly indoctrinated in white culture, something he thought briefly was happening to him. After all, he relished being part of an office environment and receiving dignity and respect. Most Black men didn't have that.

After leaving the office, he decided that a drink or two was in order. Frenchy felt the moment's weight expanding inside but knew he still worked better under pressure. Maybe some cards with Boppie and his friends would deflect his thoughts. Being on swing shift, he could party all night if need be.

Boppie, Grover, Pudgy, and Love were ready, willing, and able to come over for a proverbial poker game. Frenchy picked up some cigars and a bottle of Harvey's Bristol Crème, one of his favorites. Once Frenchy got home, it didn't take long for everyone to congregate in his garage. There was a card table, radio, and a huge James Bond 007 "Dr. No" poster tacked on the wood beams to set the vibe. Bond had captured everyone's attention, and the fellas found the 007-character cool and relatable.

Around 2 am, everyone, dispersed, and Frenchy had to face the music with Tipy. Knowing he could not quickly resolve this issue, how to approach it was the key. If only she could hear Malcolm's words and understand the dynamics of this country's history. More importantly, Blacks were taught to believe dark is ugly, and just because they are both fair-skinned, they are still Negro and should embrace fighting for racial justice. Somehow, he knew convincing her would be nearly impossible and a battle he probably could not win.

When he entered the room, she peacefully slept with a cute soft snore, like a Tweety bird. Feeling a little buzzed from the wine, he watched her for a few minutes until suddenly, a hysterical whaling sound raged from the other room, waking her up.

"Frenchy, why are you just staring at me?"

"Can't I look at my wife?"

"It seems a little strange," she said, getting out of bed. "Is everyone gone?"

"Yes."

The screams got more intense, so Tipy rushed out. Frenchy began peeling off his clothes and got into his flannel pants and a t-shirt. He put his head on the pillow and drifted off before he could talk to Tipy.

When morning arrived, he awoke to the sweet bread-like smell of buttermilk pancakes blended with Farmer John sausage links. Tipy never let him down with her cooking, and because of her breakfasts, he didn't mind swing shift so much. Casually, he picked up the paper to see what they wrote about the inquest.

> *Citizens News – May 15, 1962*
> **Shooting of Muslim Held Justifiable**
> A Coroner's jury says the police shooting of a black Muslim in a riot April 27 was justifiable homicide.

Although he knew the verdict, the headline sparked a touch of anger still burning in his body. Deciding not to read the article, he wanted to put the case behind him and get back to work.

The office was bustling when Frenchy arrived. There was a case involving two white 6-year-old girls that died after getting locked inside a refrigerator in their home on April 23. Ruled a double-sex homicide by Curphey, Frenchy had already closed the file and was confused why it was sitting on his desk.

"Alvaro!"

"Si, Que Paso?"

"Why is the Hanna/Cram file on my desk?"

"No se. I don't know. Curphey put some stuff on your desk. Maybe it was him."

"Alright, thanks."

Immediately Frenchy was on guard that Curphey was lurking around his desk. 'Here we go,' he thought. Just then, his phone rang.

"Deputy Grandison."

"Grandison, can you come to my office?"

"Sure, Dr. Curphey. Be right there."

He just knew he was about to get fired after the inquest stunt. Walking down the hall seemed eerier than usual as Frenchy prepared himself to face the consequences of yesterday.

"Grandison, an issue has come to my attention, and I need to speak to you about it."

"What is that, sir?"

"We have a case that has an incorrect ruling. The medical examiner was wrong."

"How could the doctor get that wrong?" Frenchy asked.

"That doesn't matter. We need to fix it."

"I don't understand."

"The manner of death and cause need to change, and we need to explain it."

Perplexed, Frenchy assumed he was talking about Stokes, which was Curphey's case, but the request didn't make sense.

"Sir, Stokes was your case."

"Stokes? I'm talking about the Hanna/Cram murder. New details have emerged proving it was accidental, not a murder."

"The report said the girls were sexually molested, beaten, and stuffed into the refrigerator. Are you saying that didn't happen?"

"It looks that way. A witness came forward claiming they saw the girls climb into the icebox."

"You're asking me to reopen the case and change the information?"

"Yes."

"Alright. How do I explain that huge discrepancy?"

"We're issuing a press release, and I need you to be able to answer questions. You need to reaffirm we conducted a comprehensive and exhaustive investigation and now believe the girls themselves may have been responsible. Their actual injuries apparently were minor when they occurred, then aggravated by the confinement of the two girls in the refrigerator."

"O…kay," Frenchy said, thinking that was a huge stretch.

"There's more. The temperature reached a high degree while they were inside, which created the impression of more serious damage than actually occurred. We have ruled out any man's participation and believe the bruises were caused by the pressure of one girl against the other. Here is the press release for your reference."

"That's a mouthful, but I will relay if anyone asks me."

That meeting solidified the incompetence and deceit of the coroner's office. Frenchy knew that Curphey's explanation was nearly impossible. How do you accidentally deem something a homicide involving sexual molestation in a case like this? *Why would anyone do that?* There was no way it was an honest error; of that, he was sure. Nevertheless, Curphey was twisting like a pretzel and delegating the dirty work.

Those girls lived in the city of San Fernando, which bordered Pacoima. Frenchy's thought process haunted him for thinking this could have been a more devious and sinister intentional act. The only reason to deem this a murder is that you want a suspect. There is no other reason. There was no monetary advantage since insurance was not involved. *Could they be so conniving to potentially set up an innocent Black or Mexican for murder? Was he overthinking?* The world could not be that cruel, but the implications of this case seemed evil, more than Frenchy could comprehend. He concluded the power of the coroner's office was limitless, and there was nothing they could not do. The bottom line is Curphey was scum, dangerous scum.

Nothing else seemed to come from the Stokes case in the coroner's office. Everyone was uncharacteristically quiet about it. The Grand Jury was now investigating, and it would likely end with the same results. While in the file room, he felt compelled to ask Alvaro.

"Hey, hombre. What's the word around here? No one is talking."

Alvaro began laughing and put his arm around Frenchy.

"Amigo, they are talking plenty. Just not to you."

"What are they saying?"

"Longhorn wanted you fired, but of all people, Curphey told him no."

"Serious?"

"Si. He said you were doing a good job."

"Ha. I wish I could say the same about him. Guess I'm lucky to still be here–but it's hard to believe he likes me."

"Compadre, do not feel so lucky, and never let your guard down around any of these men. None of them. Nada."

Frenchy knew Alvaro kept it real and appreciated his candor.

* * *

One of the months Frenchy always looked forward to was July. Having children made him see things through a magical lens he never knew existed. Whereas watching the kids open presents on Christmas morning was exhilarating, the amazement of fireworks in their eyes on the fourth was equally rewarding.

Last year was tough because they made the massive mistake of heading to San Fernando Park too early. As a result, the kids did not take their naps and had severe meltdowns. By the time the fireworks show started, they were insanely cranky. But the mood quickly changed when the spiraling, blazing lights appeared in the sky. The amazement in their eyes allowed Frenchy to feel immense joy through his two and three-year-old offspring's reaction.

This year he decided to prep Tipy so they could head to the festivities when he got home.

"Hey, babe."

"Hi, sweetie, how's work?"

"Same ole, same ole. I just wanted to remind you to make sure the kids take their naps."

"Crystal is out like a light, and Lonnie is fighting it. Lance slept all morning. He's sitting up now, but tiring out."

"Well, I'm getting off early. The office is closed for the holiday, but someone still had to be here. So, I should be home by 3:30 ish."

"Good. Everyone should be at the park by the time we arrive. Are we going to get some sparklers from San Fernando?"

"I gave Boppie some money to pick us up a pack."

"Ok. We'll be ready when you get here."

Like clockwork, Frenchy arrived at the house as promised, and everyone was ready. Tipy had the kids dressed nicely, and she was beautiful as ever. The hot July day had begun to cool off, and they piled in and headed for the park.

Both sides of the family were there. The redolent air was filled with the aroma of barbecue chicken and ribs, along with the chatter of women arranging platters on the picnic tables.

The men played cards and reminisced about high school while kids scattered everywhere. Most of Frenchy and Tipy's friends married shortly after them, and they all had children the same age.

Boppie, Grover, Love, and Pudgy had set up a card table and made a spot for Frenchy when he arrived. Dennis and Printes, who had just graduated high school, scouted out the females with their hormones raging.

"Hey Den, you want in on this game?" Frenchy asked.

"You know I'm not a card person. I brought my guitar to play for all these foxy girls," Dennis replied.

"Do you play guitar too, Printes?"

"Naw, I just listen and check out the chicks drooling over Dennis and settle for his leftovers."

"What do you cats plan to do now that you're out of high school?" Frenchy asked.

"Air Force for me," Printes bragged.

"Navy," Dennis said.

"Wow, both you playboys are going to work for Uncle Sam? There aren't many ladies there. You two know that, right?"

"We both want our own pads. GI is the best way to go."

"I see."

As the sun began to set, Frenchy looked for Tipy, who had her hands full. She had spread out a blanket and was hitting a hammer and peg set for Crystal with Lance in her lap. Frenchy left the card game to join them.

"I was going to make your plate, but I don't have extra hands," Tipy smiled.

"How about I make yours?"

"I would love that, my handsome prince."

"You're amazing, Tipy. I don't know if I tell you enough."

"You don't," she snickered.

"Be right back."

After they ate, everyone settled down to watch the fireworks. Frenchy lit a sparkler for Lonnie, who was incensed when he saw all the other kids with one. It burned slowly, emitting sparks with bright, intense color flames. Copying the other kids, Lonnie twirled it in circles until it went out.

Thinking Crystal would enjoy it, he tried to hand her a lit one crackling with gold sparks. She immediately ran to Tipy, somewhat afraid. Then a big pop shook the park, and red, orange, and green formations spread across the sky. Almost immediately after, a bigger, brighter, colorful, dazzling burst fanned over the sky in a rhythmic motion. Lonnie and Crystal froze in place, mouths wide open, looking with amazement.

"Ooooh," came out of both mouths.

Tipy and Frenchy's eyes met with a unifying gleam, capping the moment, as the fireworks extravaganza went on for nearly thirty minutes. The finale had multiple explosions releasing a smell of gunpowder throughout the park, ending in darkness and complete silence. A few seconds later, clapping, whistles, and cheers planked the park.

They bid their farewells to everyone and headed home feeling complete. All the young ones were exhausted and went instantly to sleep. Frenchy lit a candle in the bedroom and poured them a glass of wine. It was a perfect holiday for the Grandison family.

PHOTOS

Frenchy joined the Boy Scouts of America as a youth during the early 50s. His step-grandfather, U.S. Army vet. Thomas Williams attended meetings with him.

Frenchy (age 12), Mo, Ora (Nana), and Dennis at the new Pacoima house on Filmore St in 1952

Tipy, in pigtails at age 12, in front of her home on Louvre St in Pacoima. Frenchy thought she was the most beautiful girl in the world

Tipy (right), Johnny (Skip), and Betty hanging out at the Sorrell's home on Weidner Ave in Pacoima

Frenchy and Tipy's prom picture at San Fernando High in 1957

January 10, 1959, Frenchy and Tipy were married at the First United Methodist Church of San Fernando

Frenchy's groomsman were Love, Dennis, Scratch, and Boppie (front)

Frenchy's and Tipy wave goodbye to the guests

Frenchy and Tipy on vacation during her second pregnancy, with his mother Ora (right) joining them

Frenchy and first-born son, Lonnie, in 1960

Frenchy enjoys Easter Sunday at Mo's house with Lonnie and baby Crystal in 1962

Tony, Lonnie, Crystal, and Danny terrorize the house on Montford Street

Ora (Nana) holding baby Lance, giving Tipy a break, in 1962

1962 Los Angeles County Coroner's Inquest - Malcolm X (center) sits with Ronald Stokes' wife and Attorney Charles Brody

6 Muslim men were shot, then handcuffed, after exiting their masjid including Ronald T. Stokes who was killed

13 – The Connection

On Sunday, August 5th, Frenchy arrived at the office early because there was no weekend traffic. Forecast to be a double-digit hot day, Frenchy liked the slightly cooler city temperatures more than the valley, which was scorching all summer long. Although he was used to it, there were never enough fans to contain the sweat his body created.

Schwartz oversaw assigning cases and had worked for the coroner's office for 25 years. He never mentioned the Stokes case to Frenchy in the three months since it happened, and things seemed business as usual. There were about ten cases from the previous night, but Schwartz greeted Frenchy as soon as he arrived.

"There's a hot and very high-profile case that I want you to handle," Schwartz said urgently.

"Sure, and good morning to you too," Frenchy said, laughing as he looked at the brightly lit-up phone lines. "I guess this is going to be a busy day."

Frenchy looked at the high-priority paperwork that Schwartz mentioned while sitting at his desk. The name Marilyn Monroe leaped off the page like a frog barreling towards him. His jaw dropped in disbelief that Schwartz assigned him this case instead of golden child Goldstein or taking it himself. Frenchy knew he handled the press and public exceptionally well, but a veteran would have been more appropriate. Nonetheless, he took charge with the tenacity this case required.

"Hey, Goldstein. Marilyn Monroe died last night. Holy cow!"

Being on a phone call, Goldstein didn't immediately respond. The police notes indicated a drug overdose and that 20th Century Fox Studio signed a release for Marilyn's body. However, Frenchy knew they couldn't do that without a family member or approval from the coroner's office. Goldstein hung up the phone and gave Frenchy an odd look.

"Did you read my notes?"

"Yes, but I don't see who authorized the body's release. Who was the next of kin? I don't see any name."

"20th Century Fox said Westwood Mortuary has a pre-need agreement, and they have legal authority."

"Was that confirmed?"

"I don't know," Goldstein said, irritated. "LAPD and the biggest studio in the world are involved. So why would they lie?"

Rolling his eyes and shrugging his shoulders, Frenchy said each word definitively. "Why would they?"

Frenchy immediately began dialing the number on the paper, which indicated it was to Marilyn's house.

"Sergeant Byron speaking."

"Hi, I'm Deputy Grandison from the coroner's office. I need to speak with the police official in charge."

"You're speaking with him. I'm Sgt. Robert Byron."

"Hi, Sergeant Byron. I'm trying to verify authorization for release of Monroe's body."

"Um, that's no longer necessary. Westwood Mortuary just took it."

"On whose authority?"

"Her friend Peter Lawford, and 20th Century Fox."

"Well, who is the next of kin or the person responsible for her estate?"

"The only information we have about a next of kin is her mother, Gladys. However, she is currently in a sanitarium and unable to assume responsibility. But the studio said it had an agreement."

"Did you verify it?"

"There was no need. We believe them to be credible."

"Sgt. Byron, can you hold on just a moment."

In a death such as this, California State Law prohibits the release of a body without next of kin authorization and, or release from the coroner's office. This was not good, Frenchy analyzed. The police were handling it entirely wrong.

"Sgt. Byron, I'm going to call the Mortuary and let them know I'm sending a deputy over there to retrieve the body."

"Why are you doing that?" the Sergeant exploded.

"You should never have released that body without our authorization. In this type of death, under these circumstances, the law says the coroner's office takes possession of the remains."

"You know, some people won't be happy about this."

"I'm sorry, there's nothing I can do about that, Sergeant. I'm dispatching a coroner's unit now."

Immediately Frenchy called the backroom, and Deputy Danbacker answered. He was in his late 30s with a thick Irish accent and curly black hair and was generally reliable.

"Danbacker, I need you to pick up a body. The deceased is Marilyn Monroe."

"Who? You're joking, right?"

"No, I'm not. She's over at Westwood Mortuary."

"Roger that."

The next call was to Westwood Mortuary to fix this debacle.

"This is Deputy Grandison from the coroner's office. Can I speak to someone in charge, please?"

"One moment."

"Hello, how can I help you?"

"Yes, this is the LA County Coroner's Office, and you have a body in route to your facility without proper authorization. So we are sending our guys over to pick it up."

"Is this for Marilyn Monroe?"

"Yes, it is."

"We have pre-need…."

"Sir, that is only for funeral arrangements. The body's removal was against state law. We're dealing with a high-profile case, and her body must be authorized for release by us."

"But …"

"You, of all people, know the law. This is not a debate, sir."

"Alright," the mortician said, obviously caught off-guard.

Rubbing his head, Frenchy realized things were moving extremely fast. Then, Alvaro walked over with a half-smile.

"This is loco," he squinted, pointing to the lights on the receiver. "All these calls are about Marilyn Monroe. Television stations and newspapers everywhere want us to confirm her death."

"Alright, Alvaro. I know you worked graveyard, but I need your help today."

"No problem."

One by one, Frenchy started taking the calls. Some were from London, Italy, and France, wanting to know if it was suicide. From the beginning, detectives seemed to push that theory without toxicology reports or an autopsy. That, in itself, was bizarre and suspicious.

Fox Studios issued a press release and held a press conference describing her death as a suicide, and the body was still warm. The studio, mortuary, and police actions eerily reminded him of Kovacs' case, where he later discovered insurance money was involved. He never connected the dots with Reeves, but the association with a big Hollywood studio was beyond coincidental. This case was already following a similar path.

An hour later, Danbacker arrived back from the scene.

"It was like a zoo at the Mortuary. The press was everywhere.

"Did they have any information on a next of kin?"

"She has a mother alive in a sanitarium but no kids or family members. Representatives from the Studio couldn't produce any document that authorized them to handle her affairs. But clearly, they wanted to control her body."

"Where did you put it?"

"Downstairs in room 1. I've been doing this for a while. If you ask me, it looks like her death occurred much earlier than reported. She's been dead for a while."

"I need you to do something else. Head over to her house and get all information regarding recent prescriptions and take every pill container into custody. And find out if any next of kin showed up."

"You got it."

"Also, search the house for any personal items that may contain helpful information and see if there was a suicide note. Her address is 12305 Fifth Helena Dr. in Brentwood. You'll be contacting Sergeant Byron."

"How nice. I get to see where the Hollywood stars live."

"Well, no sightseeing. Get back soon as possible."

After Danbacker departed, Frenchy decided to walk over to the dimly lit morgue. Marilyn's body was on the gurney, partially covered, so he pulled the sheet back to peek. Her body was naked with bruises while she lay there pale, cold, and stiff.

The sound of silence resonated while standing alone in this depressing room, a seemingly surreal moment. She was such a beautiful Hollywood starlet and only 36 years old. He then gently replaced the sheet as he found it and exited.

While filling out the forms to process Marilyn's body, Danbacker returned from the star's home.

"Here's what I retrieved, but there wasn't much," Danbacker said, placing a box of Marilyn's personal property on the desk.

"I took possession of about 15 prescription pill bottles, which were all empty, a few papers, some receipts, and a purse containing a small wallet and some kind of notebook underneath. Here you go."

"Was there a suicide note?"

"Nope. But someone had forcibly opened a file cabinet containing some papers. The housekeeper, Eunice Murray, said there was no will anywhere."

"Thanks, Danbacker."

Frenchy began looking through Marilyn's property. He sorted through the empty pill containers and unfolded a piece of paper that appeared to be a press release. He put it down and picked up the purse. Inside the bag was a small wallet, and underneath, a little red book. He placed the handbag down and began flipping through the pages.

"This is for all the people who ever called me a dumb blond. I may be insecure, but not stupid. I only want to twinkle."

Looking intently through the passages, he realized this diary was her life in her own words. But some keywords stood out and were alarming. FBI, Bay of Pigs, Jimmy Hoffa, and the president of the United States.

Goldstein walked up from behind and placed his hand on Frenchy's shoulder, making him uncharacteristically jump and instinctively snap the book closed.

"Planning on being here all night?"

"Naw. Wrapping things up now. It's been a long day."

"What's that you have?" Goldstein queried.

"Nothing. Just looking through some items, trying to find her family. But it's time to get out of here. Hey Goldstein, you think it's possible that Monroe's case is something more than a suicide?"

"I don't know. Why are you asking?"

"I was just wondering. Everyone seems so convinced. It seems like a rush to judgment."

"Well, stories have circulated about her problems for years. If you believe the tabloids, she has attempted to kill herself before."

"You sound skeptical."

"I've heard rumors that Marilyn was involved with some very powerful people, and as you know, where there's smoke, usually there's fire. But nobody has seen any actual proof."

Flashes of what he had just read exploded in Frenchy's mind, wondering if he should mention this to Goldstein.

"Yes, it can get hard to know what or who to believe. I only heard about her singing for President Kennedy's birthday. Other than her movies, that's about it."

"There's a lot you don't know, young man. But you will learn soon enough. Well, goodnight."

"Good night."

The swing shift crew had arrived, so Frenchy went to lock up her belongings. He looked at this secret diary, intrigued, curious, and longing desperately to read more. The significance of the words on the page beckoned him like an itch demanding to be scratched and not ignored. This would be hard to forget. Placing it down, he slowly began to turn the lock, then Goldstein's rumors about Marilyn rang loudly in his ears. He quickly grabbed the book and tucked it into his jacket, knowing it was against the rules. *After all, the next of kin was still needed, right?*

When Frenchy got home, dinner was ready as usual. The kids ran around like wild animals, and the adults watched the evening news. The phone was piercingly ringing when Joyce answered.

"Hello," he could hear her say. "He just got home. He's going to eat dinner, then he can call you back."

"Who was that, Joyce?" Frenchy curiously asked.

"Let me tell you. This phone has been ringing all day. They want to know about Marilyn. Heck, I want to know too. Did you see her body?"

"Joycie!" Boppie chastised. "Why would you ask that?"

"I want to know, too," Tipy chimed in.

"It's been insane. So in answer to your question, yes, I saw the body, but that's all I want to say about it except this is the craziest mess ever."

"That's it?" Joyce said. "We've been waiting all day. Give us a little more."

"All I can say is her body came into the morgue, nothing has been determined about the manner of death, and everyone in the world wants to know, including myself. But here's what's really a gas, her case was assigned to me."

Tipy froze with wide eyes, "Really, Frenchy? You oversee the Marilyn Monroe case? Seriously?"

"Yes."

Putting her hands over her mouth, Tipy continued.

"Let me get this straight. My husband is in charge of the Marilyn Monroe death?"

"Yes, Tipy. Now can I get something to eat. It's been a long day and I'd like to lie down?"

After eating, Frenchy glanced at the notepad on the counter with all the messages. He slightly rolled his eyes and then rubbed his face with both hands. With a deep exhale, he headed toward the bedroom. He had to read that red book.

When Tipy came into the room, Frenchy was reading intensely. He glanced up, noticing how she stayed looking good no matter what her day endured. She kissed him on the cheek, smelling like Este Lauder's youth dew fragrance, her hair in a flip, and a soft, friendly smile on her face.

"I thought you were going to rest. Are you okay, sweetie?" Tipy lovingly asked.

"It was rough today. Really rough."

"Well, that would be expected with a death like Marilyn Monroe."

"It's worse than that. I'm not convinced she committed suicide, but the police, Curphey, and Fox Studios say it was. Tipy, they are forcing it without fully investigating the facts. I don't know one way or the other, but here we go with lies one more time."

"You mean you're not used to it yet?"

"Actually, I am, but there's more."

"What? Don't tell me she was murdered?" Tipy said jokingly.

"I don't know, but I have her diary. It says some shocking stuff."

"What? You have her diary? You have Marilyn Monroe's diary?"

"Quiet!" Frenchy said, shushing her.

"No one can hear us. What's in it?"

"Tipy, you cannot share this with anyone. I can get in trouble for bringing this home. You're a gossiper, but this must stay between us."

"Not even my mother?"

"Especially your mother."

"Alright, what is in it?" Tipy said, rolling her eyes, knowing deep inside keeping this secret would be next to impossible.

Frenchy began reading, slowly enunciating each written word.

"The FBI wanted me to do something for America. They sent Iron Bob to ask me if Arthur was a Communist. When I told him we weren't that close, he laughed and said you could get closer. He told me I should talk to Paula."

"That sounds like gibberish to me. What do you think that means? Whose Iron Bob or Paula?" Tipy queried.

"I don't know yet. But it gets better."

"The best day of my life. I met Jack at Peter's house. He was introduced as Senator John Kennedy and the next President of the United States. I wanted to stay calm, but he was so exciting. His confidence, intelligence, and charm struck me. It lit a fire. We started seeing each other."

"Got to see Jack every time he came to New York City. I was close to Arthur and working regularly too. I was with the next President of the United States, and we made violent love."

"Frenchy! She wrote about the Kennedys. Oh my gosh! She was sleeping with him! This is better than 'As the World Turns.'"

"There is so much here. Some of this concerns the country."

"The spy boys were really serious about killing Castro. Big Jim and Eduardo were actually involved in the Bay of Pigs. Jack never let them forget about it."

"The war against communism tore our industry apart. I'm sorry they used me to get him."

"Hum. I have no idea what she's talking about, but communism is bad, right? What are you writing?" Tipy asked.

"I'm taking notes. I must return this tomorrow and pray no one sees me."

"I'm still stuck on Marilyn sleeping with the President. I wonder if Jackie knew?"

"Tipy. This is not one of your soap opera stories. It's real."

"I know it's not a soap, but it's so interesting. Who would have thought?"

"Let's go to bed, honey. I'm going to have a long day tomorrow. But check this out:

"Hollywood was such a crazy place. It didn't matter how many movies I made, the studios still treated me like I was nothing."

"Wow!" Tipy rumbled with eclectic eyes, amazed that her husband had a connection with the most famous woman in the world.

Heading to work on day two of the Marilyn saga, Frenchy listened to morning news on the radio as usual. The only discussion was Marilyn Monroe's death on every station. Newsstands were flagging cars and pedestrians pushing the morning edition for a quick sale.

"Get your paper here! Marilyn Monroe dead from suicide."

Not knowing what to expect, he engaged in a fast-paced stride from the parking lot, mentally preparing himself for pandemonium with the goal of staying focused.

As suspected, inside the office, the feeling was that of the New York Stock exchange with people galivanting around at a frantic pace. Folks were at the counter wondering if Monroe's body was there, anxious to get any information about this famous actress they could. Marilyn's death had consumed the world.

Before speaking to anyone, Frenchy jetted to the property room and discretely returned the diary. Upon heading back, he stopped by Schwartz to ask for any updates, who rambled off a stream of peculiar happenings in his typical civil service-style voice.

"There were two men here at about six this morning searching for you. They didn't identify themselves, but some of the guys from downstairs said they were Secret Service agents. They were shuffling through papers on your desk and asking for details about her property. Any idea what they might be looking for?" Schwartz asked.

"All my files are right on the desk, and her property is locked up. I have no idea."

With his mind wondering if the diary was the object of their search, a deep concern pulsated as he rubbed his lips together. According to Danbacker, many people were at her house, and someone appeared to have rummaged through her file cabinet. But clearly, they didn't find what they were looking for, and after what he read last night, the logical answer was the diary. One question plaguing him was how Danbacker got it and not them.

"Hey, Danbacker. How are you today?" he asked after dialing his extension.

"I'm grand, and you?"

"I'm hanging in there. It's pretty insane. So let me ask you, where exactly did you find this diary?"

"It was on her closet floor in a bag."

"Did it look like anyone searched in there?"

"That's hard to say. It was a mess. I don't know if she kept it that way or if someone ransacked it. I just know from experience to check inside old purses."

"What did her room look like?"

"It was pretty messy but smelled like cleanser."

"Cleanser? That's strange. I wonder who cleaned up?" Frenchy said, scratching his head.

Needing more details about Marilyn, Frenchy decided to pick the brain of the one person who seemed to know a lot.

"So, Goldstein, what else can you tell me about Ms. Monroe?"

"You got all day?" he laughed.

"I need a crash course, and you seem to know a little about everything."

"Well, she was married to baseball legend Joe DiMaggio and playwright Arthur Miller, but I don't know if she was legally divorced. She signed a new contract with 20th Century Fox in 1955. They were furious when she left the set to sing for Kennedy at that fundraiser in New York a few months back."

"What broke up her and DiMaggio?"

"Well," he said with a chuckle. "Rumor has it, her antics with her dress blowing in the air in front of everyone was the final straw. Joe was extremely upset over her sexualizing herself."

"I can imagine. It would be hard seeing my wife like that. Sounds complicated."

"And that's not even half of it."

After making a quick restroom visit, Frenchy returned only to find a note from Curphey wanting to speak with him. *Ugh, the dreaded office.* In addition, the toxicology lab wanted more information from the physicians regarding prescription label discrepancies on the pill bottles. *Take a deep breath, Frenchy* thought.

Despite making the toilsome journey to Curphey's office countless times, traipsing down the corridor still resembled the feel of a horror movie, and today it felt magnified. He sat in Curphey's office, preparing for a lashing from his A-moral boss.

"Hope you realize the kind of pressure you put on this office with your rash decisions."

"Excuse me, sir?"

"This case shouldn't have been difficult because it was an obvious suicide. Now, everybody is breathing down my neck for information, and I don't need this crap! I told you before about questioning our authorities."

"Sir, I'm following the law. The mortuary or the studio had no verifiable rights to the body's release."

"Well, because of you, I have to take this step. I'm assigning the Suicide Investigation Team to the case, so get them anything they need. Anything! This case MUST come to a quick conclusion, understand?"

"Is there going to be an inquest?"

"No!" he snapped brutally, sending an indescribable disdain down Frenchy's spine.

Frenchy wondered why he always felt sucker punched whenever in Curphey's presence. According to Alvaro's spying, this man was supposed to be the one who defended him. Yet Frenchy felt like an abused child trying to get praise from a parent, which he was positive would never happen. Undoubtedly, Curphey was a cancer metastasizing in front of his eyes.

Leaving the office, he noticed two FBI agents waiting outside. He nodded, continuing to think this was a nightmare and, even worse, only the beginning.

Before Frenchy could close this out, he had to get all the official findings. The toxicology report would come from Dr.

Ralph Abernathy, who oversaw the Medical Department. The police report should be typed-up soon, but he couldn't do anything to speed things up besides be a thorn in their side. The autopsy was still pending too. Frenchy sat at his desk, still reeling from Curphey, when Alvaro appeared.

"You look like someone shot your dog," Alvaro commented.

"If you only knew."

"I have something for you."

"What is it?"

"The preliminary toxicology reports. Just what you wanted."

"'Perfect. Thanks, amigo."

Looking carefully at the report, Frenchy was baffled. *No poison in the stomach.*

"Did you confirm this?"

"Sure did. I double-checked with Abernathy. He said he took her blood samples and found no poison or traces of other medication that Marilyn could have swallowed to contribute to her death. They're ordering microscopic tests that will reveal more. We need to send them the list of prescription containers we recovered. Should we log them?"

"Let's do that right now. Go get them from the property safe."

"No problemo."

Staring at the report, Frenchy realized this would be a setback for Curphey. Ruling her death a suicide would be nearly impossible if this finding held. It would have to be accidental, undetermined, or homicide. Immersed in his thoughts, Goldstein waved at Frenchy to get his attention after hanging up the phone.

"Grandison, I talked to Marilyn's lawyer. He said there might be a will, but he didn't create it."

"How can we get ahold of it?"

"We need to check with her business manager. Her name is um…." Goldstein looked down at his notes. "Inez Melson."

"That would be great. A will identifying someone to handle her affairs would solve all my problems."

"You know there's a funny rumor going around that Robert Kennedy was in town the night she died and may have been at her home. The word is she was planning a press conference. That's crazy, right?"

"Yeah, crazy," Frenchy said, creasing his forehead lines.

"How's everything going with the case?"

"I just got the toxicology report."

"Yeah, the preliminary said no poison."

"You know, that rules out suicide."

"We'll see," Goldstein smugly said.

After that conversation, Goldstein departed the room, leaving Frenchy to reflect on what he had read about Robert Kennedy and the press conference. He knew tensions had flared with Marilyn and thought about the diary entries.

"Bobby was really mad. Acted crazy and searched all my stuff. Told him it's mine. I'll never let him have it."

"Bobby came back with Peter. Shook me until I was dizzy and threw me on the bed. Should call the doctor...."

Diving into deep concern, Frenchy drew in a long bottomless breath. This was entirely out of his league. *Would it be better if someone else discovered the contents of her diary?*

Unexpectantly, Alvaro's voice jolted him from his thoughts.

"Here are the containers."

Frenchy removed all the pill bottles and her purse, noticing the diary was still inside. He shuffled through the papers and found the flyer.

Press Release

Subject: Marilyn Monroe Reveals All

For Immediate Release: Marilyn talks about diary of secrets

Place: Los Angeles Press Club

Date:

Time:

Studying it intensely, the plot had drastically thickened. Her revealing the diary would have expeditiously increased the list of people who may have wanted her dead. But apparently, Marilyn was about to make it public and wrote about it.

"Peter called. Bobby is coming tomorrow. They want me to call off the press conference. Too late."

Tapping his head, it was blatantly clear this diary was a ticking time bomb. Marilyn was a loose cannon and a threat. *But how far-reaching was the danger?*

Frenchy logged all the containers and called Alvaro back over.

"I need you to drop this list off to Abernathy. I'm gonna lock up her property, then check the autopsy room to see how it's going."

"Be careful down there. I hear the paranormal spirits are in rare form."

"I'll try to steer clear."

Frenchy walked into the autopsy room, which was always unnerving and cold. He instantly saw Marilyn's nude body lying on the grey gurney. Dr. Thomas Noguchi, scheduled to perform the procedure, was standing near her in a shirt and tie under his white doctor's blazer. He weighed something on a balancing scale while talking to Deputy District Attorney John Miner, head of their medical-legal section.

Though not uncommon for Miner to be there, it was usually during the autopsy procedure. Marilyn's wasn't scheduled until tomorrow at 8 am, and Dr. Noguchi was the best in the county. Frenchy liked how he interacted with family members and the coroner's office staff. He was excellent at explaining things.

Miner and Noguchi discussed a bruise on Marilyn's hip, which looked oddly out of place. Staring at it carefully, Frenchy wondered how that would happen. It didn't look like a fall, which should be circular and larger. Instead, the bruise was small and puffy, like when Frenchy got his vaccination shot. Her face was discolored, typical for postmortem, but she looked oddly at peace.

"Excuse me, Dr. Noguchi, will you be needing anything from us for your final autopsy? I won't be here tomorrow."

"No, deputy, I think we have everything."

"How are you today, Mr. Miner?"

"I'm doing well, deputy."

"Can I ask you a question, Dr. Noguchi?"

"Sure,"

"Those bruises on Marilyn's hip, what caused them? Deputy Danbacker thought maybe someone dropped her body. But that bruise seems different."

"Perhaps, but this bruise could be the result of body handling. The others may be from it getting dropped. Unfortunately, that happens all the time."

"What about her time of death? He also thought she died much earlier in the evening."

"It's difficult to say, but the police reports and her doctor's statements seem fairly consistent. I have no reason to doubt them."

"OK, thank you, doctor. I'll let you gentlemen get back to work."

It was nagging Frenchy that Miner was in with Noguchi before the autopsy, which didn't feel quite right. However, the bruises raised his eyebrows more than anything. Noguchi was wise and trustworthy, as Frenchy knew, but sometimes seemed a bit passive. At best, things were bizarre, but Frenchy didn't have much time to worry about that. He had more questions for Danbacker, so he stopped at his work area.

"Can you run by me exactly what you saw when you got Monroe's property?"

"The bed was in disarray with papers, books, and stuff on the floor. People were all around, so things could have been moved. It was overbearing," he explained with his thick Irish accent. "The empty pill bottles were on the nightstand. One was still on the bed, so I grabbed them all. It felt staged, but who knows?"

"Really? That's fascinating. Why would she have a bunch of empty bottles? She could not have taken them all. And her housekeeper would have cleaned that up. This is crazy."

"Where I come from, we would call her house manky."

"Manky? I never heard that before."

"Their kitchen is manky. You'd be safer eating in the jacks."

"I'm not even going to ask what the 'jacks' is."

"It means toilet."

"I knew I didn't want to know," Frenchy shook his head. "So, tell me, what part of Ireland does your family come from? You have an interesting accent."

"That's funny you say that. To me, everyone here has an accent."

"Good point. I guess all of us have dialects that are only normal to us. I never thought about that."

"I'm from Northern Ireland. My family left because of how they treated Catholic Irishmen and came here to the land of freedom."

"We have similar issues here, but there's no place like the good old USA."

"This is my home now."

"You're a good guy Danbacker, I can tell."

"Thank you, Grandison. I think you are exceptional. You're my favorite person here."

"Ah, stop, you're making me blush," Frenchy said lightheartedly.

Back at his desk, Frenchy received the initial typed police report, which was a summary of the statements. He carefully read each word so he could understand what exactly transpired.

"Marilyn Monroe, on August 4, 1962, retired to her bedroom at about eight o'clock in the evening; Mrs. Eunice Murray of 933 Ocean Ave. Santa Monica, Calif., noted a light in Miss Monroe's bedroom. Mrs. Murray was not able to arouse Miss Monroo when she went to the door, and when she tried the door again at 3:30 am when she noted the light still on, she found it to be locked."

Frenchy had arrived to work at 8 am that day, and the body was on its way to the mortuary. That's an unusually large gap from the time they discovered her body. He surmised they rushed while typing this report since they spelled Monroe wrong.

"Thereupon, Mrs. Murray observed Miss Monroe through the bedroom window and found her lying on her stomach in the bed, and the appearance seemed unnatural. Mrs. Murray then called Miss Monroe's psychiatrist, Dr. Ralph D. Greenson, of 436 North Roxbury Drive, Beverly

Hills, Calif. Upon entering after breaking the bedroom window, he found Miss Monroe possibly dead. Then he telephoned Dr. Hyman Engelberg of 9730 Wilshire Boulevard, also of Beverly Hills, who came over and then pronounced Miss Monroe dead at 3:35 am."

Red flags instantly flew like hurricane winds in the Florida Keys. *How did the maid see the light was still on in Monroe's room at 3:30 and both doctors arrive by 3:35 to pronounce her dead?* He also wondered why the maid called the doctor instead of the police for appropriate help. Frenchy squinted as he continued reading this report.

"Miss Monroe was seen by Dr. Greenson on August 4, 1962, at 5:15 pm, at her request, because she was not able to sleep. She was being treated by him for about a year. She was nude when Dr. Greenson found her dead with the telephone receiver in one hand and lying on her stomach. The police department was called, and when they arrived, they found Miss Monroe in the description described above, except for the telephone, which was removed by Dr. Greenson."

Frenchy was trying to tie in what Goldstein said about Kennedy in this timeline. Marilyn's doctor's appointment was at 5:15 and she was in her room by 8 pm. *Where would Kennedy fit in, and wouldn't the maid have known if he was there?* Frenchy found the phone in her hand interesting. Maybe she was calling for help. *But what time did they call the police?* That was nowhere on this report.

"There were found to be 15 bottles of medication on the night table, and some were prescription. A bottle marked 1 ½ grains Nembutal, prescribed by Dr. Engelberg, and referring to this particular bottle, Dr. Engelberg made the statement that he prescribed a refill for this about two days ago, and he further stated there probably should have been about 50 capsules at the time this was refilled by pharmacist."

The bottom of the report read:

Occupation: Actress
Probable Cause of death: Overdose of Nembutal, body discovered 8/5/62 @ 3:25AM
Taken to county morgue- from there to Westwood Mortuary

Report made by SGT RE Byron LA Detective Division
Next of kin: Gladys Baker (mother)
Coroner's office notified. The body was removed from
premises by Westwood Village Mortuary.
(8/5/62 11AM WLA hf J R Brukles 5829)

Re-reading this, Frenchy had serious concerns. If there were 15 bottles, why did they zero in on just Nembutal? He was also troubled by the confusing information at the bottom of the report. It said the body was taken to the county morgue and then to Westwood Mortuary, but it was the opposite. This was ridiculous.

Giving it thought, his experience was that in overdose cases, the body reacts with vomiting or gagging. Frenchy had handled numerous suicides, and that was fairly consistent. It wasn't his job to find a killer but to gather the facts about the manner of death, and this was a puzzle with pieces scattered across the table. He took out his notepad and began listing things of concern. Most importantly, how did everything happen in only five minutes?

1. Unrealistic timeline
    a. Doctor appointment 5:15
    b. 8:00 bed - Lights on-door locked
    c. 3:30 am maid was concerned & called doctor Greenson.
    d. 3:35 pronounced dead by Dr. Engelberg???
2. When was LAPD called?
3. Who called Westwood Mortuary? Authorized body removal?
4. Prescriptions? Doctor who prescribed Nembutal assumed she took all 50 capsules without vomiting. What about the other prescriptions?

This definitely needed immediate clarification. Frenchy called officer Byron requesting they reinterview the maid and doctor because the timelines were concerning, information was wrong, and some was missing. Quickly he cleaned up his desk and headed home with his head more bogged down than the day before. There was no way this would be as expedient as Curphey demanded. No way.

Glad he had the next two days off to process this overwhelming development, Frenchy was curious about what Marilyn planned to disclose. From what he read, numerous people would not want her talking. Day two felt like a murder investigation without a doubt, but Curphey's words were clear to close out this case.

The hot August sun sizzled through the car as Frenchy headed home down rural San Fernando Road with the windows down. When purchasing his 1960 Pontiac Bonneville brand new after landing the new job, he opted out of factory air conditioning, thinking he could tough it out. Very few cars had it, and he thought it an unnecessary expense, a decision he now regretted. However, concerns were mounting because his extensive commute accumulated so many miles. The threads on his tires were in dire condition, and his budget had been tight since the last baby. He tried to learn simple things like changing oil, but that didn't work either.

The drive home went quicker than usual, with his mind wholly bombarded. As he pulled into the driveway, the kids were in a little plastic pool, splashing and laughing in the front yard. It was 6:30 pm, yet the temperature felt like triple digits.

Lonnie and Crystal jumped out of the pool as soon as he exited the car, screaming "DADDY," like they hadn't seen him in decades. Their wet bodies had no regard for his work clothes as Lonnie grabbed his leg, and Crystal raised her arms to get picked up. He did this while appreciating the simplicity of childhood.

"Daddy, we missed you," Crystal smugly revealed while puckering her lips for a kiss.

After the hug, Lonnie ran straight back to Cousin Tony and jumped in the pool, splashing water in his face and causing Tony to seek revenge with a boyish wrestling maneuver. The two tussled relentlessly as usual. Finally, Frenchy put Crystal down and couldn't deny that getting drenched felt good.

"Hi baby," Tipy yelled out.

"Hey. You guys look like you're having fun."

"We must try to stay cool. It was too hot to be outside earlier. The fan broke, so it's like a sauna in there. It's been miserable."

"That's not good. I'll pick up a new one tomorrow," Frenchy said. "Hi Joyce, how's it going?"

"Three offspring is more work than I ever imagined."

"You're doing a great job," Frenchy reassured her putting Crystal down.

Still sticky, despite the cool-off from Crystal, Frenchy jumped into the shower. The streaming water on his body felt like heaven, yet his mind seemed overloaded as thoughts of not visiting Mo and Tom in a while came to him because he usually checked on them. Then surprisingly, he quickly snapped back to Marilyn Monroe, needing answers and wondering what would occur at the office while he was gone.

Dinner with the family was frenzied as usual. Lance was five months old and still suffering from colic, constantly screaming relentlessly with nothing to soothe him. Tipy tried a pacifier, warm baths, and rocking, but still, he cried nonstop, forcing her to place him in the crib during dinner so they could eat.

Boppie and Joyce were easy to live with, but with six kids in the house, Frenchy wasn't sure this was a sustainable situation, even though he and Boppie were like brothers. He wasn't used to this loud atmosphere because his household was small and quiet growing up. The noise was overbearing, and he couldn't think at times.

After breakfast the following day, Frenchy stood up and kissed Tipy on the forehead.

"I'll be back in a little while."

"Where are you going?"

"The library."

"I was hoping you could stay with the kids so I could run some errands."

"I won't be too long."

"Why the library?"

"I have to look some things up on microfiche."

"For work?"

"No. For knowledge."

"You're the smartest man I know. What knowledge do you need?"

"How do you think I got smart?"

"But Frenchy, I need a break."

"Can't you call my mother or Veda?"

"It's Tuesday. They all work," Tipy said, visibly upset and tearing up.

"Babe, I have some important stuff going on."

"I'm not important? I'm with the kids 24 hours a day, and Lance constantly cries. I'm going crazy."

Frenchy opened his arms, gave her a loving embrace, and then tenderly caressed her cheek before planting a caring kiss.

"I know it's hard. Believe me, I know. I will help tomorrow, I promise. Just let me do this, babe. It's important."

"It feels like we've been here before. Now, it's your job. When am I going to be important? I have been changing diapers or potty training for three years nonstop with no break."

"Tomorrow, I promise you can have a break," he said sympathetically. "It's only one day. Hang in there, baby. Just know what I do is for us."

"Tomorrow, you promise?"

"Yes, and I will pick up a new fan after I leave the library."

"Okay," she said, taking a deep tear-filled breath.

The Pacoima library had just opened on Van Nuys Blvd last year. When he entered the new 200,000-book establishment, he was impressed. There were no other people of color inside, but everyone was friendly. This side of town had a different demographic. After showing his card, he asked the librarian where the microfilm area was, and she pointed to a corner. Sitting down with his notepad and diary excerpts, Frenchy hoped for clarity. First on his list was to look up Dr. Greenson, who was in Marilyn's diary.

"Frank introduced me to Doctor Greenson. He was able to get me some pills that relaxed me. I wondered if Frank knew Greenson was a party member."

It seemed strange to Frenchy that Dr. Greenson, a psychiatrist, was also prescribing medications. The police report only mentioned Dr. Engelberg and Nembutal. Moreover, Marilyn believed Greenson was a member of the communist party.

"Dr. Greenson spent hours with me discussing world politics. Jeanne and Terry think he has some kind of control over me."

This intriguing entry seemed to suggest people in Marilyn's life didn't like Greenson. Scrolling through the microfilm he jotted down what he found on the doctor.

Birth name - Romeo Greenschpoon

Family immigrated from Russia

Anglicized name in 1937

Enlisted in army after Coming to Los Angeles

So, Greenson's family were definitely communists. That confirmed what Marilyn wrote. However, another shocker stood out when posted real estate records revealed that John and Eunice Murray sold a home in Long Beach to Ralph and Hildi Greenson in 1946. *Are you kidding me?! The doctor and maid have known each other for 17 years!*

Frenchy wrote it down, then noticed Greenson also had a heart attack in 1955, causing him to begin working from home. There wasn't anything else on Eunice Murray, but now, he understood the reasoning behind her calling Greenson first. Time had forged their relationship over many years, and this housekeeper was clearly under his control.

His next concern was Marilyn's entries about Fidel Castro. Being somewhat up on the news, Frenchy knew this was big. *Why would a Hollywood starlet be in the know with Kennedy and the Bay of Pigs?*

Frenchy remembered in 1959, Fidel Castro overthrew the American-backed Cuban government led by General Bautista. But Frenchy did not know that the CIA and the Kennedy administration were plotting to overthrow Castro until they failed miserably with the Bay of Pigs fiasco. The CIA launched an attempt to remove him with a definitive strike and full-scale invasion by 1400 trained American Cubans. To their surprise,

Castro's troops badly outnumbered the invaders, who embarrassingly surrendered in less than 24 hours, leaving Kennedy with egg on his face.

Marilyn wrote in her diary:

"The spy boys were really serious about killing Castro. Big Jim and a guy named Eduardo were actually involved in the Bay of Pigs. Jack never let them forget it."

"We attended a meeting with the spy boys and mafia gangsters. They were discussing how to kill Castro. Johnny Roselli boasted about the Mafia's ability to infiltrate anybody's security to kill them. They had a pill to cram up Castro's butt."

So, JFK took Marilyn to meetings with spies and mobsters discussing how to kill Castro? *Is that what this says?*

Frenchy got a chill thinking this woman knew top-secret happenings in real time. Not surprisingly, he had no clue who the spy boys were, Eduardo, Johnny Roselli, or even Big Jim. Still, he knew the big fish was Fidel Castro, and this was top government information.

Baffled why the President of the United States would involve Marilyn with these people, he realized that any of them could have wanted her dead because of what she knew. His eyes fixated on his notes where she wrote about the two's relationship.

"The thing with Jack was getting hot. I love all that real-life drama. Just think, I'm in on it."

"My life is very confusing after Jack became President. I want to go to the White House all dressed up like when I met the Queen, but I'm not his damn wife. That's so depressing."

"Jack stopped taking my calls. He even had the nerve to change his phone number. Peter told me Jackie was raising hell and would divorce him if he saw me again. Wish she had left him. I could have been his wife. I'm not afraid of these aristocrats."

After looking up JFK, the first article he came across surprised him. JFK ordered Bobby to pursue a strong attack on organized crime, who then established a "Get Hoffa Squad."

"Bobby was on the phone most of the night talking to Jack. It was something about putting that guy Jimmy Hoffa in jail."

"I met Hoffa at Frank's party. Made a big fool of myself. Drank too much and smoked too much. Sam and him were asking about Bobby. What did I say?"

Scratching his head and twisting his mouth, Frenchy felt the nerves in his stomach twitching. There were a lot of names Marilyn mentioned in her writings. *Could she be referencing mafia boss Sam Giancana? Was Marilyn involved with him as well?* And that name, Frank. It popped up several times. *Could it be Sinatra?*

He noticed his hand slightly trembling as he began writing down information about Hoffa, a well-known Teamster with Mafia ties.

Hoffa - Teamster president

1957 arrested for bribing select committee aide

Acquitted

Currently on trial for bribery in Nashville

At that moment, Frenchy recognized a bomb ready to explode. Marilyn had placed herself in the middle of a war between the Kennedys and organized crime. Bobby was leading the charge, and public enemy number one was Jimmy Hoffa.

The paradox was that Kennedy's father, Joe, was said to have mob ties. Moreover, Frenchy could not ignore Bobby and the many diary entries in his notes.

"I finally met his brother Bobby. It was fun but didn't work out."

"I love being with Bobby. He says we're going to make America the most powerful country in the world."

"Bobby found out about my diary. Can't believe he raised holy hell for writing about us. Told me to destroy it. Never thought he would react like that."

"Couldn't reach Bobby, and he won't call back."

"The dirty bastard changed his number. He thinks he going to do me like his brother did. I'll fix them all."

The only thing stranger than Bobby Kennedy being in town when Marilyn died was that she wrote her last diary entry about him. Undoubtedly, with all this information, an investigation by law enforcement was warranted. However, Frenchy had some tough decisions when returning to work. *If he kept the diary's existence to himself, how would he explain when they found out?* One thing he couldn't avoid was the reality that someone may have murdered Marilyn Monroe. He felt a drop of sweat drip down his face wondering why fate put him into this hornet's nest.

At the end of the day, the suspect list was long. After sitting for hours, finally, with a growling stomach and the thinning of readers, Frenchy realized it was time to leave. Staying much longer than planned, he picked up his notepad and headed to his car.

When he got home, a rush of heat slapped his face like a fireball after opening the front door. Frenchy realized he had forgotten something. *Oh, crap, the fan!*

Oddly the house was soundless, with only a neighbor's dog barking in the distance. There was no food aroma letting him know dinner was in the works, nor could he see any running, jumping, laughter, or crying. *Was he in the correct place?* Slowly creeping to the kitchen, a note on the refrigerator read, 'Gone to the Sorrells to swim.'

Joyce's parents, the Sorrells, lived on Weidner Street and had the first house on the block with a built-in pool. He assumed they would also be eating there, so he would be on his own for food. Unfortunately, the icebox had no leftovers, but he noticed it badly needed defrosting. Piles of packed frost hovered around the plastic swinging door resembling mold growing on cheese but now invading outside its borders.

There was frozen beef and chicken, but they needed hours to defrost, so he opted for a ham sandwich with fresh Dairy milk. While eating, Boppie came home.

"Hey man, how's it going?" Boppie said.

"Hot!"

"Try being in a big rig all day."

"You've been with Western Carloading for a while now. I know that's hard."

"Yeah, but check this out. I just got another raise. The teamsters are looking out for us. They call my boy Hoffa a gangster, but he's pulling some deep shit stopping nonunion workers from messing up our money."

"What are they saying about him at the union meetings?"

"Everyone loves him, and I'll tell you what, Kennedy better quit messin' with both Hoffa and the Mafia. Them boys don't play."

"I'm beginning to get that impression."

"Where is everybody?" Boppie asked with a frown on his face.

"Your in-laws."

"Hum. I'm hungry."

"You see what I'm eating. No telling when they'll get back."

"Dam. I'm going to my mother's. She always has something cooking."

"I'm sure they'll bring some food home."

"I'm hungry now. Catch you later."

"Alright. Later."

Frenchy put on a pan of water to boil for the defrost. Maybe if he did something domestic, a rarity for him, Tipy would forgive his absence and lack of a new fan. He took all the frozen food out and placed it on the table. After setting boiled water inside, he turned on the television set. A few minutes later, he could hear ice plopping from the freezer roof. It took about an hour and a little scraping, but he got it done and replaced the food. He decided not to say anything and see if she even noticed.

Shortly after, the posse returned with all the kids in tow. Tipy walked in without a word, with Lance asleep in her arms. She placed him in the crib and went back out the front door.

"Are you not speaking to me?" Frenchy asked, wondering if she was still upset.

"I gotta get Crystal. She's sleeping. The sun and swimming wore her out," Tipy whispered.

"I'll get her," Frenchy said as Joyce entered with her daughter Patricia, sleeping in her arms.

"You two know how to tire out kids," Frenchy commented with a smirk.

"Tony and Lonnie never get worn out. They are still going at it," Tipy said, shrugging her shoulders.

The boys jumped out of the car, causing Crystal to flop limply on the seat. Frenchy carefully picked her up and placed her in the room.

"Come on, boys, bath time," Joyce called out.

With Tony and Lonnie having endless energy, the bath should finish the job before bedtime. Frenchy was always impressed at how well Joyce and Tipy managed the kids and husbands.

"Sweetie, we brought you and Boppie a plate. Where is he?" Tipy asked.

"He went to Veda's for food."

"I should have known that spoiled brat couldn't wait," Tipy snarled, knowing her brother was particular about his meals.

"I made myself a sandwich, but he wanted real food," Frenchy explained. "So, are you still mad at me?"

"I'm just exhausted. I talked to your mother today. She said she'll take Lance on her days off, so I can get a little reprieve. Mo said she'll help on the weekends, so you have been saved by the bell."

"How did that happen?"

"I asked. With the Marilyn Monroe case, you are of zero help. Parenting is hard work, and I'm going crazy. But thanks for defrosting the freezer."

"You noticed?"

"Yeah, there's a pot sitting out next to the mayonnaise. I saw the freezer when I put it up."

"Oops," Frenchy said, chuckling.

"How did the library go?" she asked.

"I got a lot of interesting information. It's going to help me understand what we are dealing with. I'm gonna be slammed when I get back to the office."

"So, relax now. Let's see what's on TV."

Flipping through "TV Guide," they had a choice of "Combat," a World War II drama series, or "The Virginian," a western that Frenchy liked. Luckily, they received a 19-inch RCA Console set, resembling a box on sticks, for a wedding present. To the right were channel, volume, and contrast knobs on a mesh/wooly type fabric. The top had a Martian-like antenna, also called rabbit ears, to adjust the signal. Television had only been popular in homes for the past ten years and not every household had one.

'The Virginian' won the coin toss, so after the kids were in bed, the couple cuddled, watching a gunfight-filled western with cowboys and plenty of action. Tipy cooked some popcorn kernels in her stainless-steel pot with oil so they could have a snack with the show.

The next day Frenchy woke up early, somewhat refreshed. Despite the forecasted heat, he knew mowing the lawn was on today's schedule. Moreover, he needed to do it before the blazing sun barreled down like a torpedo, melting everything in its path. In the garage was their push mower which he grabbed and began his laboring task.

The smell of fresh-cut grass was cathartic to Frenchy, despite his allergies. He pushed and pulled, hoping his house measured up to the older neighbors, who were all in their 40s. He was the youngest homeowner on the block but respected, nonetheless.

Creeping slowly down their quiet street was a black 1961 Ford Galaxy. Two white men in suits stared intensely at the house. It was strange and definitely out of place for this African American community. The four-door, official-looking vehicle slinked by as the driver looked intensely at Frenchy through his dark sunglasses.

While continuing to push the mower, a strange sensation pulsated through his body as a loud inner voice screamed a warning. After he finished mowing, Frenchy proceeded with the dreadful grass raking. Then, to his surprise, another sedan with two white men appeared, driving slowly just like the other. *What did this mean? Who the heck are these men?*

With crazy thoughts swirling through his mind, the only thing that made sense was the diary, but it was hard to know with certainty. So, upon entering the house, he grabbed Tipy and gave her an impulsive kiss.

"What are you doing?" she laughed. "Baby, next time, can you shower before plowing me with your sweat? I love you dearly, but…Ewww."

"I'm sorry. I just felt a sudden urge. Things are getting weird. I just saw two odd cars driving by. They definitely weren't from this neighborhood."

"Who do you think they were?"

"I don't know. They were wearing suits and sunglasses. Could have been anyone but unquestionably not from this area."

"Maybe detectives? I could ask Veda."

"No, they were not detectives. I can smell a detective from a mile away."

"Come on, how can you tell the difference?"

"We've been to police picnics, babe. I know all the detectives at Foothill Division and what their cars look like. These guys were different."

"You think it has to do with Marilyn Monroe?"

"It's hard to say, but maybe. Just stay on alert while I'm at work."

"What's that in your hand?"

"I got the crowbar from my car so you can protect yourself."

"Really, Frenchy? What the heck am I going to do with a crowbar?"

"Babe, if you need to swing at someone, this will knock them out."

"My mother works for LAPD. I doubt they want me. You probably need that thing more, but if it makes you feel better, sure, I'll take it. I just hope Lonnie and Tony don't get ahold of it. That's more dangerous than any random men coming in here."

Boisterously, the kids came crashing out of their rooms.

"Mommy, we're hungry," Lonnie peddled.

"Okay, tell everyone the food is ready."

After showering, Frenchy decided to call the office and see if there was anything new. He spoke with Schwartz, who told him to relax; there was no need to worry. Usually, when someone told Frenchy not to worry, it was time to worry. However, at this point, there wasn't much else to do but relax for the rest of the day. Those cars driving by were not easy to dismiss but fretting about it was not helpful either.

As promised, Tipy got to run her errands for a couple of hours. Lucky for Frenchy, it was nap time after he played with the kids for a bit. When 5 pm came around, Frenchy decided to check the evening news while Tipy was cooking. To his surprise, Marilyn's funeral was on every channel.

"Tipy, it's on TV!"

"What? More of the Virginian?"

"The funeral."

Being shocked was an understatement, forcing Frenchy to remain in Marilyn's world. It was only three days since her death, and the services were as rushed as everything else thus far. Without a next of kin, it would be difficult to have a funeral before resolving the manner of death or having a death certificate. *Why didn't Schwartz give him a heads-up?* Minute by minute, things became more complicated.

Tipy and Frenchy sat down with their eyes glued to the rectangle box, curious about the memorial service. Crossing his arms in anticipation, Frenchy watched as the camera panned to a sign that read, Westwood Memorial Park Village Mortuary.

News coverage showed guests entering the chapel while mostly looking down. Women wore various hats with purses hanging off their lower arms as they proceeded inside. At the same time, the men stepped in stride, making eye contact with each other and giving a slight nod of recognition. The chapel had glass doors and walls with beige drapes on either side cascading together with a small opening for guests to enter.

When Joe DiMaggio, her ex-husband, entered, the depth of his grief was in plain view. All eyes were focused on the famous major league baseball player, and the camera followed him until he entered the chapel. The guests piled in, and the shot revealed a massive audience behind ropes with an enormous law enforcement presence. The commentator's low somber voice drew the viewers painfully into the deepness of this heart-wrenching tragedy.

At that moment, a rush of questions plagued Frenchy's mind, and they were all unanswerable. *Did they find the next of kin?* Many bodies in Los Angeles remain unclaimed and get cremated, with their ashes scattered across the lonely ocean. He felt relieved for this iconic woman as the grainy New York Jewish accent of Lee Strasberg, an acting coach, and director, rang throughout as he emotionally read Marilyn's eulogy.

"Marilyn Monroe was a legend. She created a myth of what a poor girl with a deprived background could obtain. For the entire world, she became a symbol of the eternal female, and I have no words to describe the myth and legend, nor would she want us to do so. I did not know this Marilyn Monroe, nor did she. We gather here today for only Marilyn, a warm human being. Impulsive and shy and lonely, sensitive and in fear of rejection, yet ever avid for life and reaching out for fulfillment.

I will not insult the privacy of your memory of her, a privacy she sought and treasured by trying to describe, her whom you know, to you who knew her. And now the memories of her remain alive, not only a shadow on the screen or a glamorous personality.

For us, Marilyn was a devoted and loyal friend—a colleague constantly reaching for perfection. We shared her pain and difficulties and some of her joys. She was a member of our family. ... It is difficult to accept the fact that her zest for life has been ended by this dreadful accident. Despite the heights and brilliance, she had attained on the screen, she was planning for the future. She was looking forward to participating in the many exciting things she had planned. In her eyes and in mine, her career was just beginning. ...

The dream of her talent, which she nurtured as a child, was not a mirage. When she first came to me, I was amazed at the startling sensitivity which she possessed, and which had remained fresh and unhinged and struggling to express itself despite the life to which she had been subjected. Others were specifically as beautiful as she was, but there was obviously something more in her, something that people saw and recognized in her performances and with which they identified. She had a luminous quality. A combination of wistfulness, radiance, and yearning that set her and made everyone wish to be part of it—to share in the childish naiveté which was at once so shy and yet so vibrant.

This quality was even more eminent when she was on the stage. I'm truly sorry that you and the public who loved her did not have the opportunity to see her as we did and many of the roles that would foreshadow what she had become. Without a doubt, she would have been one of the great actresses of the stage.

Now it is all at an end. I hope that her death will stir sympathy and understanding to a sensitive, honest woman who brought joy and pleasure to the world. I cannot say goodbye. Marilyn never liked goodbyes. And the peculiar way she faced reality, I will say Au Revoir for our country."

With tears streaming down her face, Tipy looked over at Frenchy, whom she had never seen cry. Today was no different, but clearly, this aroused emotion in him like she had never seen. His face was stoic as he gazed at the six pallbearers in black suits rolling the coffin out of the mortuary. They ambled past uniformed officers that stood at attention on the grass that led to the hearse. A line of men and women followed as the cameras caught the massive number of onlookers and media cameras, all trying to understand why this legend had to die at only 36. Rope separated the uninvited guests as tall landings stood all around with large cameras on stands vying for usable footage.

The grey casket was placed carefully in the vehicle and proceeded, followed by a procession of people walking behind until they reached her mausoleum and crypt. Curtains lined the vehicle's window, not allowing any view of Marilyn. When they arrived, pallbearers carried the casket to the tomb—a single curtain, second from the bottom, identified where Marilyn's body would rest.

Officers stood side by side with their backs to the casket, watching the enormous crowd gathering everywhere, including bushes and rooftops. People, young and old, packed the landscape of the mortuary. A set of metal chairs were to the side of the 12-

foot-tall structure that housed rows of crypts with beautiful white floral sprays behind Marilyn's casket. Then, finally, the coverage ended, leaving Frenchy more confused than ever. Tomorrow would go one of two ways. Either all his questions would get answered, or many more would linger. He feared the latter.

Nothing could have prepared Frenchy for the mess on Thursday morning. His desk was in complete chaos, not how he had left it, and no one even took the time to stack the new paperwork neatly. It looked as if someone was going through his things because items like the stapler and clips were not in the correct places.

The revised police report he requested was there, as was the preliminary autopsy that showed Dr. Noguchi found 30 Nembutal tablets lodged in her throat, but the stomach was empty. He thought this further weakened the suicide theory; however, Dr. Abernathy's microscopic tests were still pending.

Goldstein was sitting at his desk dressed in his usual suit but had a different demeanor than usual. He usually said good morning and was personable but appeared distracted.

"Good morning, Goldstein," Frenchy chirped despite his dissatisfaction with the condition of his desk.

"Hey, Grandison," Goldstein forced out.

"Tell me, what's going on? How did Marilyn get buried without closing her case?"

"She's not buried," Goldstein blurted out.

"Okay, placed in a crypt," Frenchy said sarcastically.

"She's not in a crypt either. Her body is here. It was on loan for the service."

"Say what? Loan? I've been here for two years and never heard of that. I saw it on television."

"Let that be a lesson, don't believe everything you see on TV. All I can say is I'm glad Monroe isn't my case."

"It should have been. Would have saved me a big headache. Do you see my desk?"

"A sharp guy like you can handle it."

"So let me ask you, what was the big rush for a funeral?"

"That's a million-dollar question among many. Unfortunately, there are no answers right now, but Dr. Curphey has instituted a new policy. He wants all information about Monroe, whether coming in or going out, cleared with him."

"I don't understand. Why would he do that?"

"There is a gathering of eagles hovering over this particular case. An Associated Press reporter told me that Kennedy was not only in town but also at her house. LAPD and the FBI are crawling all over the city, looking for some important evidence. What it is, I don't know, but Curphey is meaner than usual, if that's even possible."

Welcome back to work, Frenchy. At that moment, he decided to retrieve the diary and give it to Curphey. He could no longer deny his duty as a sworn officer. This diary offered evidence that could help law enforcement with her case. If they are looking for her killer, this book has all the suspects wrapped in a little red cover.

So, he headed to the property room, carefully placing his key in the slot. The file cabinet drawer shrieked as he pulled out the Monroe bin labeled 81128, thinking how everything was about to change. But, unexpectantly, it felt incredibly light, and to his surprise, nothing was inside. Her contents were gone, every single item. Immediately he checked the sign-out log, and there was no entry. All property required logging in and out, with only three people having keys, Curphey, Schwartz, and himself. Frenchy rubbed his head and decided to report the missing property to Schwartz, following protocol. He didn't particularly want to do this, already having a full plate, but decided to see it through.

"Good morning, Schwartz. How are you today?"

"Busy. What's going on?"

"The question is… what's not going on?" Frenchy chuckled, trying to lighten the mood. "We have some property missing, and it wasn't logged out."

"Whose property?"

"Monroe."

"I'm sure it will turn up," Schwartz said nonchalantly.

"You're not bothered?"

"When I'm reduced to taking these Monroe calls, I lose focus. We can't be concerned about that now. Maybe Curphey has it. He's not one for following his own rules."

"If you're not concerned, then neither am I. Why didn't you tell me about the funeral when I called yesterday?"

"It was complicated. But I wouldn't worry about that if I were you. Just look at your work pile."

"Not worry? Right," his voice dropped to a sarcastic baritone.

When Frenchy returned to his desk, he picked up the revised police report and slowly began reading.

'Upon reinterviewing both Dr. Ralph F. Greenson (wit #1) and Dr. Engelberg (wit #2) they both agree to the following time sequence of their actions.

Dr. Greenson received a phone call from Mrs. Murray (reporting person) at 3:30A, 8-5-62 stating that she was unable to get into Miss Monroe's bedroom and the light was on. He told her to pound on the door and look in the window and call him back. At 3:35A, Mrs. Murray called back, and stated Miss Monroe was lying on the bed with the phone in her hand and looked strange. Dr. Greenson was dressed by this time, left for deceased residence, which is about one mile away. He also told Mrs. Murray to call Dr. Engelberg.

Dr. Greenson arrived at the deceased house about 3:40A. He broke the windowpane and entered through the window, and removed the phone from her hand.

Rigor Mortis had set in. At 3:50A, Dr. Engelberg arrived and pronounced Miss Monroe dead. The two doctors talked for a few moments. They both believe that it was about 4A when Dr. Engelberg called the Police Department.

A check with the Complaint Board and LA Desk indicates that the call was received at 4:25A. Miss Monroe's phone, OR 61890, has been checked, and no toll calls were made during the hours of this occurrence. Phone number 472-4830 is being checked at the present time.'

The report was signed by R.E. Byron.

The first impression after reading this was the math didn't add up, much the same as the first report. At 3 in the morning, if your engine didn't warm up, the car would be sputtering, no matter what model. He questioned that it only took five minutes to get there, but that was the least of Frenchy's concerns. As a doctor, Greenson appeared more concerned with Marilyn holding a phone than calling the police. If Rigor Mortis had already set in, why remove the phone from her hand and wait for Dr. Engelberg? That question rang loudly in addition to not notifying the police for almost an hour.

Looking at the police photos, Frenchy closely examined the pill bottles on the nightstand. He agreed with Danbacker that the scene appeared staged. In addition, images showed no cups or liquid for taking even one pill, let alone fifty.

Frenchy picked up the receiver and called Dr. Noguchi to clarify the autopsy findings.

"Good day Dr. Noguchi. This is Deputy Grandison."

"Yes, hello. Good day to you as well."

"I wanted to ask you about the Monroe autopsy."

"Yes, yes."

"The preliminary lab results showed no poison, and the autopsy revealed the pills had lodged in her throat, and her stomach was empty. So is the manner undetermined instead of suicide?"

"No. We are sticking to probable suicide while we wait for test results from her liver and bodily tissues."

"We have reason to believe someone may have been with her that night but isn't on the police report."

"Deputy, we do not use gossip in the coroner's office to make our findings."

"I understand. But there wasn't any water or liquid to take the pills."

"That was not noted in the police report."

"But it's in the photos. There was no cup anywhere."

"Deputy, this is not Dragnet. We do only pathology here, and I suggest you practice the same."

"But doesn't the body react by vomiting or convulsions?"

"That may be true, but that doesn't mean it happens all the time. Now I have work to do. Good day, Mr. Grandison."

Extremely confused by Dr. Noguchi's attitude, Frenchy's quest for the truth left him empty and feeling alone. Perhaps he was too emotionally vested, but common sense demanded answers.

There were about twenty messages regarding Monroe's case as he sorted through his papers. He returned all calls with the same response, "her case is still under investigation."

After making the last call on the list, Schwartz stood next to Frenchy's desk.

"Dr. Curphey wants you to arrange a press conference. He wants to assure people that our office is doing everything possible to shed light on Marilyn's death."

"Are we doing everything?"

"What do you mean by that?" Schwartz sternly belted.

"Nothing."

Schwartz let out an exasperated sigh while looking Frenchy in his eyes.

"Listen, deputy. Our office is under extreme pressure to close this case. Right now, that's all any of us need to know. If you have any personal issues with that, tell me now."

"No issues. What does he want the press release to say?"

"The statement should confirm that the Suicide Investigation Team is examining her case and the coroner will guarantee a thorough investigation, utilizing their full subpoena power for witnesses, and calling for an inquest if necessary."

"Alright."

Frenchy reluctantly began drafting the document, holding his head down, wondering why forces were holding him back. They could easily rule her death 'undetermined' and throw the ball into law enforcement's hands. He looked at the autopsy report to help him draft the press release. One thing that immediately stood out, it was dated August 5, 1962. Frenchy was in Noguchi's office on the 6th, who had scheduled the autopsy for the following day.

The report boldly said: Acute Barbiturate Poisoning Ingestion of Overdose.

He then flipped to the case report dated 8.5.62 at 5:25 am, and then (7:45 am) next to it said Barbs overdose.

That report was dated 8/7/62, but Noguchi's name was handwritten with a circled date of 8.5.62. *So what's going on here?*

Trying to understand the sequence of events, he regretted having those two days off. Frenchy decided to ask 'Mr. Know-everything' to get a better understanding.

"Goldstein, when did Noguchi do Monroe's autopsy? They have more dates than you had last week."

"They were supposed to do it on the 7th, but they changed it to Monday night."

"Why does almost everything say it was the 5th?"

"Don't ask."

"The documents are all wrong and information inaccurate."

Goldstein rolled his eyes and shrugged his shoulders. Then Frenchy had a thought, and he dialed Officer Byron, who he had spoken to before.

"Sergeant Byron please," Frenchy requested. "Hello, Byron? This is Deputy Grandison from the coroner's office. How are you doing today?"

"It's a day. How can I help you?"

"I wanted to discuss the Marilyn Monroe case."

"Oh, I'm not on it anymore."

"Can I speak to the person handling it now?"

"I honestly don't know who's handling it. Sergeant Jack Clemmons was the first on the scene, but they took him off too."

"The biggest case in the country, even the world, and no one knows who's in charge? Isn't that special?"

"Sorry."

"Thanks," he said, feeling like he kept hitting brick walls.

When his stomach growled, Frenchy realized he didn't bring his lunch. He grabbed Alvaro to join him as his perspective was usually straightforward and the only one

Frenchy trusted. They walked to a burger place down the street.

"Al, are you feeling the same tension as I do?"

"I got to tell you; the phones won't stop ringing. I put those messages on your desk because Curphey doesn't call anyone back. Then guess what? They call again on top of our new calls."

"There are so many unanswered questions. I honestly believe this case has seriously damaged the credibility of our office."

"Yeah, even the media is sweating us. But Curphey doesn't care. He doesn't want an inquest, either. That dude is like a rock. He ain't budging."

"You know, it's kind of sad. Somebody told me last week that we should all be team players, but where do we draw the line? Marilyn Monroe was a real person. Doesn't she deserve the truth? Don't we owe that to her?"

"Well, mi Abuela used to say, a lie might hide the truth today, but the truth will hide a lie forever. One day the truth about Marilyn Monroe will come out. But, señor, the vibes inside this building are dark. Very dark. I have never seen it like this before, and it's not the spirits of the dead. It's the evil of the living."

"I feel you. Have you heard anything?"

"That's the problem. They are too quiet. I usually hear everything, but they're tight-lipped, hands in pockets and looking away. Those are signs of serious deception. Something is very wrong."

"So, it's not just me? I thought I was losing it."

"No, my man. You ain't losing nada. You are the only real person in here. Well, besides me."

"You're a good guy Alvaro."

"You too, amigo."

Other cases needed Frenchy's attention, and it was time to get to them. However, there was a nagging concern about the autopsy report still. He was usually excellent at puzzles, but this was ridiculous. He stared at the autopsy diagram a little closer and noticed it omitted the bruises he, Dr. Noguchi, and Deputy DA Miner saw on her hip. They all saw it together. *How could that be?* Since Noguchi had been dismissive of him, he channeled his inner Joe Friday and decided to call Miner.

"Hi, Mr. Miner. This is Deputy Grandison from the coroner's office. We met in Noguchi's room before Marilyn Monroe's autopsy."

"Yes, hi deputy. What can I do for you?"

"Listen, I just got the preliminary report with the body drawings. Do you remember the bruises we saw on her hip?"

"Yes."

"It's not on the autopsy diagram."

"That's strange."

"Everything about this case is strange. Has your department investigated anything?"

"Different people are doing different things. I interviewed Dr. Greenson, and he even shared some tapes of his sessions with Marilyn. He verbally claimed she was depressed. But what I heard was an optimistic, happy woman. She was joking with the doc and upbeat, obviously not suicidal. I filed two reports stating my opinion."

"Who's in charge of the DA's investigation?" Frenchy asked. "LAPD doesn't have a contact person."

"I gave my findings to McKesson's office. He's the elected District Attorney, so it should get included with everything. Greenson's timeline and actions were very suspect. I'm not officially assigned to this, but nothing he said added up."

"He seemed sketchy to me too. So did the housekeeper. Their stories changed multiple times."

"Well, McKesson has both my reports. I'm hoping our office will announce an investigation soon."

"That would be great. Thanks, John. Take care."

"You too."

Frenchy felt a burst of optimism with things possibly headed in the right direction for the first time. This gleam of hope inspired him to proceed to the neglected cases stacked untouched in the tray. There was a stabbing, car accident, and natural death on top of the pile, which he took one by one, chipping away at the backlogged deaths. One thing he learned working there, your off days only meant double or even triple the work when you returned. Your cases sat like starving pets waiting for food. Of course, the pay structure should have considered that minute detail.

As much as he understood the workload, pecking order, and politics, Frenchy never once considered doing anything else for a living. Each case represented someone's life and needed him to assume personal responsibility for ensuring it was right. That included the famous blonde actress who may have been murdered.

On the morning of August 10, Frenchy felt strange isolation that he didn't understand. When he entered the office, it was like a ghost town. All the desks were empty, leaving him wondering if he had missed something important. Never before was this place quiet and vacant like this. It was like a holiday, but he didn't get the memo.

While trying to figure it out, he suddenly heard Curphey's door open down the hall and saw people exiting, which included Goldstein, Schwartz, Rayban, and Longhorn. Their faces were somber as if someone had just died, but he couldn't help but wonder why the meeting didn't include him. Goldstein's face was ashen and out of character. Schwartz avoided eye contact, and the other deputies looked down at the ground. Finally, Alvaro came out of nowhere and tapped Frenchy on the back.

"Hola, amigo."

"Hola, Alvaro. Where did you just come from?"

"File room. Schwartz sent me down there on a wild goose chase. These people are losing their minds."

"I thought we were closed, and nobody was allowed to die."

"Anything you need me to do?"

"Yes, can you go to Abernathy and see if he has any updates on the toxicology report? He was waiting on more test results. If he has something, I need it for the file."

"Isn't Curphey handling everything on that case now?"

"He is, but I still need to sign off on it. He can't do that."

"You are walking a fine line. Are you sure you want to continue? They are loco with everything, Marilyn."

"I still have to do my job."

"Okay, I'll be right back."

Despite orders, Frenchy knew closing out the case would still be up to him, even if Curphey was involved. Although he was the chief and made all high-level decisions, Curphey knew very little about the inner workings and mechanics of the coroner's office. Frenchy wasn't going to get blamed for a botched Monroe file. If nothing else, he will include all pertinent reports before closing the case. At least, that was the plan.

The tension felt so thick in the office that you could cut it with a knife. Nevertheless, Frenchy proceeded with his other cases despite the strained atmosphere and closed out several. Chatter was minimal until Goldstein casually walked over to Frenchy's desk.

"How's it going, Lionel?"

"It's goin'. Just trying to stay on top of things."

"Do you have any plans for lunch?"

"No, nothing special. I haven't thought about it."

"Good. I got a great spot. Let's go."

Goldstein had never addressed him as Lionel. It was always Grandison. They were colleagues but definitely not lunch buddies, so Frenchy found this request surprising. Goldstein was wearing a very expensive-looking watch and what appeared to be a new suit with a handkerchief folded in the breast pocket. As usual, his hair had massive hairspray, and he smelled of English Leather cologne.

Being a person of class and privilege, Goldstein chose Cole's restaurant on east 6th street at the bottom of the Pacific Electric Building. Frenchy had never been there before and was amazed at the wallpaper and Tiffany lamps. Unfortunately, it reeked of pricy meals, which Frenchy's budget did not include.

"This is on me, so don't worry," Goldstein said as they waited to be seated.

Breathing a sigh of relief, Frenchy smiled curiously, wondering why all this was happening.

"Thanks, man."

The host sat them near the window, not even batting an eye that Frenchy was a person of color. Many high-end establishments were not color-friendly, something he knew through everyday chatter. Perhaps this place is more progressive, or his shirt and tie made a difference. He wasn't sure. The table settings featured folded linen napkins with two forks, a knife, and a spoon lined to the right, unlike any restaurant he had dined at before. His experience was usually one fork, spoon, knife, and straw.

The host poured them water and handed them menus referring to Goldstein by name, with a "Mr." preceding it, which let Frenchy know he was a regular.

"The waiter will be with you in a minute," the host said.

Frenchy opened the menu, and the sticker shock made his toes scrunch up as the numbers scrolled slowly toward his unsuspecting eyes. While focusing intently on the exorbitant prices, he was utterly oblivious to the food choices, trying not to reveal he had never been to a high-end restaurant. He never knew a salad could cost the same as a pair of shoes.

The waiter presented himself in a white dress shirt, a red vest, bow tie with a white apron wrapped around his waist. His mannerisms were slow and delicate while looking at each customer directly in the eyes.

"May I offer appetizers, gentlemen?" he said with a slight British accent.

"We are on a time limit, so we need our food as soon as possible," Goldstein demanded.

"Very well. I will give you a minute to make your selection."

"I know what I want. The original French dip sandwich, please," Goldstein abruptly said.

"Would that be full or half?"

"Full."

"For you, sir?"

"I will have the same," Frenchy added to keep it simple even though he was unsure what a French dip was.

"Very well. Good choice," the waiter said, scooping up the extra silverware.

"And to drink?" the Britt asked.

"I'll have cranberry and lime juice," Goldstein replied, looking at his Rolex/Panerai black watch that had Roman numerals combined with standard numbers for telling time.

"The same?" the waiter asked, looking at Frenchy.

"Root beer, please," Frenchy responded, wondering what the cranberry mixture tasted like. Regardless, Goldstein undoubtedly grew up on the right side of the tracks.

"So, what brings us here for lunch?" Frenchy point blank asked.

"I wanted to talk to you about the Monroe case."

"I hope you have some answers. Unfortunately, I keep hitting dead ends."

"As you know, Curphey is under a lot of pressure with this," he began. "Washington is on him, Fox studio, the press, CIA, and the FBI. This is bigger than us."

"That's more the reason to get it right, isn't it?"

"We, I mean, I, am in awe of how you approach your job with such vigor while seeking the facts. It's noble and admirable. But in this case, we must all take a step back and let it flow."

"So why choose me for this case? Someone like you seems far more experienced at going with the flow. Me? Curphey has reamed my butt several times for being overzealous with the job. The Kovacs' case in particular. If they didn't want me doing it my way, then why not you? They could have put anyone else on this case."

"I have no idea, but we are where we are. It just makes sense, at this point, to get it out of the coroner's office and put it to rest. You need to take a step back."

"You mean, overlook the truth?"

Goldstein picked up his fork and inspected it's cleanliness, twirling it around like a carousel. After receiving the seal of approval, he meticulously placed the white linen napkin in his lap as their waiter appeared with the food.

"You're a family man Lionel," Goldstein said, pouring the *Au Jus* on his sandwich. "You have a wife and kids to consider. So, I feel for you."

Frenchy leaned forward and looked intently at Goldstein, slowly taking a bite of his sandwich, then swallowing.

"What do you mean? Why would you feel sorry for me? I'm just doing my job. If there are unforeseen consequences, at least I can go to sleep at night knowing I did my best."

Focusing his eyes in the distance, as if retrieving data from his brain's hard drive, Goldstein picked up his linen napkin and carefully patted his mouth.

"Good for you, my man. We all need sleep. Look, I noticed your tires are looking worn," Goldstein said, pulling out his wallet. "Take this and handle your car. It's on me."

Goldstein flipped out his Standard Oil credit card and casually tossed it on the table.

"Just give it back whenever you're done getting your ride up to speed. That's a nice car, and I'd hate to see it stranded on the road."

Frenchy stared down at the card with wide eyes, then glanced at Goldstein.

"I can't take this from you."

"Sure you can. I see everything you are going through and have always been on your side. I've never told anyone this, but it was you that added those names during the Stokes inquest, right? We might have disagreements, but were on the same team and must stick together. Helping you is something I want to do. Besides, my folks are well off. Now, don't go buying diamond rings or anything."

"I'm speechless. That's pretty cool of you."

"Don't get mushy on me," Goldstein laughed. "Alright. We have to get back to work. How did you like the French dip?"

"Very tasty. I might have to come back here."

"My parent's friend owns this."

"Must be nice."

When the two returned to the office, Alvaro had placed the toxicology report on Frenchy's desk. It had a new conclusion contradicting the earlier findings. This one revealed two drugs in her bloodstream: Phenobarbital, the generic name for Nembutal, listed at 13 mg, and Chloral Hydrate at 8 mg.

Frenchy looked at his notes because he did not remember seeing a prescription bottle for Chloral Hydrate, the oldest sleep medication. Doctors used it to induce sleep before surgery. He was glad he kept a copy of the log sheet since all her property items were still missing.

Frenchy double-checked the list, and none included Chloral Hydrate, causing him grave concern. So now there's a drug with no prescription and path to how it entered her system. It did not show up in her stomach and was not in the preliminary tests. *So, where did the Chloral Hydrate come from?*

Frenchy stared at the report feeling a headache coming on as questions continued to multiply. The stench of this death infected every aspect of its growing complexity.

Driving home down San Fernando Road, Frenchy thought about the credit card Goldstein gave him, still confused about his intent. Nevertheless, he was grateful for lunch and appreciated the friendly gesture, being his first time eating at a place like that. Frenchy loved the ambiance of fine dining and wanted to take Tipy to experience a high-end eatery while being a true gentleman. He envisioned opening the door, pulling out her chair, and treating his wife like a queen. For their anniversary in January, perhaps he could save up and spoil her as she deserved.

Since it was Friday, thoughts of getting together with his friends sounded especially good. Their mortgage was paid, and this check only had a few bills, plus groceries. The car note wasn't due until the 17th, so his next payday could cover that. Getting compensated every Friday was good but required careful budgeting. However, LA County was changing soon to bi-monthly pay, an idea Frenchy hated.

Suddenly, the steering wheel began violently shaking as he got closer to home. A rumbling noise began vibrating the entire car, forcing him to the side of the road. The area was mainly open land, with scattered fruit stands and railroad tracks to the right. Whiteman Airport was on the other side of the tracks near the hills where he chased jackrabbits when he was young.

To his dismay, the front passenger tire was flat as a deflated balloon. He popped the trunk to get his spare tire and suddenly remembered his crowbar was home. He now questioned that rash decision of giving it to Tipy.

Looking both ways down the long road, Frenchy tried to see if there was a call box anywhere, but nothing. Seeing them often while driving, he had never used one before and was unaware of how exactly they worked. While contemplating his next move, a big rig truck roared by, sounding off its loud air horn and startling him. The blowing noise of the compressed air faded away the farther it got.

Up ahead a mile or two was Del Gaudio's Market, which he frequented often. The owners were an Italian couple, Salvatore and Esther Del Gaudio, who treated each customer special. They served the best Italian submarine sandwiches on the planet, much better than the expensive French dip he had earlier. It was a small storefront with 'Knudsen Dairy Products' painted in big letters below the store name. Their house was right behind the market, painted with white trim and a chain-link fence protecting it. They knew Frenchy by name because he stopped at the stand outside the store to get a fresh cup of orange juice each morning.

The walk to the market was blistering, especially in his work attire, so he loosened his neck button. It didn't take that long to reach the store, but being hot and thirsty, he first took a drink from the fountain because juice didn't quench thirst better than H2O.

"Hi, Mrs. Del Gaudio," Frenchy said, wiping his face with his handkerchief.

"Frenchy! How is everything?"

"I got a flat down the road. I need to use the payphone but wanted to hydrate first."

"Oh no, that's too bad. Today is a hot one." Mrs. Del Gaudio said, with her pseudo-Italian accent. Dressed in an apron and hair in a bun, she picked up a toy and tossed it towards the back.

"How are Tipy and the kids?" she asked.

"Everyone is good. The baby is getting big," Frenchy boasted.

"It seems like she just had him. We never get a chance to chat in the morning. You're always so rushed."

"You know I can't start my day without your fresh juice. So anyway, let me go make this call real quick, and I'll come right back."

"Sure!"

Frenchy stepped out the door where the phone booth stood, disappointed he was leaving the smell of Italian meatballs that the fan blew in his direction. He reached in his pocket for a dime but realized he didn't have one, forcing him to return inside. Mrs. Del Gaudio smiled with her palm out, holding two nickels.

"Thanks."

He called the house, and luckily, Boppie would bring the crowbar. While waiting, Frenchy went back inside and exchanged small talk with Mrs. Del Gaudio.

Boppie arrived quickly in his white Ford Fairlane with a big smile.

"Man, you know you were playing with fire riding on those tires. You're lucky not to get stuck in the boondocks."

"Man, this Monroe stuff has my mind detached."

While driving to the Pontiac, hot air blew through the open car windows making a whisking noise.

"There it is on the other side," Frenchy pointed. "You gotta make a U-turn."

"Got it."

"I'm gonna put on the spare, then head over to the Mobile station on Woodman and get all new ones. Can you follow me?"

"You got it like that? I always have to get mine one at a time."

"You're not going to believe this, but one of my coworkers gave me his credit card to get some tires."

"You lying!"

"No, I swear. This cat and I have never gone to lunch together, but he invited me to join him today. He took me to Coles, of all places. I didn't even know if they let Blacks in there, but I got treated like a king. Then he pulled out a credit card and told me to get my car straight."

"Man, talk about timing!"

"The Gods are looking out for me, or maybe it's Marilyn's spirit since I'm the only one that seems to care how she died."

"How's that going?"

"Let's just say it's messy."

As Frenchy took off the old tire, he chucked it to the side. Boppie went to pick it up and put it into the trunk.

"Hey Frenchy, where is the air cap? No wonder you got a flat."

"What are you talking about?"

"The cap is gone, and the stem is jacked. Looks like somebody got you. Maybe they really didn't like Black people at Coles," Boppie joked. "When your stem is sliced like that, it's only a matter of time before it all leaks out."

"Naw. I didn't take my car to Coles. Probably went flat because it was bald as an eagle."

"Looks a bit odd to me. We used to do that as a prank."

"Guess I'm lucky. At least I got this credit card."

Boppie followed Frenchy to the Mobile station on Woodman Avenue. He would have preferred Elias Brake & Tire because he knew Elias well. However, the card required use at one of the Standard Oil subsidiaries. The two dropped the black Pontiac off and then went home. They had a few hours to kill, so they began rounding up the crew for their card game, which they played well into the night, missing the closing time to pick up the vehicle.

"Hey man, can you drop me off in the morning to get my car?" Frenchy asked Boppie.

"I figured once the game started, we weren't going back this evening. Now I gotta get up early on a Saturday. I should let Tipy take my car, and I can watch cartoons with the kids."

"I have never seen a 24-year-old man love cartoons like you. You're such a square."

"Hey, love me some Bugs Bunny."

"What is it about Bugs Bunny that you like, man?"

"You just gotta pay attention and listen. Bugs is a philosopher. He says, 'Don't take life too seriously–you'll never get out alive!' Words to live by."

"I never thought of Bugs bunny like that. I don't want to interrupt your Saturday morning Zen session, but I really need that ride."

"Don't worry, I'll take you," Boppie said.

"Cool."

The following morning at 7 am, Boppie drove Frenchy to pick up the car as promised. He got out with him to check things out.

"This baby is like brand new," the gas station attendant said. "New tires, shock absorbers, and lube job. We washed it too."

"I think I'll bring mine here next time," Boppie expressed.

"I've put a lot of miles on it driving to LA every day. I feel much better now."

"That will be $307.16," the attendant said.

Frenchy reached into his wallet and pulled out the credit card. The attendant had a small black card imprinter and placed a three-part charge slip inside. He took the card, positioned it in the reader, then slid it across, leaving the credit card imprint on the paper.

He returned the card to Frenchy without even looking at the name. After filling in the total, he wrote down the license plate number, and had Frenchy sign his name, then returned the card with one of the carbon copies and a smile.

"Thank you, sir," the attendant said.

"Thank you. You have a great day," Frenchy responded before turning around.

"Time to head to work and see what lay ahead in the world of death and power. The good news is no traffic today. Thanks, man. I appreciate your help."

"Alright. I'll catch you later."

"Later."

The drive to work was incredibly smooth, as Frenchy enjoyed the light traffic. He felt extremely grateful to Goldstein for his unexpected kindness. There were still generous people in this world, and who would have thought one of them would be Goldstein.

When he walked into the office, his mind went straight to Monroe. The magnitude of what Deputy DA Miner said was the first thing that came to mind when he looked inside the Monroe file to assess where it stood. The deputy heard a happy, not depressed Marilyn Monroe on the tape, which did not align with the suicide narrative.

Casually shuffling through all the documents, he quickly noticed the initial autopsy report that said 'no poison' was missing, along with the preliminary police report. So, he flagged down Alvaro to see what he knew.

"Que paso Alvaro?"

"Hola Jefe. Same ole, same ole."

"Have you seen anyone rummaging through my files lately?"

"If you count Schwartz, he's been like a fly on poop around your desk."

"That's normal. Anything else going on?"

"Somethings up, but I don't know what? Curphey is acting loco, always slamming stuff around. More secret service guys were lurking about. They went into Curphey's office last night and stayed a long time. Put him in an even worse mood. I got the hell out of here."

"What do you think it was about?"

"Had to be Monroe," Alvaro said. "Her press agent came by asking for her belongings. I referred her to Curphey, and he was hotter than a firecracker at me. He warned me not to send people to him again. What was I supposed to do?"

"You handled it right. He did say everything must come through him. What a hypocrite. So, what happened?"

"Curphey told her no and made her leave empty-handed. He was rude too."

"When was this?"

"Yesterday when you went to lunch."

"Never a dull moment. Now I'm missing some things from her file. Things are getting really weird around here."

"You're telling me? Yesterday at lunch, I thought someone was following me. Then when I got off, they were standing by my car. It was spooky," Alvaro said.

"Really? It sounds like we both should be watching our backs."

Just then, Goldstein walked in wearing an olive-green suit.

"Good morning, Goldstein," Frenchy chimed.

"Morning," Goldstein responded without making eye contact.

"Here's your card. Thanks a lot. It came in handy yesterday."

Goldstein gave Frenchy a strange look and sat down nervously, rearranging things on his desk. Frenchy stood up, placed it in front of him, and then walked toward the restroom. Alvaro followed.

"Señor Tightwad gave you his credit card? That vato doesn't even tip the shoeshine guy. I wonder what got into him?"

"I don't know, but he seems different this morning. Nothing like yesterday."

"He's a special kind of psycho. I think the hairspray leaks into his brain."

"Alvaro, you always make me laugh."

Frenchy decided to head downstairs and talk to Danbacker one more time. The questions were nagging him like a buzzing fly you can't ward off.

"Hi, Danbacker, how are you doing today?"

"I'm grand. Just another day at the office."

"I have a question for you. The pill bottles you collected at Monroe's house. Did any say Chloral Hydrate?"

"Definitely not. I would have remembered that. Why?"

"It showed up in her last toxicology report."

"None of the containers listed that. You might want to ask her doctors if they prescribed it."

"I already thought about that. Thanks."

The property room was Frenchy's next stop to check if anyone had returned Monroe's items. Unfortunately, everything was still missing, including the correlating log sheets. This presented a real problem because the only person who could have everything was Curphey.

Frenchy bit the bullet, needing to have this discussion with him no matter how painstaking. He knocked rapidly on the door with Marilyn's file in hand and entered when beckoned.

Curphey wore the oddest shaped glasses on top of his beak-like nose, reminding Frenchy of a buzzard. He contorted his face and seemed oblivious to looking like Groucho Marx while sending spit bubbles every time he spoke.

"Deputy Grandison. What brings you here? I hope it's a closed Monroe file."

"That's what I need to talk to you about."

"Talk? Talk about what? I need this case closed."

"I still lack all the necessary information to sign off on this case, and her property is still missing."

"Don't worry about that. I'll add everything else to the files later. Is that it? Come on, Grandison."

"That's not just it. The first police report is missing from my file, and the original tox results are too."

"That doesn't matter because we know she had Barbiturates in her blood," Curphey blared, seething. "What is your problem? Your handling of this case has been reckless and ridiculous! I'm losing my patience with you, boy."

Blood rushed quickly to Frenchy's head when he heard the word boy. Despite the pressure, one thing that had previously held was an element of professionalism in the office. Yes, Curphey was an ass but had never gotten personal. Frenchy hesitated, then cleared his throat to compose himself.

"I'm still waiting for the suicide team report and answers about the Chloral Hydrate. These things are not within my control, sir."

"Grandison, you have nothing but excuses. I'm giving you until the end week, and that's it. We should have that report, and you will close this out. Understand? That's all, Deputy!"

Never had Frenchy's skin crawled like this before. Curphey's thirst for power and lack of morals seeped through the pores of his pastie skin. Calling him 'boy' sent a gut-wrenching feeling making Frenchy despise the ground Curphey walked on. Yet, he knew allowing this negative energy to consume him would not be constructive. He had to be bigger than that.

Stomping to his desk, he questioned if he was the person for this job. His hand trembled in anger, wishing he could tell Curphey what he thought.

Alvaro saw Frenchy's flushed face and stepped over to him.

"The look of Curphey is written all over your expression."

"I consider myself a reasonable man and treat people the way I want to be treated – giving respect even when it's not warranted. I do my job with knowledge and precision, never taking shortcuts. No one has worked here a shorter amount of time, yet they handed this Monroe case to me, and I have followed all the rules while working harder than anyone. No comprendo, Alvaro. I don't get it."

"I do. You are a newbie, and they thought they could play you. Or maybe a sacrificial cordero."

"Alright, Alvaro, what is a cordero?"

"I'm going to let you find that out for yourself. But sometimes, you can't see what is right in front of you. You know who Curphey is. The question is, how malo is malo?

"Superbad."

"Listen, I am transferring to another county agency. I wanted to let you know first."

"What? You're the only one I can talk to."

"Sorry, amigo, but El diablo lives here. I feel him, smell him, and I need to get away from him. I've been having nightmares, and mi esposa told me it's time to vámonos. The dead spirits got nothing on this gringo. I told you that before."

"You always have to do what's best for you and your family, my friend," Frenchy sympathized, placing his hand on Alvaro's shoulder. "In a way, I'm struggling with the same issue. And you know what makes this bad?"

"What's that?" Alvaro asked

"I love my work. I'm good at it. I know the rules, I'm good with people, and dead bodies don't bother me. But more importantly, I need this job."

"I hear you. You gotta do what you gotta do."

"So, when are you leaving?"

"Two weeks."

"We can go to lunch on your last day. On me."

"Gracias, señor. I would like that."

"How about the Pantry on 9th & Figueroa."

"Sounds like a plan."

For some reason, Alvaro's news felt like a real loss to Frenchy. Without him, nearly everyone at the coroner's office would be superficial. He rubbed the nape of his neck and then sat at his desk, trying to figure out what he was missing with this fast-paced case.

Curphey decided to hold updates for the press and public. Frenchy felt he was setting the stage for a suicide ruling by detailing a partial analysis based on questionable sources. He stated, *'death was due to a self-administered overdose of sedative drugs,'* something with serious flaws. It wasn't clear it was self-administered. It would be almost impossible to take that amount of poison without water or vomiting. This bothered him as an objective person.

Curphey also claimed Marilyn made suicide attempts in the past. However, Frenchy could not find any hospital documentation or medical records to collaborate those claims. This was sloppy at best.

He added she called for help and was previously rescued, which led Frenchy back to the housekeeper and Dr. Greenson emphasizing the phone in the first police report. He found that odd from the onset.

In his specific explanation, Curphey announced:

"The high level of barbiturates and chloral hydrate in the blood, which, with other evidence from the autopsy, indicates the probable ingestion of a large amount of the drugs within a short period of time. The completely empty bottle of Nembutal, the prescription for which was filled the day before the ingestion of the drugs; and the locked door which was unusual leads to the high probability of suicide."

This statement left Frenchy completely numb.

At work the next day, Frenchy was on a mission because he knew time was working against him. He racked his brain, which still bothered him about how Marilyn was lying in bed with the phone in her hand and what Danbacker said about the house smelling like cleanser. Detective Byron had only offered minimal information, so he wanted to contact Officer Jack Clemmons, who was first on the scene.

He rarely asked his mother-in-law for help, but her working for LAPD was his only hope for contacting Clemmons, so he placed a call.

"Mrs. James speaking."

"Hello, Veda. It's your favorite son-in-law. How are you today."

"You're my only son-in-law," Veda said, laughing.

"How is work going?"

"No murders today, so I guess that's a good thing. Anything new with the Marilyn Monroe case? No one around here seems to know anything."

"Actually, that's why I'm calling you. I need your help."

"What can I do you for?"

"I need the phone number of the first cop on the scene, Jack Clemmons."

"Hum. Frenchy, Tipy spoke to me about the strange things with this case. You gave her a crowbar for protection. Why didn't you come to me? I could have had squad cars watching out."

"I don't think they will harm her or the kids."

"She told me about the diary too. This is dangerous stuff, Frenchy. She said it mentioned the Kennedys. You must be careful. Your family is the number one priority. You've got a job most colored men would love to have. Why would you slander the Kennedys when it looks like they're going to do something good for this country? The Police Department will handle it."

Damn! Tipy blabbed. Frenchy wasn't surprised because he knew his wife, but now this conversation was more difficult.

"I'm not slandering or even dealing with Bobby or John Kennedy. They are the least of my worries. I'm just trying to close out the case. The first police report is missing, and LAPD doesn't list anyone in charge, so I am at a standstill. I only need a statement from him."

"Sounds simple enough. As long as you're not stirring the pot, I'll help. Sometimes you must let the powers that be, do what they do. There are big forces out there, and you must walk a fine line for both yourself and Tipy, not to mention the kids."

"The only thing I want is Marilyn Monroe off my desk. She has been a thorn in my side for way too long."

"I'll see what I can do."

After taking a deep breath and exhaling, Frenchy hoped this path worked. Veda was a brilliant woman, who became the first female to work in LAPD's detective unit. It was because of her that he sought out this job, hoping to provide security for Tipy. He could tell she loved bragging about him and his title with the Foothill Division staff, and he loved feeling worthy of her respect.

About an hour later, she phoned with Clemmons home number, allowing Frenchy to set up a lunch date. They met at Tommy's Hamburgers on Rampart and Beverly, which had recently expanded from only a small stand to accommodate their fast-growing popularity. Frenchy loved the homecooked chili they put on their burgers with its seemingly mustard-like taste intertwined. He always got extra chili with onions and cheese.

After they got the food, Frenchy found a quiet corner for them to talk. Clemmons was in his mid-forties with white hair and very thick glasses. His face was pale, almost translucent, except for his pink nose.

"Sergeant Clemmons, thanks for taking time to come meet with me."

"No problem deputy. I love eating at this place," he said, unwrapping his burger dripping with chili. "What's on your mind?"

"Like I mentioned on the phone, I'm trying to close the Monroe case and find myself confused by two conflicting police reports, amongst many other things. So I wanted to get accurate information straight from the source. Tell me, what was the scene at Marilyn's house the night she died?"

"Well, to put it in one word deputy, mindboggling. I was on-duty as watch commander when Dr. Greenson called the station at 4:25 am, and I went to the house. Mrs. Murray greeted me at the door and took me to the bedroom where Marilyn's body was stretched out, with her head lying face down, buried in a pillow, arms down by her side."

"What were your first thoughts? Did it look natural?"

"Nothing looked right, especially her body. No one would be in that position."

"Really?" Frenchy asked, pinching his chin. "Sounds like you have some reservations about what happened."

"Let me break this down to you deputy. According to what they told me, her body was discovered around midnight. They were in the room with her dead body for four hours. Four hours! I asked why they didn't call sooner than 4:25. Nobody wanted to answer. They tried to ignore me. I pressed them and finally, Greenson told me they had to get permission from the studio's publicity department before notifying anyone."

Frenchy shot up an eyebrow. "That's what they said?"

"It was rank nonsense. That wasn't an answer and had no truth to it."

"You know what always bothered me? Two doctors in the early morning are instantly there. What did you think about that?"

"That's exactly what I thought. It bothered me too. But I decided to let it pass because I thought the detective in route would investigate."

"So, what happened with the detective, because it seems that investigation never took place?"

"Both doctors suspiciously changed their story from midnight to 3:30 am when Sgt. Byron took their statements."

"That's why their timelines on the police reports didn't make sense. Those doctors would have been more accessible at midnight, rather than miraculously appearing in five minutes at 3:35am. I never bought that story, so I requested a second interview."

"Yeah, but they managed to get away with it. Nobody said anything else about it."

"What else did you notice at the scene?"

"Like I said, nothing seemed right. Dr. Greenson pointed out to me the nightstand by the bed and there was about 8 prescription bottles that contained various types of prescription drugs and they were all empty. I can still see the doctor standing there pointing and waving at the table saying 'she must have taken all these!' He directed my attention to them so I stuck my head over there and they were all empty."

"That is staged if I ever saw staging."

"But here's the kicker, I went to the bathroom just outside her room, and there was no glass. No water glass anywhere."

"Man, that's what I noticed in the pictures. There was no water to take the damn pills."

"There wasn't a suicide note either. But deputy, the strangest thing was the attitude of Doctor Greenson. He was cocky, sarcastic, and derogatory. He treated me contemptuously, and I couldn't figure out how this psychiatrist, who had just lost a patient, acted so callous. It just didn't fit. No remorse or sadness."

"How did the other two behave?"

"Ms. Murray was depressed and very quiet. Timid. Dr. Engelberg seemed dejected also. The thing is, this case needs a thorough investigation, and instead, they take everyone off the case. Nothing is being done. I don't understand."

Scooping the last bit of chili from his wrapper, Frenchy stared into the bustling traffic on Rampart Blvd with the midday sun's reflection bouncing off the cars, processing this revelation.

"Do you know who's handling it? I just get the runaround."

"I'm treated like a leper now. It's like, how dare me do police work. I smell something rotten and don't quite know what to do. I have no clue who's handling it."

"Did you hear about Bobby Kennedy being in town and maybe at her house?"

"Yeah, there's talk at the station about that. But Bobby is friends with Chief Parker, who will quash anything that implicates the Kennedys."

"I read her diary, and there are many persons of interest. I don't do police work, but I know how to classify the manner of death. This is bordering homicide, not suicide."

"Is that what you're going to rule it?"

"I think there needs to be an inquest at the very least."

"I hope so."

"Well, thanks for the info. At least I know I'm not going crazy."

Knowing to trust his instincts, a feeling of vindication and validation was a needed bonus. After returning to the office, Frenchy added his conversation with Clemmons to the file.

Shuffling through the mounds of reports and notes, he reread the toxicology results. Dr. Abernathy only performed microscopic tests on the liver and blood. *What about her other organs?* After observing hundreds of these reports, this stood out immensely. The stomach and kidney were missing. Frenchy dialed Abernathy to get some answers.

"Hi, Dr. Abernathy. I have a question for you."

"Sure, what's going on?"

"I was looking at the microscopic report for Monroe and wondering why you didn't perform any test on the stomach."

"We had time constraints. Those would have taken longer."

"But that was the only way to determine what drugs she actually ingested. The preliminary results said her stomach was empty, and no poison was present."

"It was in her blood and liver. That's all that mattered."

"Could that still be done?"

"That's never going to happen."

"Why?"

"Two reasons. One, Dr. Curphey would never allow it. Two, her organs are no longer here."

"What do you mean they're not here?"

The line was silent for a few moments.

"If you want to know anything else about that, I suggest you talk to Dr. Curphey."

Placing down the receiver, Frenchy felt like an insect getting squashed by forces out of his control. He had never, ever had organs disappear. Frenchy smelled the stench of something rotten, and like Sgt. Clemmons, he did not know what to do.

The beginning of the new week brought a sense of despair and confusion to Frenchy. Schwartz was almost as snarky as Curphey, while the office tension never ended.

"Grandison, Curphey wants you to set up a press conference this morning for the findings of the suicide investigation team and the medical examiner."

"Did they find the lost tissues?"

"What is that supposed to mean?" Schwartz scuffed.

"It means we still have unanswered questions. There are missing reports, log sheets, and property logs. Now there's a revised toxicology report that said there were enough drugs to have killed her ten times when the first one said no poison in her stomach. That one is missing. To top it off, I personally saw bruises, but the autopsy diagram shows none. Are we running a sham organization here?"

"Listen to me. Either you are a team player, or you're not. This case is bigger than you or me. But you need to ask yourself if you still want this job."

"I want the truth, that's all."

"Do you? At what expense? Think about it, deputy."

"I have no doubt Curphey is going to spew that same nonsense just like the last one, highlighting what fits the suicide narrative and omitting what doesn't. That's not how you trained me, sir! No, I don't know what happened to Marilyn Monroe, but what I do know is people are being deceptive and lying. That's what I know!"

"Well, what I know is Curphey wants the death certificate signed right after the press conference and this case out of our office. I've worked here a long time, and I understand your passion. Sometimes things just don't work out the way we want. And when you accepted that badge, you accepted all that comes with it."

"But doesn't that include the truth?"

"Who knows what the truth is? You, me, Dr. Curphey? This case is just one of many. Take my advice, close it out and move on. Live to fight another day. That's what's best for you and your family. Trust me."

The forces were methodically closing in on him, so Frenchy made one last trip to Noguchi, who was in his office downstairs.

"Hi, Dr. Noguchi. How are you today?"

"Deputy Grandison, I'm fine. What brings you down here?"

"I have the death certificate. You signed it saying suicide. Is that really what you concluded?"

"Based on many variables, it does appear to be so."

"You have always been one to explain in detail your decisions. It seemed different with Monroe. Why?" Frenchy asked.

"Haven't we had this discussion before?"

"Doc, do you really think she committed suicide?"

"Let me see the death certificate."

Frenchy pulled it out of the file and placed it on his desk. Noguchi scratched his neck and slightly fidgeted while staring intensely at the document. He then circled the words' probable Suicide."

"It says probable," handing it back to Frenchy.

With no argument, the word 'probable' left a little wiggle room, but Frenchy was still uneasy.

"Well, what about the missing tissue samples? Anything on those?

"No," Noguchi said calmly.

"So that's it?"

"Lionel, you are good man. We face many battles in life. Some we can win, some we lose. But there's an old saying:

He will win that knows when to fight and when to not. But he who's in battle slain will never rise to fight again. Think about it. I believe we both have work to do."

After leaving Noguchi's office, he headed to the press conference. Noguchi was a wise man that Frenchy respected but struggled to understand his actions with the case of Marilyn Monroe. Perhaps he felt this was a losing battle. Frenchy proceeded to watch the press conference knowing it was total bull.

There was a short table with about a dozen microphones where Dr. Curphey, along with Dr. Litman and Dr. Farberow from the Suicide Investigation Team, squeezed behind. Reading from a prepared statement, Curphey sat in the center and began the press conference, while smoking a cigar.

"Now that the final toxicological report and that of the psychiatric consultants have been received and considered, it is my conclusion that the death of Marilyn Monroe was caused by a self-administered overdose of sedative drugs and that the mode of death is probable suicide. The final toxicological report reveals that the barbiturate, previously reported as a lethal dose, has been positively identified as Nembutal by the toxicologist. In the course of completing his routine examination, the toxicologist, Dr. Raymond Abernathy, discovered, in addition to the Nembutal present, a large dose of chloral hydrate. Miss Monroe had often expressed wishes to give up, to withdraw, and even to die. On more than one occasion in the past, when disappointed and depressed, she made a suicide attempt using sedative drugs. On those occasions, she had called for help and had been rescued. From the information collected about the events of the evening of August 4th, it is our opinion that the same pattern was repeated except for the rescue. It has been our practice with similar information collected in other cases in the past to recommend a certification for such deaths as probable suicide. On the basis of all the information obtained, it is our opinion that the case is a probable suicide. The Suicide Investigation Team."

Listening to this statement was painful as Dr. Curphey attempted to wrap Monroe's case into a neat, pretty package. However, the press was very aggressive and, at times, contemptuous, asking questions that validated some of Frenchy's concerns.

Press: Due to this ruling, what legal impact will this have on the life insurance policy on the estate of Ms. Monroe?

Dr. Curphey: I have no idea. This is not our primary concern.

Press: Dr. Curphey, what is the nature of that Chloral Hydrate?

Dr. Curphey: Well, it is prescribed as a sedative. Therapeutically prescribed as a sedative.

Press: Was it prescribed to her?

Dr. Curphey: It is a prescription drug.

Press: Did she have a prescription?

Dr. Curphey: That hasn't been determined yet.

Wanting clearly to avoid specific details about the Chloral Hydrate, Curphey abruptly ended everything and left. Frenchy found his reaction telling. They have no idea how it got into her system, which should have prompted an inquest. The other doctors at the table exited as well, leaving reporters frustrated.

Since it was Monday, Frenchy looked forward to the next two days off. He felt like he had been through a typhoon and was concerned about how to handle signing the death certificate. He sighed exasperated, wiping his hands on his pants as they felt unusually clammy. This wasn't right, and he knew it.

The summons to Curphey's office was swift. He felt the need to speak his mind despite knowing his boss had already decided the matter. But unfortunately, it was determined from the beginning with no regard for the facts. He slowly walked to Curphey's office with Marilyn's file, dreading what he knew was to come.

"Deputy, did Schwartz tell you what I need from you?"

"Yes, he did. We need to talk, Dr. Curphey."

"Talk about what? Do you have the death certificate?"

"I still don't have all the necessary information to sign off on this case."

"Whatever you don't have, I will add later."

"Missing documents, switched reports, destroyed tissue samples? How will you add those? Better yet, why are they missing to begin with?"

"Grandison, I've told you what to do, and you're going to do it. You've been warned about this, and you're in way over your head. Now sign that death certificate or else!"

"Sir, I have seen a lot here. I never understood why you called an accidental death a murder, a police killing justified, or refused to investigate when it's clearly warranted. I'm only 22 and not going to pretend I know your motives, but I do know the rules. I know right from wrong. And mostly, I know we should all be better than this."

"Just sign it!" Curphey screamed.

Thoughts of Noguchi's words rang inside Frenchy's head. He wasn't going to win this battle, so he bent over the desk, signed the certificate, and immediately walked out of the room feeling compromised. When he got to his desk, he grabbed Alvaro's arm and headed toward the door.

"Let's go, buddy. It's lunchtime."

The two jumped in Frenchy's car. Alvaro saw Frenchy's face embedded with a frown while staring intently at the road and pressing hard on the gas pedal.

"I've never seen you angry before."

"It's not anger as much as frustration."

"You cannot change people, compadre. Only they can change themselves. We are fighting a well-oiled machine of deception. I've heard stories that would make your toes curl. The latest is that Curphey started the Suicide Investigation team."

"What do you mean started by Curphey?"

"It's his operation. It is not independent."

"So, everything from top to bottom is a sham?" Frenchy summarized.

"You are not a sham. I am not a sham."

"Then we are in the way."

"I would give that a yes."

"We are not a part of the good ole boys club," Frenchy conceded.

"Definitely not. The question is, what do we do about it?"

"I should not have signed," Frenchy said, shaking his head. "I should have followed my gut."

"What's done is done. It can't be changed now."

They pulled into the parking lot of the Pantry Cafe. Numerous people were in line outside the front door. It had red and white striped awnings over each window, protecting customers from the brutal sun rays. Frenchy just stared, drifting into deep thought before getting out of the car.

"You know, Marilyn dined here. Isn't that ironic?"

The café was loud and busy. The two chose to sit at the counter to avoid waiting in line. Frenchy got a Philly cheese steak sandwich, and Alvaro a BLT.

"So Curphey rigged the suicide investigation team, huh?" Frenchy rehashed.

"Hermano, a lot is going on. We are guppies in murky water with sharks circling us. That's why I'm leaving, and you should do the same. I told you before. They have no morals."

"I like my job. Besides a few, I get treated with respect. That says a lot for a young Black man."

"I get it, but they are rummaging through your desk non-stop. Goldstein asked me to get the property room key for him with no explanation a while back. He's above me, so I had to do it."

"I wouldn't worry about Goldstein. He got me some new tires, so he's fine by me."

"All that glitters ain't gold."

"You don't trust him, huh?"

"The loudest man in the room is the weakest. He comes in flashing expensive suits and watches but works in the coroner's office. He feels like a plant."

Alvaro's words made Frenchy briefly question Goldstein's motives. *"But, how could new tires ever be a bad thing?"*

"What have you heard?"

"He keeps a low profile, but I don't need to hear anything. Most snakes hide in the grass blades until they strike. Just watch him, man. I'm telling you."

"I get it. Things are just so messed up with the Monroe case. I talked to Noguchi, and he circled 'probable' in the suicide determination. It's like he was trying to tell me something."

"Let's think about that. If it's 'probable suicide,' then it's not accidental," Alvaro analyzed.

"Well, it couldn't be accidental with that many pills. You do not accidentally take 30 or more tablets. There's no way. The only other option is that somebody killed her, but they don't want that. So 'probable' leaves that open, doesn't it?"

"Yes, it does. Think about it. Either it's determined to be suicide, or it's not. Probable means likely to be or to happen, but not necessarily so."

"So, what it means is her death is undetermined. That's what it should have said."

"Instead, everyone wants this to go away. Why?"

"That's the million-dollar question. I keep going back to her diary and the press conference she was planning. If it's that high up, then I'm a little fish in the way."

"Bingo."

"I let Curphey have it. I'm probably going to get fired."

The two were silent for a moment with the sound of meat sizzling, grease popping, and plates clanking in the background. They observed the chiefs hustling over the counter, rushing plates to the waiters slapping them down for pick up.

Alvaro finished his BLT and took a sip of his coke.

"Do you know how hard it is to get fired from the county? Then all your grievances would come to light in the process. Curphey wouldn't want that."

"You're a smart man Alvaro. I guess they would just make my life miserable then," Frenchy said with a smile.

"I wouldn't mess with these people, which is why I'm leaving. They play low and dirty."

"I won't take what they say personally and just stay focused on my job."

"You're a better hombre than me."

"Let's get back to the snake pit. You enjoy your new job. I'm going to miss you, man."

After paying the bill, they returned to the office only to be greeted by two district attorney investigators standing by Frenchy's desk. Although not uncommon, the look on their faces told a strange story.

"Mr. Grandison?"

"Yes."

"Lionel Grandison?"

"Yes."

"You are under arrest."

"Excuse me?"

"Hold your hands out."

Those words crept down Frenchy's spine like a throbbing chill he could not shake. Before he could comply with the order, he felt pressure on his arms, violently spinning him around. Suddenly a jolt pierced his shoulders while simultaneously, his hands were grabbed and pulled behind his back. The chilling sound of clanking and clicking and the feel of metal gripped his wrists. Frenchy saw the wide eyes of his co-workers while they observed his most humiliating moment. Alvaro was the only one with a sympathetic face.

While feeling embarrassed, Frenchy had no clue what this was about, and investigators felt unobligated to share the law he had allegedly violated. As they reached the squad car, a hand was felt on his head, pushing him into the back seat with force, as if he was an animal. No respect. No consideration. No explanation.

The car radio and the two men's silence were deafening. *What did he do?* They made a mistake, and he would explain it when he got to the station. Speaking up to your boss isn't a crime! The timing was ironic, but he was confident he could clarify this misunderstanding.

Placed in an interrogation room, Frenchy sat for what seemed like hours before a tall bald man appeared.

"Mr. Grandison. There was a credit card missing from one of the bodies at the coroner's office. We have reason to believe you took it."

"What? I have never taken a credit card from anyone."

"Well, we have a receipt with your license plate number from a Mobile station. It looks like you helped yourself to some new tires."

"Yes, I bought some tires, but my co-worker gave me his card."

"You're trying to say someone at work likes you so much they bought tires for you? Come on. Surely you can do better than that."

Frenchy could not move or breathe as his splayed fingers covered his eyes and the shocking realization hit him quickly and hard. Alvaro was right about Goldstein. He was not the cool guy Frenchy thought. Frenchy exhaled, poking his lips out, deciding he needed to tell the whole story. Indeed, they would understand.

"My co-worker Lenny Goldstein gave me the card and told me to buy some tires."

The investigator smirked, pursing his lips in an odd sarcastic manner.

"Don't play me stupid. We will lock you up for a long time, boy."

"Call him and ask him."

"We don't have to. We already know the card was stolen from the property room, and you had the key."

"Why would I steal a credit card and sign my name to a purchase? Not to mention I'm in the middle of the biggest investigation in the country. I just signed Marilyn Monroe's death certificate."

"Monroe was buried weeks ago. What, were you working from her crypt. A darkie signing Marilyn Monroe's death certificate. That's the funniest thing I've heard all day?"

"I'm a Deputy Coroner's Aide, with a badge. You should already know that."

The investigator slammed his chair across the room, pounding his fist on the table.

"I ain't got time for no games. You need to confess to stealing the credit card and forgery," he yelled, getting directly in Frenchy's face.

"I did not forge anything! I signed my name because I had permission."

"The name on the card was Harold F. Wallace. He died on August 10th. You took the card from the property room and used it. Didn't you!"

More perplexed than ever, Frenchy realized he had never looked at the name on the card. Instead, he just signed his own name, thinking it was Goldstein's. *Why didn't he look at it?* His head spun in circles thinking back. *How could he be that trusting?*

"I did not take the credit card," Frenchy said softly.

"Let me tell you something, boy. When you go to jail, I'm going to make things extra hard on you."

The investigator left the room, leaving Frenchy's mind swirling, trying to figure this out. He had no defense. None. It looked like he stole the card and used it, period. His emotions ranged from embarrassment to anger. This day went from bad to disastrous.

A different man entered the room about an hour later. Unlike the first guy, his demeanor was a little more personable.

"Can I get some water, please?" Frenchy asked with a dry throat.

"So, you say Goldstein gave you the card. We checked with him, and he doesn't know what you are talking about. He denied ever giving you a card for anything."

Frenchy dropped his shoulders and took a deep breath. Then, he closed his eyes, unable to process this situation.

"Look, I signed my name and used my car. If I stole it, why would I do that? That makes no sense. A lot was going on at the office with the Marilyn Monroe case. I told your partner the truth about everything. He didn't believe a word I said."

The deputy left for a second and then came back with some water.

"You told my partner you signed Marilyn's death certificate. What else can you tell me about the case."

"What do you want me to tell you? That I didn't want to sign it? That the coroner's office and LAPD investigations were raggedy? That I ruffled a lot of feathers because I wanted to follow procedures? That's probably why I'm here now."

The first investigator then walked back into the room, but remained silent.

"Tell me, what made you think she didn't commit suicide?"

"The doctors lied, reports went missing and her property disappeared. There were just too many unanswered questions."

"What property?"

"She had a purse, pill bottles, and some papers."

"What papers?"

Not knowing if he should mention the diary, he wondered why all the sudden interest. After all, these people should be familiar with the Monroe case.

"Just stuff to help me find her next of kin."

"There were rumors of the coroner's office being in possession of some sort of diary. Do you know anything about that?"

Frenchy paused to think, surprised by the question. Unsure what to say, he remembered Veda's warning.

"Yes, we had a book like that. During my investigation, I glanced through it, looking for her next of kin."

"Did you find anything?"

"No."

"What did you find in there?"

Thinking of everything he read, that question felt like a nuclear bomb ready to explode in his face. Does he tell everything or play dumb like he saw nothing? It was apparent this was all about Marilyn, not a credit card. *But how can he get out of this?*

"Look, a lot was going on. I was strictly concentrating on doing my job. There were long pages of notes written in there. Most of which I had no idea what she was talking about. Just a bunch of rambling."

"Are you the only one that saw it?"

"I don't know, but Deputy Danbacker brought it in."

"Since you stole credit cards, are you sure you didn't steal this so-called diary?"

"It was locked in the safe and disappeared on my days off. And like I said, I didn't steal anything."

"Any idea who supposedly took it?"

"The Secret Service was lurking about. Maybe you should ask them."

"You getting smart with me?"

"Look, this is a complicated case, and now I'm sitting here for something I didn't do. Smart? I'm trying to figure out how I got set up."

"Set up, huh? Who else knows this?" he calmly asked.

"Nobody."

"Are you sure?"

"Yes, I'm sure. I guess I need to get an attorney?"

"That's up to you. We are going to book you for grand theft and forgery. Let's go."

All Frenchy could think about was what Tipy and Veda would say. *How could he be so careless and naïve?* Sheriff's deputies hauled him off to take a mug shot, standing in front of a height chart. One deputy held a sign in front of him with booking number 596062. He thought that was demeaning until he went to get printed, and while rolling his fingers on the black ink, things became real. The clerk grabbed each one separately, placed it on the pad, and pressed it from one side to the other. Then processed his palm the same way. The smell of the ink was distinct and something he would never forget. He thought the formaldehyde was repugnant, but ink also had a bad feeling attached to it. What came next exemplified humiliation to its core. He had to strip, get sprayed, and shower in a cage with other men. He stood there buck naked, numb, and ashamed.

After being placed in a cell, Frenchy listened to men cry, yell, and tout each other. When the cell door closed and the sound of the lock turned, he knew, without a doubt, life as he knew it was gone. Noises echoed off the walls with an eerie vibe of the unknown. He looked at his black and white jumpsuit, rehashing the nightmare engulfing him. He needed to call Tipy so she wouldn't worry. His car was at the office, and there was no telling how long he would be there. Finally, he was able to make his one call.

"Hi honey," he said.

"Frenchy, detectives came and wanted to search the house. I asked for a search warrant, and they said they would be back. What's going on?"

"They arrested me."

"OH MY GOD! For what?"

"First, let me tell you, baby, I did not steal anything. They charged me with theft and forgery. It's a setup."

"They were looking for Boppie. Is he involved?"

"Remember when I told you Goldstein gave me his credit card? I never looked at the name. I just got the tires like he told me and returned the card to him the next day. Boppie took me to drop off the car and picked it up. I'm not sure why they are dragging him into this."

"Okay, what should I do?"

"I need a lawyer."

"How can we afford a …, oh my gosh. Okay, I'll take care of it."

"I love you, baby. I need you to believe me. I did nothing wrong. I promise you; I'm innocent."

"I know."

Now staring at the ceiling, his mind drifted to Veda. Since they involved Boppie, surely, Tipy would call her mother. Frenchy wasn't sure anyone would believe him, but he knew Veda would protect her son. After all, she worked at LAPD for 17 years and knew almost everyone, but this would also put her in a shameful position. She worked often with the DA and knew the chief of police William Parker, who Frenchy believed was in on this Monroe conspiracy. Either way, this was bad.

As predicted, Tipy called Veda.

"Good afternoon, Mrs. James speaking."

"Hi, Veda."

"Hey, sweetie. What's going on?"

"I'm surprised you don't already know. They arrested Frenchy."

"No, I haven't heard. What are the charges?"

"Theft and forgery. They are looking for Boppie too. Frenchy says it was a setup. We need a lawyer."

"Let me make some calls. I'll get back to you."

"Wait, some District attorney investigators came by too. They wanted to search the house, but I told them not without a search warrant."

"Good job, but they will be back with one. Just let them in."

"Okay."

"Bye, sweetie."

No matter what, Tipy knew Veda would handle things like she always did. It wasn't long before investigators knocked on the door, just as predicted. Tipy smiled and let them in, offering them a cold drink, which they refused. Lonnie and Tony played cowboys and Indians with cap guns and holsters. Tipy said nothing to calm down their rambunctious behavior.

The investigators seemed to be looking for something specific: under the mattress, inside pockets, drawers, and up in the cupboards. They left empty-handed.

Spending the night in jail gave Frenchy time to assess his situation methodically. He couldn't get Goldstein off his mind. Alvaro was on point because that man was a tightwad. When he took Frenchy to lunch, it was way out of character, and like a fool, he took the bait, thinking he didn't want to look a gift horse in the mouth. Then thoughts returned to Marilyn and the diary. *Did he cross the line by questioning things? Did Noguchi send him a hint? What really happened to Marilyn Monroe?"* His mind rummaged through the complex web that led him to this place.

After getting no sleep, he again heard a metal-turning grinding sound.

"596062, your lawyer is here," a southern voice belted.

Looking at the number on his shirt, Frenchy stood up and followed the guard to a booth with glass windows and a phone, which he slowly picked up.

"Grandison?"

"Yes."

"I'm Kevin Blackston. Your mother-in-law sent me."

"Hi, Mr. Blackston. Are you going to help me?"

"I'm going to try. I spoke to the District Attorney investigator, and you are in deep trouble."

"I don't understand. I didn't do anything. And did not steal that credit card."

"You never noticed it wasn't your co-worker's name?"

"No. I was just happy to get some new tires. The drive from the Valley to LA was killing my car."

"What name did you sign on the card?"

"I signed mine since I had permission."

"They are charging you with forgery too."

"How can I forge my own name?"

"It doesn't matter. It was a stolen card."

"Why would I let them get my plate number if I was committing a crime? I'm not stupid!"

"Well, they want to make a deal with you but have requested to speak with you alone."

"Without my attorney?"

"That's what they said, and it's highly unusual. But I need to advise you–this doesn't look good. You are looking at five years if it goes to trial for theft and forgery. It's up to you."

"Five?"

"Yes."

"No way. I can't do that much time."

"Either way, your risks are tremendous."

"I'll listen to them. I have nothing to hide, so why not?"

The lawyer signaled a guard to take Frenchy to the interrogation area where they placed him in a small room with a table in the middle. With his brow furrowed from worry, he folded his arms over his chest while he waited. Then a balding man in his late sixties entered the room with thick glasses and a clean-shaven face. Frenchy instantly recognized him, wondering why he was talking to the actual District Attorney, not a deputy.

"Mr. Grandison, I'm District Attorney William McKesson."

"Mr. McKesson, I'm very familiar with you. I've seen you at the coroner's office many times."

"Yes, I have a deal for you, but first, I need to hear your story."

Knowing his gift of gab usually worked, Frenchy tilted his head with a slight curvature of his jaw.

"Yes, sir. So, like I told your investigator, my co-worker Lenny Goldstein took me to lunch. Has anyone spoken with him?"

"I ask the questions," McKesson snapped. "Continue."

"Goldstein commented on how hard I worked. Then, he pulled out a credit card and told me to get some new tires on him. After that, he treated me to lunch as well."

"You didn't find that odd?"

"For him, it was very odd, but we were all under pressure from the Monroe case. Nothing was normal."

"Go ahead."

"I took the card, then oddly, on my way home that day, I got a flat. The air stem had broken and…," Frenchy paused. *Son of a bitch. They caused the flat.*

"The air stem broke, and what?" McKesson snapped.

"I put on my spare and drove to the gas station. I purchased four tires, replaced my shocks, and got an oil change. The following day, his card was returned."

"We found the card in your desk drawer."

Frenchy's eyes widened, and his brows raised while suddenly words eluded him.

"Grandison, what do you have to say about that?"

Trying to think, he closed his eyes momentarily before speaking.

"Goldstein must have put it there," he painstakingly said.

"Goldstein again?"

"He's setting me up for this. And I believe it's all about the Marilyn Monroe case. That's the only thing that makes sense."

"Speaking of Monroe, tell me what you told my investigators about her diary."

"My guy brought it in with her property. I locked it up before going home, and then it was gone."

"Did you read it?"

"After your deputies asked me earlier, I thought about it. Marilyn wrote some strange things about working for the FBI and her relationships with the Kennedys. It seemed like it might have been a movie script or something. It was all a little far-fetched. But after everything that has happened, it's all beginning to make sense and what I can tell you is this. One of Hollywood's biggest stars might have been murdered, and that diary was the key."

"Who do you think took the diary?"

"With the problems I was having with the case, it could have been anyone. The diary was in the property room just like the credit cards."

"Well, you have the key, don't you?"

"I'm not the only one."

"Well, here's what I'm willing to do for you. You plead guilty to receiving stolen property, and we will recommend probation. But there is one condition. You would be banned forever from discussing this plea deal with anyone or any details regarding Monroe's case and we mean anyone."

"My family will have questions."

"Let me repeat myself. Do not discuss this deal with anyone, or everything will get rescinded. Do you understand? You will do the full five years."

"Can I think about it?"

"No, this is a one-time, take it or leave it, offer."

For most of his life, Frenchy dealt well with pressure, making quick decisions with his logical mind, which now screamed for his attorney. But facing jail time was another matter; probation seemed like heaven's gift and his best option.

"Alright," Frenchy responded. "I'll take it."

"I'll have the deputy bring the paperwork for you to sign. The gag order is effective the minute you walk out that door. I promise you'll do the full five years if you violate it. One more thing. We need your resignation from the coroner's office."

"They can fire me. I'm not going to resign."

"Grandison, that is part of the deal."

Exhaling, Frenchy couldn't believe this. He cocked his head back and stared at the ceiling.

"But why? This is my livelihood!"

"Because all of this stays right in this room. We are looking for discretion. Of course, you can give up five years of your life and still lose your job."

Crossing his arms, he slumped, trying to think. That jail cell was torture, and five years was unthinkable.

"Tell you what," McKesson said. "If you agree to the terms, we will go to the judge today and recommend letting you out on your own recognizance. No bail."

With a huge sigh, Frenchy conceded. "Alright,"

Blackston was mystified why the DA handled this case in the dark. However, he realized this may be out of his league, having never even met McKesson, only his cronies. Still, this petty crime was obviously a shield for something much bigger, and Blackston was hesitant to get any deeper involved. He offered to drive Frenchy to his car, back at the Hall of Justice. They made small talk as Frenchy appreciated freedom now more than ever.

"I'm told I can't discuss this case. Not even to my wife."

"You're going to have to tell her something."

"I know."

"You could just tell her you can't talk about it per the agreement."

"You don't understand. We talk about everything and don't keep secrets. I can talk to you, right?"

"They cannot stop you from talking to your lawyer. Our conversations are protected, but to be honest, I have never seen a deal like this before. Never. I also certainly, at no time ever, saw the DA himself plea deal on a $300 offense."

"It's because of the Marilyn Monroe death. They just released her body to the crypt yesterday, and it's already haunting me."

"But her funeral was weeks ago."

"Yes, her body was on loan for the funeral services. She didn't have a death certificate until I signed it. And that was…."

"Don't tell me yesterday. What was so interesting in her diary? I can't help but think that's why the big guns are involved."

"That would make sense. This woman was a web of mysteries buried in the deep blue sea."

"What deal did he offer you?"

"Probation for my silence and resignation."

"Hmmm," Blackston said with reservation.

Frenchy leaned in while moving closer. "What does that mean?"

"Well, that's only a recommendation. Let's hope the judge honors this deal."

"You mean this deal isn't solid?"

"Plea deals are still in the hands of the judge. The DA has to make his case and explain why the court should be lenient. Sometimes it's a slippery slope."

"Well, McKesson said if I hold up my end, I'll receive probation. Right now, that's good enough for me. It has to be."

They pulled up to the parking lot where Frenchy's Pontiac sat with a shiny glow and polished new tires. Surprised it was unlocked, he turned to look at the humongous Hall of Justice building. Just like that, Frenchy was out. For a moment, he debated whether to collect his personal items. Still, the humiliation of the arrest, coupled with his pride, wouldn't allow him to. He waved bye to Blackston and sat in his car thinking.

Since August 5, so much has happened. Now he was waiting for a judge to sentence him with no income and significant life disruption. It would be a countdown until his court case, but for now, he had to face Tipy.

The road home had a lonely feel, looking at the empty dry land on the other side of the railroad tracks. No longer would he be making that commute, and it felt surreal. When he got to the house, he realized he looked a bit raggedy, with wrinkles in his shirt and a tinge of body odor. Also, the dents in his hair gave him a disheveled appearance, and he couldn't wait to shower. His number one son, who rarely took time from play, had other ideas and greeted him with questions.

"I didn't see you last night. Where were you, Daddy?" Lonnie asked.

"Son, one day, you will have a little boy, and he will ask you where have you been. And you know what you will say?"

"What?"

"You'll say, one day, you will have a little boy, and he will ask you where have you been. And you know what you'll say?"

"Dad!!!!!" Lonnie chanted and ran off.

Frenchy chuckled, greeting Tipy with a soft kiss.

"Are you okay? What happened?"

Explaining to Tipy was more complicated than he thought. The look on her face when the reality of their financial situation hit home was heart-wrenching. She was happy being a housewife and never thought of doing anything else.

"Baby, I will get another job," Frenchy promised. "It won't pay as much, but we will make it."

"Boppie and Joyce are moving out. We will have to pay the full mortgage ourselves," Tipy informed him.

"What?"

"Yep. He found a house on Eustace Street."

"I can't be mad at him for that. This place is a madhouse with six toddlers. We'll figure it out."

Deciding to look for a local job, Frenchy first went to Olive View Hospital, which still didn't accept people of color as patients, much-less employees. Holy Cross was the same reaction. Then, feeling discouraged, he decided to try General Motors, where many of his high school friends worked. It was manual labor, but he needed something and couldn't be picky. The following week his buddy Skip, who worked at there, got Frenchy an entry-level position making a minimum wage of $1.15 per hour. It was better than nothing.

Being a math whiz, Frenchy calculated he would get a weekly wage of $46 minus taxes. That would mean two of his paychecks would go towards the $89 mortgage and one for his car payment. That left $45 for food, gas, and utilities. He was already behind on the mortgage after expecting his county check to cover that, but then this happened. *How was he ever going to catch up?* He began working, nonetheless.

GM was a car manufacturing company on Van Nuys Blvd that mostly made Chevrolet pickup trucks. It was huge, with high ceilings and multiple assembly lines, and the atmosphere was nothing like the coroner's office. The Mexicans grouped together, mostly speaking Spanish, while the Blacks were all mainly from Pacoima. The white workers seemed to have more cushy inspection-type positions or were supervisors.

It felt demeaning for him to wear overalls instead of a shirt and tie and be primarily a gopher taking orders. How people spoke to him was bothersome, but he had to grin and bear it. Then, while sitting in the lunchroom a few weeks later, his supervisor Chris Berg called him into the office.

"Lionel Grandison, something has been brought to our attention."

"What is that, sir?"

Berg pulls out a Los Angeles Times paper and points to an article.

Los Angeles Times – September 13, 1962
Credit Card Trips Ghoul Suspect: Friend Sought

A 22-year-old aide in the county coroner's office was arrested by district attorney investigators and accused of using a dead man's credit card to buy auto supplies.

Lionel Grandison of Pacoima was booked at county jail on suspicion of grand theft and forgery.

Police say that on August 10th, they brought in the body of Harold F. Wallace, 76, who had died of natural causes in his apartment in Los Angeles.

Grandison, who handles the booking of property of deceased persons, said he took a Standard Oil Credit Card belonging to Wallace. The next day he and a friend reportedly took his 1960 Pontiac to a service station on the intersection of Woodman and Van Nuys Blvd, Pacoima, and bought a new set of tires, two sets of shock absorbers, and had the car lubed and oil changed--- a total bill of $307.16.

He signed for the purchases then returned the card to the coroner's office safe, where Wallace's property was picked up by Mrs. Margaret Holben of Highland Park.

When the bill came to Wallace, Mrs. Holben pointed out he couldn't have made that purchase since he died the day before.

District Attorney investigator Francis D. Ratay began an investigation which ended in Grandison's arrest. The friend with him at the time is being sought, Ratay said.

Slowly reading each word, a knot developed in the pit of Frenchy's stomach. His head felt dizzy from a sense of utter betrayal by the District Attorney, who claimed this needed to stay quiet. Not knowing how to explain things to Mr. Berg, Frenchy stood up, dropping his chin to his chest, unable to look this man in the eyes.

"It was a pleasure meeting you," he humbly forced the words out.

"You don't have anything to say about this?"

"It's complicated, sir. It's complicated."

"You can get your last check on the way out."

"Thank you."

After getting his check, Frenchy glanced at the total of $33.56 and took a deep breath realizing this disclosure just crushed his chances of finding employment. He stared blankly at the steering wheel with no regard for the time while his mind tumbled with a ball of worry that twisted in his stomach like a fist ramming inside his ribcage. Was he angry? Yes. The bills were mounting, and he saw no viable solution.

Instead of going home, Frenchy just drove around. Second thoughts about his decision to take that credit card poked and jabbed him like a Kidney dagger. Unable to change anything, reflecting on his actions was all that remained. His tires were bald! *Who wouldn't accept a much-needed gift? But why did Goldstein set him up?* The man literally knew everything about Marilyn and the Kennedys. He's the one that said Bobby was in town when Marilyn died. *So what skin does Goldstein have in this game?* Frenchy thought about him and the others coming out of Curphey's office that morning. *Did Curphey, Schwartz, and Longhorn also play a role?* They must all be involved; if that's the case, he was the proverbial fly in the ointment. It was all too much for Frenchy to wrap his weary head around.

After driving around and sorting through his situation, Frenchy knew Tipy and her family would have seen the article because they were newspaper junkies. But Mo and Tom were not. He hadn't spoken to them about the situation, but with it being in the press, he felt obligated to give them a heads-up. After all, they lived in a small town, far from gossip-free.

Tom greeted him at the door with sweat dripping on his dark skin and a cigarette hanging out of his mouth. Being Frenchy's only father figure, they had an unspoken bond. He remembered Tom taking him to boy scout meetings and teaching him masonry skills.

"Well, look what the cat drug in," Tom said, smiling, then calling out. "Mo, Frenchy's here!"

"How's it going?" Frenchy said, giving him a man hug.

"It's all good."

Mo could not contain her excitement and stepped out with wide beaming eyes, a house dress, and hair in a bun.

She squealed with her arms extended. "Baby!"

Frenchy tenderly embraced her.

"How have you been? You never come by to see me no more. Where is the babies?"

"At home. I know I haven't come around much but look at you. You changed your hair."

"Aww, come on now, only the gray," she said, stretching a strand.

"I have something to tell you both," Frenchy announced.

After studying his face carefully, Mo's demeanor changed.

"I knows you not having another baby. Something is wrong."

"This is unpleasant. I don't know where to start."

"Baby, what is it?"

"You two sit down," Frenchy motioned with a creased forehead. "Something happened at the coroner's office. They claimed I took a credit card, and I got fired. But it was a setup. Somehow it got in the newspapers, so soon, this town will be talking."

"Oh, Lord have mercy," Mo chanted.

"I just wanted you to know."

"Bud, you know if you need anything, we are here," Tom propositioned.

"I know."

"You haven't been over for Sunday dinner in a while. You, Tipy, and the kids need to come after church," Mo pleaded.

"Since I was working on weekends, we stopped attending church, but we will come over this Sunday."

"I miss you, baby, and don't let this get you down. Nobody betta not say nothin' to me. I will cuss them out in a minute!" Mo said, waving her finger while crinkling up her face.

"You haven't changed one bit. I'm sorry for not coming by more."

"We'll see you Sunday," Tom said happily.

When Frenchy got home, he saw the newspaper on the coffee table with the article about him front and center. Concerned with how Tipy reacted, he first looked for her in the kitchen. When she wasn't there, he checked the bedroom where she was lying down, quietly weeping. He could see her back rising in quick motions, so he touched her gently, slowly sitting down while guiding her to roll over. She looked at him with puffy eyes, a red nose, and a tear-drenched face.

"Frenchy, I was humiliated today. I thought this was going to stay quiet. Everyone knows you were arrested."

"Yes, I know," he hesitantly said. "I also got fired today."

"No!!" Tipy scowled. "Can this get any worse? What do these people want from you, from us, our blood?"

"I've been driving around trying to figure this out. They lied to me."

"I was at the store, and it was brutal. They said Mrs. Goody Two Shoes is married to a criminal. They think that I think I'm better than them."

"You're beautiful, and they're just jealous."

"I thought they were my friends."

"Tipy, now we will see who our true friends are. You need to stay strong."

"Veda is not pleased with this. It affects her too."

"She is the strongest woman I know. If anyone can handle this, it's her."

"I can't believe you are so calm. You just lost your second job; we are behind on the mortgage, and the town is disowning us."

"I have a plan for our finances. Just trust me."

"Really?" She said, sniffling. "You have a plan? What?"

"I can't tell you, but it will work out. Sometimes you just have to take a few risks. Don't worry," Frenchy explained, rubbing the tears from her face.

"You're not going to do anything illegal, are you?"

Squinching his face, Frenchy kissed her on the forehead and continued rubbing her cheek.

"Babe, please. You know me. I would never do anything to make this worse. I'll be back in a while."

"Where are you going?"

Frenchy's words were delicate and elusive as he purposely avoided giving Tipy more grief.

"I'm going to take care of business. We have to reset."

"What does that mean?"

"It means I love you."

Their life was at a crossroads, and the pendulum was swinging in the wrong direction. Leaving her like that was never good. Nevertheless, Frenchy headed to BB's, a house turned club, where guys gathered regularly to play cards and shoot dice. On the weekend, they partied all night, but gambling was the main activity during the workdays.

The smoke-filled structure wasn't the place for a married, family man, but Frenchy felt the walls closing in on him with few options. He had $33.00 from his paycheck and hoped he could double or triple it. The question was, which one had the best odds? His luck with poker was decent, but the dice seemed to call out to him like a decadent dessert with extra frosting, holding his eyes hostage.

He could put all the money on one throw and double it. He had seen that happen before, so he knew it was possible. But he concluded he had to win this time, and losing was not an option.

By the crap table were three older men looking a bit scraggly. Frenchy felt extremely young next to them but watched while they threw the die, hoping luck would come. The table was nothing like what he played on the streets with his friends. Instead, it had markings on a refurbished pool table with pictures and numbers. The most visible words on the left and right said: "COME." Underneath said, "pays double," which intrigued him. But then he saw bigger payouts in the middle, where specific numbers had better odds. For example, a five and six (eleven) paid 15 to 1 odds. That's what he wanted to do.

The ashtrays lined the table while the men seemed immersed in the game's fast-paced action. One regular put his paycheck on the line every week until his wife finally threw him out. Still, he never stopped gambling, finding the pull powerful. Rigidly postured with a grim face of intensity, it seemed his life depended on each roll of the dice.

"You got some ID?" a deep bass voice said from behind.

A dark-skinned man with a tilted hat and yellow teeth stood there.

"Uh, sure," Frenchy said, raising his eyebrow.

Not knowing if this man was the owner, or a helper, he extended his hand with a smile.

"They call me Frenchy, and you are?"

"They call me BB."

"Pleasure to meet you, BB. I heard a lot about this place."

"Well, Frenchy, got any ID?"

"Oh, of course," reaching in his pocket.

BB looked carefully at the driver's license, then glared at his face.

"Why do they call you Frenchy?"

"I guess because I look French," he said, twisting his jaw.

"Maybe so, with those avocado eyes. What are you doing in a place like this, young man."

"I just wanted to check it out."

"Lionel Grandison, huh? I just read about you in the paper. You're Tom Williams' grandson."

"Yes, I am."

"He comes through here every now and then. Good man."

"Yes, he is."

"How did you get yourself in trouble with the law? You had a good job."

"Man, it's a long story that I just want to forget."

"What's your game?"

"Me and my buddies play poker. But I'm ready to check out other things. Which one pays out the most."

"Young brother, don't come in here thinking you gonna win. The house usually wins. Remember that."

"But I know some folks win."

"Not as many as you think. I'm just being straight with you. These men are hooked on this, and you don't want to be a gambling junkie. You too young."

"Junkie? I don't do drugs."

"Gambling is a drug. It's addictive and dangerous. One win and you're hooked."

"That's all I need is one win."

"My brotha, then you can't quit. Your grandfather can tell you all about it. Trust me. It's like bad heroin."

"Are you saying Tom has a gambling problem?"

"Everyone here has a gambling problem. As I said, it's hard to quit. That's why business is so good."

"Naw. It's all in the mind. It can be controlled," Frenchy said, finding that hard to believe.

"You're a bright young man, but you still have much to learn. I tried to warn you. How many chips you want?"

"$30.00."

Watching the game, he figured people simply didn't know when to quit. When you are ahead, you should walk away, he thought.

He observed, trying to get a feel while placing his chips in front of him.

"You know what you doin', young man?" a familiar voice said.

"I'm learning," he said, turning to see Tom was standing next to him. "Hey, what are you doin' here?"

"This is my home away from home."

"BB told me you came here."

"So, you wanna play craps? This your first time?"

"Naw. I played with my posse. This looks different."

"It's basically the same, but you have different ways to win and lose."

"It is still 7 or 11 on your first roll you win. Anything else is your point."

"The difference is you can bet on the roll or against it. Let me explain what all this means. Most important is to go with your gut."

Tom explained the crap table options and what he thought was the best way to win. Listening with eager ears, Frenchy absorbed it like a sponge until his turn came to roll, and so it began.

After placing two chips in the "CRAPS" box, Frenchy shook the square porcelain dice and watched while they spun frantically on the table. The first die twirled, settling on a three. The second rolled over and over, teetering on the five but landing on four. Frenchy couldn't believe it and knew things would go his way from there. Players chanted and began to bet for him. He won four times the wager.

He was able to roll again, this time two 5's. He had to hit ten to win; seven was the enemy this time. After a few tries, the dice landed on 6 and 4, subconsciously telling him lady luck was in the building.

"I gotta get in on this," Tom chimed.

"I knew I felt lucky!" Frenchy boasted.

Adding the last 20 chips to his bet, Frenchy calculated the winnings in his mind. His current win was $40. If he played the other 20 chips, his victory would be $240. He fantasized about what that would mean. The mortgage would be caught up, his car note up to date, and Tipy happy.

"Young man, you sure you wanna do that?" BB asked.

"Yes, why not?" Frenchy replied.

"Leave him alone," Tom belted.

A worried expression marred BB's face as his eyebrows raised. Ignoring BB, Tom encouraged Frenchy to go the distance while throwing five chips on the table himself.

"Come on, buddy. Let's get this dough!" Tom's baritone voice rumbled.

Kissing the dice, Frenchy stared upwards and closed his eyes. He never prayed much but needed this badly. His stomach knotted up with hope and nerves while he inhaled the stale smoke that swirled the room like a charmed snake. He began shaking his hand, feeling the dice move inside freely. He opted to put an extra spin when he released them hoping to see another seven, but an eleven would also do. Watching them roll captivated every sensory emotion Frenchy ever imagined as the first die plopped on six. A five would do it, as the second tossed over and over, slowly staying on three. Nine was now the point.

Glancing at Tom, who gave him a slight smile and a look of encouragement, Frenchy waited for the dice to get handed back. $240.00 consumed his thoughts as he closed his eyes briefly. Rubbing the holes, he focused intently on the number nine. A six and three or five and four were the only combinations that would win. If he won, he would quit, go home, and lavish Tipy with something special. He threw the dice, which landed a two, then a six.

"Come on, nine!" Frenchy energetically yelled, throwing once more.

Suddenly his world went into slow motion as a four and three rolled on the table. Frenchy's heart sank just staring in disbelief, rubbing his hands through his hair and slumping over. He could not hear the "awws" of disappointment from the others, just blackness and despair. The dots on the dice pierced him deeply while the reality of losing plunged through his soul.

"Let's go," Tom said, patting him on the back."

The two left, walked towards Frenchy's car, and stopped on the grass when they arrived. Lost in defeat, he realized he could have walked away doubling his money, but went for everything and blew it.

"How long have you been coming here, Tom?"

"A long time."

"Does it always feel this bad when you lose?"

"Only when you lose it all."

"I'm on the brink of losing everything right now."

"Ahhh. You're still young. Just remember, as long as you don't lose yourself, you can never lose it all."

"This is tough, Tom. But I'm trying."

"Let me tell you from experience. Your answers are not at BB's."

"I take it Mo doesn't know you come here."

"And don't tell her."

"Did you walk over here?"

"Yeah."

"Let me give you a ride home. Mo will be worried about you."

"Naw. She's sleeping."

After dropping off Tom, Frenchy headed home, unsure what he would tell Tipy. He promised everything would be alright, but it was much worse. It was late, so he hoped she was asleep, and luckily that was the case.

Concerned that Tipy would go over the edge from all the bad news plaguing their family, Frenchy decided to keep the loss a secret. He quietly crept inside, still overwhelmed with the sick feeling of the gambling debacle and the loss of his job. The life he had built was spiraling out of control and his pathway out was a blur.

The Grandison family dressed on Sunday and went to Mo and Tom's house. Tipy had Crystal in white pants with a cotton white shirt and Lonnie in a white shirt with black trim that matched his pants. Mo was appalled at the cheap shoes both kids were wearing.

"Frenchy, you needs to go get these kids some good shoes. Stride Rite is just down the street. I want you to go now before dinner. I can't have these baby's feet messed up."

"Mo, you don't have to do that," Frenchy said.

Mo shot out a look that was all too familiar to Frenchy. One that would stop you dead in your tracks, her eyes shooting piercing darts while never saying a word.

"Go get them now. When you gets back, dinner will be ready. Tipy, you can stay here and help me."

After Mo handed him the cash, Frenchy grabbed Lonnie and Crystal and headed straight to the shoe store, knowing instinctively not to argue or debate. Crystal had only been walking for about six months, so he understood the importance of good shoes. The main issue haunting his manliness was the inability to provide fully for their family. He relished controlling and managing the funds, even if it required budgeting.

The shoe store was not very crowded, but Frenchy wasn't used to handling kids without Tipy. Lonnie jumped from the car as soon as the door opened and ran into the street while Frenchy was picking up Crystal. A sense of panic swelled inside his stomach, fearing the looming danger from oncoming cars. His eyes bulged in shock as his firstborn's life flashed before him, causing a fright unlike any he had ever experienced.

"LONNIE!" Frenchy yelled. "Get back here!"

Immediately putting Crystal back in the passenger seat, it felt like an eternity, racing in desperation as he frantically ran to get him. Snatching his shirt and lifting him into his shaking arms, Frenchy held Lonnie tight.

"Don't do that again, son. Do not just run off. YOU COULD HAVE BEEN HIT BY A CAR!!"

"I sorry," Lonnie apologized.

"Son, you got to think."

"I said sorry."

"It's important to think before you do anything, Lonnie. Do you understand?"

"Are you gonna spank me like Mommy?"

"No. I'm going to teach you to use your brain. I love you, son," Frenchy said, holding him so close he could feel Lonnie's little heart pounding erratically.

He took the kids inside the store with weak knees and adrenalin pulsating throughout his system. Lonnie seemed unphased by the experience, and Crystal clueless, yet Frenchy's nerves remained rattled. *How does Tipy do this with them and the baby?*

A salesman greeted them with a friendly smile and encouragingly sat the kids down to get their feet measured.

The middle-aged, medium-brown-skinned man could see Frenchy's awkwardness and tried to put him at ease.

"This is always a challenge for parents."

"Yes, it is."

"This is your first time. I can tell."

"My wife usually handles stuff like this. I don't know how I got lucky this time. It's easier just giving her the money."

The clean-shaven man wore a very nice suit and had an aura that impressed Frenchy. He seemed intuitive and presented himself as if he had an inner knowledge of life.

"I'm brother Shabazz."

"Pleasure, they call me Frenchy."

"Nice to meet you, brother Frenchy. And who is this prince?" Shabazz asked, watching Lonnie squirm in his seat, fascinated with Crystal's toy.

"This is my son Lonnie."

"Hey, brother Lonnie. Can I take off your shoes? I gotta see how big your feet are?"

"I'm getting new shoes. My tister is too."

"That's right," he said, sliding Lonnie's foot out of his blue denim Keds.

"These shoes are okay but not good on the arch."

"That's what I heard," Frenchy replied. "I was sent here specifically to get Stride Rite."

"Well, someone knows shoes."

Shabazz went to the back room where they stored boxes. Frenchy could feel his body slowly returning to normal as he found this man extremely calming. He had a sense of self that Frenchy found strangely familiar.

"Well, brother Lonnie, let's see how these feel on you," Shabazz said after returning.

Lonnie was disinterested in his new shoes, but he noticed they were hard, and he could kick things with them, which fascinated him. Meanwhile, Crystal calmly let Shabazz put hers on with little resistance.

"These will work just fine. Can you put the old shoes in the boxes? We're heading to Sunday dinner." Frenchy said, relieved.

"No problem, brother. Can I give you a card? We have a Nation of Islam temple at 13209 Van Nuys Blvd, next to Ramon's Market. You should come to check us out sometime."

"Only if you got bean pies," Frenchy said, smiling.

"So, you are familiar with us."

"I met Malcolm X and a few others when Ronald Stokes was killed. I was working at the coroner's office."

"Oh, that was you? There were stories about a brotha helping us out during that nightmare."

"I tried my best."

"We appreciated it. Come on down and check us out. We are trying to get more people involved."

"Thanks. I think I will."

When they pulled into the driveway, his mother's car was there. He called her "O," which stood for Ora, and was glad to see her. Dressed in pedal pushers and a hat, Ora broke out with a huge smile.

"Lionel!"

"Hi, O. Good to see you," Frenchy replied, returning the smile. "Thank you for helping Tipy on the weekends with Lance. She needed some relief."

"Oh, it's no bother. I love getting to bond with my grandson."

The 900-square-foot home smelled of fried chicken with a hint of cornbread. Tipy was in the kitchen helping Mo while Ora engaged with the baby.

"O!" Lonnie screamed.

"Baby, where's my kiss?" Ora puckered up.

Lonnie puckered his face demonstrating his dislike for mushiness.

"How about a hug, then?"

Readily wrapping his arms around her neck, he quickly released and moved on to his next round of mischief. Frenchy put Crystal down, and without hesitation, she went into Ora's arms.

"Hey baby," Ora smiled.

"Hi," Crystal replied, creasing her lips.

Shortly after, a good old-fashioned southern meal laced the dining room table. There was a highchair for Crystal while everyone else sat in front of place settings. On the table was a platter of fried chicken, mashed potatoes with gravy, peas, and cornbread. Mo had also made bread pudding for dessert. Initially, everyone was quiet, chewing on the feast set before them. Frenchy, then, broke the silence.

"O, I didn't get a chance to tell you about my misfortune."

"Misfortune?"

"Well, I resigned from the coroner's office."

"Frenchy, why did you do that?"

"It's long and complicated, but I'm working something out to get back on track."

"I'm proud of you no matter what. I have never worried about you. Look at this beautiful family you have."

"Well, there is a story in the newspaper that says some bad things about me. Just know I pled guilty to something that I didn't do."

"You know we are always here for you no matter what. You don't have to tell me anymore. Let's enjoy our dinner."

"We gots a little surprise fo the kids. Tom picked it up," Mo announced.

"What is it," Lonnie shouted.

"You'll see after dinner," Tom smiled. "So Frenchy, I have a proposition for you."

"I'm listening."

"The construction company I work for needs help. I can show you the ropes with masonry. It's physical work," holding his hands up, twisting them from side to side. "But it pays."

"I can cut grass and do yard work, but building things... that's outside my IQ."

"It's a job that can help you take care of your family."

Frenchy took his last bite of a chicken leg, then drifted into deep thought.

"Thank you, Tom, you have always been there for me. I truly appreciate the opportunity."

"It's not a cushy office, but it's honest work."

Lonnie hopped out of his chair and began jumping up and down the minute he demolished his food. Tipy helped Crystal finish eating, then let her out of the highchair afterward.

"We ready for the surprise," Lonnie shouted.

"It's outside," Tom proudly said.

Everyone headed to the door, and once in the driveway, Tom anxiously rolled out a red tricycle and a basketball which he handed to Lonnie. Then, with a bright smile, he picked up Crystal and put her on the trike. Bouncing the ball a few times, Lonnie could not take his eyes off the shiny bike. The color was like a magnet to him.

"Lonnie, aren't you going to thank Tom?" Tipy asked.

"Thank you, Tom. Do I get a turn on the bike?"

"Crystal's on it. You have to ask her."

"Tistal, can I ride now?" he sweetly asked.

Crystal just looked at him, trying to figure out how to get her feet to reach the pedals. Unfortunately, it was a little big, but still, she was determined.

"Let me show you." Lonnie insisted, but she didn't budge until he got the ball and offered it.

"Let's play ball."

Crystal eagerly got off and began to chase the ball while Lonnie jumped on the seat, pedaling like a wild child.

While the kids amused the women, Frenchy pulled Tom aside.

"Luck must have come your way."

"Sho' did. If you play long enough, things can happen."

"What's your secret?"

"I got one rule, never gamble more than you can afford to lose."

"What if you have nothing to lose?"

"Don't play. It's a slippery slope."

An anxious feeling overcame Frenchy when they returned home. Envelopes stamped PAST DUE lined the coffee table, and uncertainty filled the house. Trying to relax, he took out his new album by the Miracles titled "I'll Try Something New," realizing buying records was a luxury he could no longer afford.

Weighing heavy on his mind was the court date tomorrow, where he had to make a plea. The sooner he got this over, the sooner he could get on with his life. Tipy came out after putting the kids to bed and tenderly sat beside him.

"Everyone is asleep except Lonnie. I don't know what to do with him. The energy is exhausting."

"That's what boys do."

"How was he at the shoe store."

"I don't know how you do it. Let me just say he gave me a run for the money."

Tipy chuckled, rubbing Frenchy on his thigh.

"Now you know how I feel."

"What I know is how lucky I am to have you."

The two embraced and finished the evening snuggling in front of the television.

The LA County Superior courtroom was very intimidating. It opened in 1959 with split-level structures and state-of-the-art architecture, a far cry from the Hall of Justice building. The eleven-foot hands and numerals clocktower stood prominent with a bronze cornerstone engraved with "Los Angeles County Courthouse 1958." It had eight robot elevators, of which Frenchy needed to ride one to the fourth floor.

When he found the correct room, a strange feeling surged through him. He questioned why he was so headstrong about Marilyn Monroe. He looked for his lawyer Mr. Blackston but didn't see him. Up front was a judge's bench facing the entrance with a big California seal behind it and a wall clock.

Frenchy adjusted his tie, then sat with other defendants waiting for the court to begin. Finally, Judge Mark Brandler entered, and everyone stood up. Wearing a black robe, he took his seat, then gaveled the court into session, causing Frenchy to tense up. Looking again for Blackston, he recognized an assistant district attorney from his old job. McKesson was nowhere to be found, making Frenchy wonder if he was in the correct place. Then suddenly, Blackston appeared.

"The People versus Grandison," the judge announced.

Frenchy stood up and walked to the table with a plaque saying, DEFENDANT.

"Mr. Grandison, you are charged with receiving stolen property. How do you plead?"

"My client pleads Guilty, your honor."

"Is that correct, Mr. Grandison?"

"Yes, sir."

"Sentencing is set for December 12th at 9 am."

"That's it?" Frenchy whispered to Blackston.

"Yep."

Relieved this drama was almost over, Frenchy left and headed home. The sky was overcast and gray, yet his optimism was holding. He was more fueled than ever to get his life, family, and finances back in order. Frenchy stared at his house for about ten minutes before going inside. At that moment, he realized you should never take your family for granted.

"So, how did it go?" Tipy eagerly asked.

"I made my plea and now go back on December 12th for the probation sentence. After that, we're back on track. I start with Tom tomorrow, so babe, we will be fine."

"We are still behind on our bills; how will we be fine?"

"Don't worry so much. Just trust me."

Working with Tom wasn't Frenchy's cup of tea; however, it wasn't nearly as bad as he first thought. He never took the time to understand what Tom did besides the construction work. Masonry involved bricks and rocks and required a special kind of knowledge, which Tom explained well.

Frenchy remembered when he helped Tom build the brick wall around the backyard during his junior high years. Tom also cleverly added a small retaining wall for a doggie run and smooth red cement pavement covering half of the yard area. He made the backyard an oasis.

When they began, Tom reminded him of having pride in his work. The job was on Foothill Blvd, where they were constructing a factory. The lead man was a slightly overweight older white man in overalls.

"Morning, Williams. Is this your grandson?"

"Yeah. This is Lionel, but they call him Frenchy."

"Welcome, Frenchy."

"This is Slim," Tom said.

"Pleasure to meet you, Mr. Slim."

"It's just Slim."

"We got the holes dug. The bricks are stacked over yonder. You know the drill, Tom."

"Yes, sir."

The two mixed a cement paste and planted bricks the entire day.

The only part Frenchy got tired of was putting the heavy blocks inside the wheel burrow and pushing them. But he did it. When he got home, every muscle in his body was sore. Subsequently, Tipy drew a warm bath and fed him his favorite meal, steak, potatoes, and green beans.

When Saturday came, Frenchy breathed a sigh of relief. He was surprised when the phone rang, and Alvaro's' familiar voice was on the other end.

"Aye vato, Que Paso?"

"Hey man, good to hear your voice. How have you been?"

"Bien. So, you pleaded guilty to forgery?"

"Excuse me?"

"Today's paper. That's what it says."

"What? I never pled guilty to forgery."

"Well, it looks like you've got some reading to do, amigo."

"I don't know if I want to, now."

"I'm sorry to be the one with bad news. But there's more. That bendejo Goldstein just got a cushy new job. He's not with the coroner's office no more."

"Where did he go?"

"The word is, he's at Mayor Yorty's office."

"Well, I'll be dammed."

"One last thing."

"Not more?"

"The headline for the story is 'Pleads Guilty in 'Ghoul' Case."

"Ghoul? Really?" Frenchy sighed. "Thanks, man. I'd say nice talking to you again, but you'll understand why I don't."

"Just keepin' it real, vato. Just keepin' it real."

"I appreciate you, man."

"Later."

Stunned, furious, and confused, Frenchy balled his fist, clenching his fingers tight while the reality of Marilyn's curse on him sunk in. He stared blankly at the two newspaper issues he hadn't yet read.

Los Angeles Times – November 14, 1962
Pleads Guilty in 'Ghoul' Case

Lionel Grandison, an assistant in the county coroner's office, has pleaded guilty in Superior Court to forging a dead man's signature to purchase $307. worth of auto supplies.

Grandison, 22, of Pacoima, was arrested August 12 on charges of stealing an oil company credit card and forging the name of the holder.

Grandison's job in the county coroner's office was to log receipt of the property of dead persons.

He has been ordered to appear Dec. 12 for probation and sentencing.

Knowing this information was released by his former employer, the inaccuracies floored him. Firstly, they did not arrest him on August 12. The arrest was the same day he signed the death certificate, August 28. *So why are they saying the wrong date?* But the real question is why they say he pleaded guilty to forging a dead man's name. That never happened. The number of untruths in the press was astonishing.

Frenchy knew his plea deal precluded him from discussing this case, but he needed to clear the false stories in the press. Everyone trusts what the press says, including his wife, and this could ruin him all across the board. No one would believe his story, and he knew it. This cannot be happening to him.

The streets of Pacoima felt like a mini Payton Place, lined with idle chat about who was doing what and the distribution of everyone's business. To a certain extent, it was always that way, as in any small town, but never did it affect Frenchy like now. Even more so, unfortunately, Tipy absorbed the brunt. Still, she gave her all to be a good wife, and he appreciated that commitment, despite her obvious displeasure.

After hard days working with Tom, Frenchy realized he missed having exciting stories to share with Tipy. There wasn't much to laying bricks, and he did not want to dwell on past misfortunes. Yet, sitting on the couch, they were closer in many ways, bound by the love of their children and the hard times.

"Honey, I have to tell you something," Tipy confessed.

"What is that."

"I put us on the waiting list for the San Fernando Gardens Projects."

"Why did you do that without letting me know? Are we keeping secrets now?"

"Frenchy, we are behind two months. How will we ever catch up? They keep calling and sending notices."

Putting his hands on his forehead, Frenchy closed his eyes and rubbed his temples. Although he thought the projects were helpful to low-income folks, he never saw his family in that category.

"I thought you hated the projects?" he asked.

"It's embarrassing, but what are we going to do? No one's house is big enough for five extra people, including a baby."

"We will get through this. I'm working with Tom, and everything will be fine."

"We both know you are not a manual labor person. What happens when you get tired of it?"

"Don't worry so much," he said, grabbing her closer.

"The projects are just a backup. Veda suggested it."

"Your mother is okay with you living in the projects?"

"She's a realist. It beats the streets, and she wants me to be a survivor."

"We will always have a home with Mo and Tom. So, I'm not worried."

When the day came for sentencing, Frenchy was consumed with both anticipation and relief that this phase would soon be over. Clean-cut and shaven, with a shirt nicely ironed, he double-checked his appearance while straightening his tie. Yet, mentally he was already scheming on a new career once this dark cloud faded from view.

The courtroom looked the same as his eyes focused on the humongous seal behind the Judge's bench. Blackston arrived, and they exchanged handshakes. When the Judge called their case, Frenchy breathed deeply before taking his seat at the defendant's table.

"Lionel Grandison, I am sentencing you today for receiving stolen property. You have pled guilty, and the prosecution has recommended probation. However, after reviewing the details of your case, I have a problem with that. The L.A. County Coroner's Office is a place of community trust. You participated in violating that trust by stealing that card from a dead man at your office. Do you understand the predicament you placed the coroner's office in?"

"Yes, sir. But…"

"There is no but. A dead man's property was stolen and his name forged," the Judge said sternly.

"Your honor, may I speak on behalf of my client? He accepted that card in good faith," Blackston interrupted.

"That's irrelevant. He pled guilty. The District Attorney recommended six-month probation; however, Mr. Grandison, you will not get away without jail time. Therefore, I am sentencing you to 6 months in the county jail and five-year probation."

Those words felt like a bulldozer plummeting over Frenchy's body. The thought of being in a tiny jail cell for six months made him nauseous.

"You will be remanded into custody immediately," the Judge said, hitting the gavel with a whopping bang.

Frenchy's pulse jittered around the 160 mark as the clicking sound of handcuffs left him stunned while two guards spun him towards the door. He glanced at Blackston, who angrily shook his head and clenched his teeth.

"I will try to appeal this sentence, Lionel. We have legal grounds," Blackston shouted to him.

"Please call my wife. Let her know."

* * *

After two months behind bars, Frenchy began to feel like his mind was playing tricks on him. His cell seemed like it was getting smaller by the day. They kept him isolated despite room for another person on the top bunk. The picture became more evident as thoughts bounced inside his head like tiny rubber balls. *They didn't want him engaged in any jailhouse conversation.*

He only left the cell to eat and was allowed one hour of community time in a large room. Nevertheless, Frenchy continued to keep his mind occupied with books. He surely would have snapped into a place of no return without them.

Routines were the same daily, and when Frenchy joined others in the activity room, he avoided inmates by reading. He tried to keep an eye out for the cruel guards with bad intentions for him. The threat was real, and the more he thought about it, the more concerned he became.

Everything was now clear as a fresh-cut diamond. He was the loose connection between Marilyn Monroe and a high-level conspiracy that infected the coroner's office. Openly questioning the suicide ruling left him a significant risk, in addition to knowing sensitive details about her case that might become public. The credit card setup effectively removed all of his credibility. After all, who would believe a criminal?

But moreover, he questioned himself. *Why did he ignore so many words of warning?* Noguchi, Schwartz, and even Goldstein all advised him to LET IT GO. *Was his own ego and stubbornness partly to blame?*

Glancing up from his corner, he watched inmates interacting with each other. There were occasional disagreements, but he wasn't aware of any actual violence. Constantly checking on the guards and managing to steer clear, he noticed them talking with two inmates. One was white, the other Hispanic, and he wondered if the guards were giving them trouble too.

The restroom was off to the left, so Frenchy headed there. It smelt damp and moldy inside, with urine spots fixated on the wall. While at the urinal, he heard the door close, looked over, and saw unflinching eyes filled with darkness staring at him coldly.

Unbeknownst to him, the two guys interacting with the guards had followed him. Quickly fixing his pants, Frenchy saw one of them had a shank in his hands. They didn't say anything and just stepped slowly toward him. He glanced around to see if there was anything he could use for a weapon, but nothing. He balled up his fist and planted his legs wide, ready to defend himself.

Suddenly the crashing sound of a door caused the two attackers to freeze. Scratch stood there, eyes staring with an unmitigated look of fury, and holding a shank of his own.

"You fellows looking for me?" Scratch said, holding up his blade.

"This ain't about you, Scratch. This is about ghoul boy here."

"Naw, you get at him–you gotta deal with me. He's a Turk, and we are one."

Without waiting for more discussion, Scratch charged at the Mexican that held the weapon. Frenchy instinctively plunged at the other guy with a spinning leap. The sound of rubber scuffing the floor signified an all-out battle. Scratch narrowly avoided getting cut but managed to draw blood on the Mexican, causing him to drop his weapon after jabbing him in the shoulder. Blood oozed from the wound, saturating his inmate scrubs. With no regard for the red plasma, Scratch aggressively grabbed him by the throat while Frenchy battled the white guy plowing him blow after blow until he hit the ground. When Frenchy saw Scratch about to stab the guy's neck, he yelled.

"Don't do it, Scratch!"

"Man, they were about to kill you."

"They have the guards on their side. You don't. Let's go," Frenchy said.

Scratch mercilessly kneed the Mexican in the groin with an infinitesimal twitch in his lips that told him he had hit the mark. He then slammed him to the ground leaving both attackers lying helplessly on the floor. Finally, Frenchy and Scratch casually bailed out, slapping five.

"Dude! What are you doing here?"

"Shit, this is my home away from home. I saw them fools checking you out. It's a cold world when you're locked up. They need money on their books, and they deal with the highest bidder."

"Man, it's good to see you, Scratch."

"I've been following your story."

"Well, don't believe what you read in the papers."

"Folks in here talk too."

"What you been hearing?"

"All I can say is your name goes high up."

Shocked at what Scratch said, Frenchy glanced away, only to notice one of the guards staring at them from across the room.

"What are you in here for?" Frenchy asked, hiding his concern.

"Same type of shit that always gets me in trouble. Man, I kinda knocked my girlfriend around a lil' bit, and she called the cops. It was just a small argument."

"You are never going to change."

"How's Tipy doing through all this?"

"It's been hard on her. I gotta make it up to her when I get out."

"If you need a hustle when we're released, hit me up."

"I'm not doing nothing that might land me back in here, even if I have to shine shoes."

The bell rang, indicating it was time to return to their cells.

"Good seeing you, man. Thanks for coming to my rescue."

"Hey, Turks are one! And Happy Birthday. Ain't you 23 today?"

"Yes, I'm getting older. Thanks, man. I wasn't expecting any birthday wishes today. I guess fate still wants me to see another year."

"Sleep with one eye open tonight," Scratch warned.

"You do the same. Some people won't be happy you helped me out."

"I ain't worried about them fools. Catch you later."

"Later, my brother."

A flurry of thoughts circled Frenchy's mind after returning to his cell. How ironic it was for Scratch to come to the rescue when he needed him most. Despite his rough edges, he was always a loyal Turk, and Frenchy was forever in his debt. However, it was now clearer than ever that Frenchy's life was in danger.

Disappointed that he didn't hear from Tipy on his birthday, he just sat on his lonely bunk, wondering what she was doing at that exact moment and if she was thinking about him. His eyes sparkled when the mail came later that week, and he saw a letter from her.

February 16, 1963

Dear Frenchy,

Happy Birthday! I hope you are doing well. I got a job at Fantastic Fair. A lady named Lina is babysitting the kids. They seem to love her. Many kids go there, and she has a swing set and tons of toys, so they have fun.

We had to leave the house since they foreclosed. Luckily a place was available and last weekend, we moved to the projects, and it's not that bad. It has two bedrooms upstairs, plus we have a lovely patio. It came with a washing machine, and the clothesline is right outside the back door.

There is a small park where the kids can play, and the neighbors seem really nice. I made a friend named Vye. She's a white gal with a son Dane that is Lonnie's age.

I hope your birthday is good. I know it's hard being in there, but two months have already been chipped off the clock. I miss you, sweetie.

Love, Tipy

Excitement quickly went to disappointment after reading the letter. Thinking of his children living in the projects put a lump in his throat. He fought back the tears as a heaviness besieged his body leading him to plunge downward on his bed and bury his head in the pillow. He just laid there for hours, not even leaving to eat.

The next few days were uneventful, and Frenchy finally found the words to write Tipy back, deciding not to share the dark side of jail, and the incident with Scratch.

February 27, 1963

Dear Tipy,

It breaks my heart you have to work, and live in the projects. My mind is still swirling around this situation. At times I feel like this is a bad dream and I will soon wake up. But you know me, I will get through this somehow. Tell Mo and O I send my love. I know they are worried about me. It makes me sad how much all the people around me are hurt. I will make it up to you and them if it's the last thing I do. You were always so proud of me and seemed to enjoy my stories from the office. I wish I had interesting stories from here, but trust me, you don't want to hear about this place. I'm counting the days. The good news is I may be released early, and when I get out, we will thrive.

I bet Lance has gotten big. I hope he remembers me when I get home. I don't worry about Lonnie and Crystal. I miss you so much. Time to go. It's chow time, and I have to eat garbage that even a dog wouldn't eat. I want a dog when I get home. Are they allowed in the projects? I love you, baby.

Love you Always,

Frenchy

The sound of metal locks turning always made Frenchy cringe. It was April, and the cell walls felt like they were inching closer to him every single day, like wolves circling, waiting to attack. He felt stagnant anxiety, anticipating his release. Then, to his surprise, the sound he came to dread was now a guard holding his ticket to freedom.

"596062, get your stuff," the gruff voice chanted.

"I'm out of here? Seriously?"

"Here are the clothes you arrived wearing. Get changed and make your phone call."

"You don't have to tell me twice," Frenchy smiled.

Deciding not to make a phone call, Frenchy opted to surprise everyone with his early release. He packed up his letters from Tipy with miscellaneous things and headed towards the bus stop. The weather had drastically changed since his incarceration, and the smell of freedom hit him like a brick as a warm breeze fluttered across his face. He shielded his eyes, unaccustomed to the ultraviolet rays of brightness that hampered his vision. As his eyes adjusted, never before had he appreciated the sun as much as he did today. Walking with an extra bounce, he began his long journey home, longing to see Tipy's lovely face.

Frenchy jumped on the MTA bus and headed toward Pacoima. He had not been on one since his teens, but today he welcomed it. Thoughts of holding Tipy, smelling her fresh perfume, and running his fingers through her hair consumed him while he contemplated his next move. The worst was finally over.

After careful thought and much reading, he wanted to get into communications. Then, Tipy could be proud of him once again. Sitting on the steel bus seats, he looked out the window at the open fields he once thought irrelevant. Somehow, the railroad tracks looked different as he watched the flashing lights blinking fast while the barriers began to lower. Dinging noises began to sound, then, suddenly, the train's horn shook all the passengers as it barreled through, rumbling like a twister. Shocking to Frenchy, he loved his hometown.

Not wanting to show up looking scruffy and raggedy, Frenchy decided to stop at Mo's house first. That house on Filmore Street represented security to him that he had never understood until now. So many things were coming into focus and clarity, to his surprise. He always thought a house was just a house until this. Four months felt like a lifetime.

Strutting up the driveway, he could see Mo sitting at the dining room table, looking out the window like she often did. Her face lit up like a Christmas tree.

"Hey, baby!" Mo screamed.

"Surprise!"

"Let me look at you," Mo said, examining him from head to toe. "You look a mess. Did they hurt you?"

"No. I'm just fine. I wanted to stop here and clean up before going home."

"Tipy has grown up a lot. She will be happy to see you."

"She better be," Frenchy said, grinning while raising his eyebrows. "What do you mean grown up a lot?"

"She is more, how you say, responsible."

"She was always responsible."

"You just see for yourself. Go ahead and get yourself cleaned up. Dennis is in the back room playin' his guitar. Ask him for his razor and some clothes. The soap is in the bathroom."

"Alright."

Frenchy looked at his old familiar house relishing in the great memories he had. The living room was pretty small, as was the kitchen, but when he inhaled the familiar smell of red beans and rice, the feeling of home warmed his soul. Now he's heading to a place he has never seen. It felt strange.

After showering and talking with Dennis, it was time to head to the projects. The excitement he felt had cast his hunger aside. Then, it dawned on him that he didn't even know Tipy's schedule or when she got home. He pulled out the letter, and the return address was 10824 Lehigh Ave which was not far. He could have waited for Tom and gotten a ride, but walking would be good for him.

He paraded down Herrick to Van Nuys Blvd, then jotted over to Lehigh. He saw building numbers on each complex, which was slightly confusing, so instead, he followed the numbers painted on some of the curbs. Finally, as he just about reached the cross street parallel to Whiteman Airport, he saw the numbers. She was absolutely correct about the neighborhood. There were people of all races living in the projects.

The first thing that stood out was the patio that Tipy mentioned in her letters. It was nice sized with a 6-foot-tall brick wall that spanned over 20 feet and wrapped around. He looked up and saw two windows on the top floor and two facing the patio. Deep inside, a sense of grief consumed him that their old house was gone. He purchased his own home at 18, and now at 23, it disappeared in the wind.

As he slowly walked to the door, he took a deep breath, surprised at the fluttering butterflies disrupting his empty stomach.

His palms were sweaty as he knocked three times and patiently waited.

"Who is it?" Tipy's sweet voice hummed from the other side.

Frenchy said nothing and tapped again, not wanting just yet to reveal his identity.

"I said, who is it?" Tipy repeated impatiently, opening the door.

Eyes fixed on Frenchy with an incredulous stare, she clutched her throat, frozen in that moment.

"Is that how you greet your husband?"

"They let you out? I didn't expect you. Why didn't you call me?"

"Can I get a hug and a kiss from my wife?"

With wide arms, Tipy melted in his chest, burrowing her head against his collarbone, tightly clinching him around the neck. Her body felt like the richness of silk to him as he took a strand of her hair and smelt it. Nothing could have prepared Frenchy for the vulnerability and emotion he was experiencing. Pulling her chin up, he passionately put his lips on hers, trying not to shed an emotional tear. His heart was pounding so hard he wondered if Tipy could feel it when his lips were on hers.

"I missed you so much," Frenchy's dry throat pushed out.

"I missed you too."

After looking into each other's eyes a few minutes longer, Frenchy stepped inside the door.

"This is nice, Tipy. The walls are made of brick, so they won't ever burn down. I like it," Frenchy admitted. "Where are my kids?"

"In the kitchen eating dinner. Are you hungry?"

"Starving."

"I guess SpaghettiOs won't work for you, huh?"

"You feeding the kids that for dinner now?"

"We just got home, and they were hungry. I forgot to take something out of the freezer."

"Hey, kids!" Frenchy hollered.

"DADDY!!" Lonnie and Crystal yelled.

"Look at you guys. You've all grown so much."

"Where have you been?" Lonnie asked.

"Don't you remember what I told you about asking that question?"

"Yeah."

"Yeah? It's yes, son. You don't say yeah."

"Okay."

"Where's my hug? You too, Crystal."

Both kids happily got up and hugged Frenchy. He then looked at Lance in his highchair.

"Hi, Giant," he spoke in a soft voice.

Lance was covered in red sauce from the food and gave Frenchy a quick look, then continued grinding the SpaghettiOs into the tray. Frenchy kissed him gently on the forehead.

"Let me see what I can find to cook for you," Tipy offered. "I think I have some ground beef to make a burger, and I can cut up some potatoes for fries. I have to put the meat in hot water to thaw out, though."

"A homemade hamburger sounds like heaven since I have been eating mush for nearly four months."

It was impossible not to notice how nice she decorated the place and how clean it was. He walked through the living room, looking at the pictures in frames. One thing that stood out was no wedding picture.

"The bedrooms are upstairs. Mine, I mean ours, is on the left and the kids to the right."

"Okay."

The kids finished eating and got up from the table while Frenchy sat patiently on the couch. Crystal eagerly jumped in his lap.

"I miss you, Daddy."

"I missed you too, princess. Where's my kiss?"

She puckered up and planted one on his cheek.

"Are you going to stay?" Lonnie asked

"Yes, I'm going to stay."

"Mommy was sad when you were gone," Lonnie added.

"I was sad being away."

Tipy walked into the living room with Lance in her arms and then placed him down. He wobbly walked about ten steps before sitting down.

"Look at you, Giant. You're walking!"

"He not Giant? He's Lance," Crystal said.

"Do you see the size of his head?" Frenchy whispered in her ear, making her chuckle.

Although Frenchy was happy to be home, something felt peculiar. He couldn't place his finger on it, but Mo was right about Tipy. She had taken on adult responsibilities and was not a dependent teenager any longer.

"So, how is the job going?"

"It's good. I am a cashier and help with customer service. My boss likes how I handle people."

"That's great," he replied, looking down at the floor.

"Do you want to see the upstairs?"

"Sure."

She took his hand and rubbed it, sensing a change in his demeanor.

"Are you okay?"

"Yes, I'm fine. It's just I feel like a stranger here. It's not my house."

"You have to get used to it. It's not our old house, but it's home now."

They headed upstairs, and when they got to the top, there was the bathroom. Tipy had a white shower curtain and colorful towels perfectly placed on the racks. It smelled like Pine-sol, something he hadn't experienced in months.

The kids' room had beds perfectly made with stuffed animals placed on their pillows. There were no scattered toys like one would expect in a children's room.

"How did you get this room so together before heading out this morning? It looks perfect."

"I have a morning schedule. First, I shower, get dressed, go downstairs, make breakfast and lunches, and then head back upstairs to get the older kids up and ready. After that, I send them down to eat while I make up the beds and get Lance ready. Then, we go downstairs, I wash up their plates, and we head out. Lance eats at Lina's."

Frenchy smiled. "I'm impressed."

"Veda helped me organize my mornings. Our room stays clean too."

They stepped into the master room, which had a familiar feel.

"This looks like our old room except a little bigger. Who would have thought the projects were larger than a single-family home?"

"It's nice here. Remember I wrote you about it?"

"I know, but we will get another house. I'm not raising my kids with a stigma," Frenchy asserted. "But, I'm glad we have this place now. You've done a great job. I'll have to go talk to the office about a few things though."

Tipy grabbed his hand. "I have to tell you something. When I got this place, I qualified as a single parent. Technically you can't officially live here, but I'm told they never check. There are 800 units, and they can't keep track of all of them."

Frenchy pulled away. "Wait, Tipy! I'm not supposed to live here? Are you kidding me?"

"It's the only way I could get accepted."

"We can't live here then!"

"What do you mean we can't live here? Where else would we live?"

"We can move in with Mo and Tom. They have an extra room."

"Frenchy, there are five of us. Do you really expect us to sleep in one room?

"I can sleep on the couch or in Dennis's room."

"I am not sleeping in a room with three kids, Frenchy! What about all of our stuff? No!"

"Tipy, you don't understand what this does to me, how it makes me feel."

"This is the deck of cards we have been dealt. First, I was happy being a housewife. Then all of a sudden, I am everything, wage earner, caregiver, doctor, and problem solver. You worked but never did you have to get kids ready, drop them off, go to work, deal with people, pick up the kids, cook dinner, bathe them, read bedtime stories and keep your sanity. All you had to do was work!"

"I know it was hard, but I'm home now."

"I don't want to be mean, but you are an expense to me when I'm already on a tight budget."

"That's why we can live at Mo's for free, and she can help."

"Squeezing me in a ten-by-ten room is not help. I would lose my mind. My life is hard, but I like it."

"You like it without me?"

"You can live here, but it just has to stay quiet."

"That's not okay with me."

"Then maybe you should go stay with Mo."

"Really, Tipy?"

"I have adjusted to this situation, and you need to as well."

Frenchy shot Tipy a furious glance, unable to believe the depth of this situation. He started to speak but huffed out of breath, consumed with feeling betrayed as a man. His head felt like it was about to explode when he headed toward the stairs.

"Are you leaving?" Tipy scowled.

"This is not my home."

One thing about Frenchy was he rarely admitted to being wrong, even to himself. Instead, he analyzed and then assessed. Tipy, up until now, was content with the sun rising and setting from his perspective. She usually gave him the win, but now, that world had crumbled into bite-size pieces. With his life spiraling downhill since Monroe died, he began to wonder when the drama would end. His heart had tragically fallen prey to this horrific sequence of events, and the pain felt like burning blades piercing his soul.

Unsure where to go, the street looked different as he began walking. His mind drifted to promising the kids he was there to stay. *But what was he going to do now?* He wasn't in the mood to see family because they would ask questions he wasn't ready to answer.

When he got to Van Nuys Blvd, he went towards Pacoima Food Market and aimlessly roamed toward the pay phones. As he approached, he saw a familiar dark face standing in front of two other guys. One recognizable person looked a little disheveled with a bottle of ripple.

"Tom, what are you doing here?" Frenchy asked, breaking into a warm smile.

Looking at Frenchy with bloodshot eyes, Tom grinned, showing his yellow teeth.

"Buddy! Hey, you got out!"

"Didn't Mo tell you?"

"I got something you should know. Mo put me out. She found out about my gambling and hates my dranking."

"Aww, I'm sorry to hear that. Where are you staying now?"

"Here and there."

"You homeless?"

Tom opened his arms and gave Frenchy a man hug.

"You don't want to hear about my troubles. Looks like you got plenty of your own. You out early, huh?"

"Feels like I should have done the full six months now."

"Naw, the less time you spend behind bars, the better. But it's hard out here too. Dealing with bosses talking to you like you are a piece of crap just gets to you."

"You seemed happy at your job."

"Well, I could lay down cement and bricks better than anyone. I built San Fernando High School. Those brick designs in the front, that was me. Do you think those crackers cared? Do you think I got credit for my work?"

"That was excellent work."

"Well, they still called me boy, and I'm a grown-ass man. I'm a man, not a boy!"

Sipping on the green Ripple bottle, Tom took a few steps back, stumbling a bit.

"They do us wrong, and we keep on. You got done wrong, and you will keep on. At least you worked in an office with a shirt and tie. You got to hob knob with management, at least for a bit. But at the end of the day, we always have to suck it up," Tom slurred.

The two other men with Tom shook their heads, agreeing with him. Frenchy looked at them intently, curious about what their story was. For a brief moment, he forgot his troubling woes, thinking about what an excellent talented man Tom was. He had never seen Tom's pain or weakness before. Frenchy bit his bottom lip, deep in thought.

"You need some money? Here are a few bucks to get you by," Tom offered.

"No, no. I'll be alright."

"Take it! And when you get yourself together, try to become yo own boss. Start your own business and don't think bout workin' fo' the man no mo. That's my 'vice to you."

Shoving the money into Frenchy's hand, Tom faltered away.

Two months later, Frenchy was at Mo's house when an older silver-haired man came to the door, asked if he was Lionel Grandison, and handed him a manilla envelope. Frenchy opened it, startled by the intimidating letters Superior Court of Los Angeles. Underneath, it read "Alithra Denise Grandison vs. Lionel Alfred Grandison." Tipy had filed for divorce.

He felt numb, looking blankly at the papers, his mind spinning in disbelief. Frenchy hoped Tipy would show up one day, ready to stay with him. But that never happened. He felt sick to his stomach, and his throat was dry. Since first laying eyes on her when she was twelve, this woman he loved would no longer be his wife.

Mo noticed him sitting on the couch, staring blankly.

"What's the matter, baby?"

"Tipy filed for divorce."

"Remember I told you she changed, but everything will be fine."

"Mo, what happened with Tom?"

"Tom's a good man, but he got them demons that I couldn't take no more. So, I'm filing for divorce too. Mrs. Wise gonna help me with a lawyer. I can see if they can help you too."

"I don't want a lawyer. I just want to get this over, so I don't hurt anymore."

"The only thing that will help with the pain is time."

"How long?"

"It's different for everyone. You just needs to keep busy."

"I think I'm going to go to college."

"Go head now!" Mo said with one solid clap.

The sense of loss was still overwhelming despite thoughts of moving forward. Frenchy couldn't help but wonder, was it really over? Something was telling him to give it one last try. They hadn't spoken since he walked out; maybe that was a mistake. After all, he could always sway Tipy to his way of thinking.

The crunch and crack of twigs railed under his feet as he walked toward the projects. This conversation had to happen, and they needed to work things out. Tipy and the kids were everything; he couldn't let them slip away without a fight.

When he got to the door, Frenchy slowly balled up his fist and thumped with his knuckles. He looked at his car on the street, wondering if she had maintained it. He knocked again, thinking about how she would be dressed today, secretly wishing she would fall into his arms and everything would be like it was before. But this time, there was no 'who is it?' Instead, Tipy just opened the door as if she was expecting him.

"Hello, you don't look surprised to see me."

"You just got served divorce papers. So why would I be surprised? Tipy said nonchalantly.

"We need to talk about this."

Frenchy bowed his head down, entering the doorway, and watched his feet step one after the other with his hands clasped behind his back to keep his cool. Then he sank to the couch, a bit nervous, reminding him of their first date.

"What are we doing, Tipy?"

"It's time to move forward, Frenchy," Tipy said in carefully spaced words.

"You sound like you've been practicing that line."

"You think this is easy for me?"

"It must be, since you found money for a lawyer."

"It's not easy."

"Then don't do it."

"I don't want to rehash where we will live again. I'm on my own, and yes, I like it."

"And you no longer like us being a family?"

"So much has happened. I've been through a lot. I finally feel important." Tipy adamantly expressed.

"What about what I've been through? Ever since Marilyn Monroe died, I lost my job, got arrested, went to jail, got humiliated by the entire town, and now lose you and the kids. How much am I supposed to take? I deserved none of this!"

"You want me to feel sorry for you?"

"No, I don't."

"I've been through a lot, too, Frenchy. I had a life that I loved. Taking care of you and the kids was all I ever wanted to do. I stood by you, believed in you, but dammit, I have my limits too."

"So, you just give up?" Frenchy blew out his cheeks.

"No, I move forward."

"That sounds like Veda talking, not you."

"Don't bring my mother into this. She tried to help you!" Tipy said, gritting her teeth in frustration.

"She never really liked me, and you know it. She just wanted a son-in-law she could brag about, and now she can't. You can't give up just because things get tough. We have to work it out."

"Don't put this all on me. You're the one who didn't want to live here."

"The management doesn't want me. I can't stay where I'm not wanted. Plus, I'm on probation. That's an entirely different subject. I'm not going back to jail for a violation."

"That is NOT my fault!" Tipy spat out, emphasizing the last three words.

"It's not mine either. I did nothing wrong," Frenchy said with a pained look marring his face. "It was all a set-up. Dammit, Tipy!"

Frenchy's posture remained still and composed as he slowly dropped his face into the palm while the room went suddenly silent. Tipy breathed in and fixed her eyes on the ceiling, trying to disguise her unmitigated disappointment in everything.

"I never said you did anything wrong. It's just that I'm different now. I can't go back to who I was. I like the new me. I'm not dependent on anyone. I'm not even asking for child support. It says $1.00 on the documents. Did you see that? I want nothing from you."

"One dollar? I can't see my kids every day, Tipy. That's nothing? New men will come and go in their lives. That will hurt worse than anything."

"So, you're jealous I might date someone else?"

"I want you to be happy, Tipy."

"Then you need to let this go."

"You mean let us go?"

"Look," she calmly said. "Instead of child support, you can have them on the weekends. I can drop them off on Friday and pick them up Sunday evening."

"What does that have to do with you and me?"

"I'm just trying to make it easy on you to see the kids."

"Wow. Hum. Alright, Tipy, I see your mind is made up. I will have to check with Mo on that, but I'm sure it will be fine."

Frenchy's whole world seemingly had fallen to pieces. He felt like this was an endless bad dream with no exit while the angry words buzzed through the room like hornets.

"Frenchy, I will never keep you from your kids. I promise."

"So, this is it? There's nothing I can say to change your mind. You know you are the only woman I ever wanted. You are the only woman I will ever marry, even though you hurt me deeper than anything in my entire life."

"I'm sorry, Frenchy. I'm a grown woman now."

"I won't interfere in your life. Just bring the kids to Mo's, and they will have everything they need. What are we going to do about my car?"

"Your car? I have been making the car payments."

"I bought that car, and it's in my name. Hell, I went to jail getting new tires for it. I want it back."

Tipy speared him with a daunting glare after being taken off guard by his request.

"I can't believe you are doing this to me. Are you being vengeful now? I still need to get to work and drop the kids off."

"Huh? I'm the one that's homeless!" Frenchy grunted. "Let's not go 'tit for tat.' It's my car."

Tipy's tone softened as she brushed her hair off her face.

"Can you give me a week to find a new car?"

"Sure," Frenchy exhaled, standing up. "There's not much more to talk about then. Tell my kids I love them."

"Why don't you tell them yourself? They are upstairs."

"I can't. I can't. I have to go. You know what? Just keep the car."

There were so many emotions circling Frenchy's orbit at this time. Not sure what to do with himself, he walked to Pacoima Park to get his thoughts together. He wanted to cry so badly, but he couldn't. Men must be strong. But if there was ever a low point in his life, this was it. After all he had been through, all the disappointment and deception, nothing paled to this. While he was in his darkest moment, he never suspected Tipy would leave him like this.

It was a perfect day for the park, but nothing seemed to matter anymore. He found a bench to sit on by the basketball courts, watching the neighborhood kids chanting and laughing, but he couldn't hear them. It was a fog, a silhouette of silence. His heart shuttered with a falling, spinning-down feeling. He closed his eyes for a minute, praying his life would improve. The last six months had been nothing but hell.

The following week, Frenchy felt strong enough to talk with Mo and O. His mother was moving into Mo's house and taking the other room. Frenchy could sleep in the room with Dennis, but he didn't want to.

"I need to talk to you two," Frenchy announced.

"What's the matter, baby?" Mo asked.

"Yeah, what's going on?" Ora concurred.

"I'm going to need your help. Tipy is not asking for child support, and if we keep them on the weekends, she won't pursue it."

"That's wonderful. We will do whatever it takes to keep these kids in your life."

"I knew you would."

"They are going to call me Nana, and I will be home every weekend. This will be fun. Don't look so down, Frenchy."

"This will be a kids' heaven!" Mo added.

"Tipy is bringing them here in a while to stay the weekend. Nana? Where did you come up with that? I like it."

"Don't laugh, but Peter Pan had a dog named Nana that watched the kids."

"Now that's funny. I remember that in the movie."

A rumbling engine noise interrupted the conversation at just the right time.

"That would be Tipy." Frenchy sighed.

Moments later, a rapid thumping besieged the front door. Happily, Nana opened it with her arms wide open for the kids.

"O," Lonnie touted immediately.

"Hi, baby. Call me Nana now. Now give Nana a big hug."

Lonnie and Crystal clung to Nana gleaming with joy. Tipy put Lance down, who walked to her and held his arms up.

"Lancy boy," she beamed.

Tipy bid her farewells soon after she arrived. He couldn't believe how the butterflies swarmed his stomach after all they had gone through together. Watching her leave was torture. He didn't know if he would ever get over her. He sensed getting used to the new normal would be an uphill battle.

"Are you guys hungry?" Mo asked.

"Yeah!!!!" Lonnie yelled.

"Lonnie, what did I tell you about yeah?"

"You said to say yes."

"Come on, guys. We are going to have a family talk."

"What's a family talk?" Lonnie queried.

"Let's go in the back room and find out."

Frenchy took the kids to the room and sat them on the bed, except for Lance, who he held in his arms.

"You guys know I haven't been around much."

"Yes," Lonnie said.

"Your mother and I have made a few changes. I won't be living with you, but I want you to know that no matter what, you can tell me anything. I'm going to start with you, Lonnie. Tell me, what's going on at daycare?"

"Daycare? I got in trouble, but it wasn't my fault."

"What happened?"

"Enrique kept the bike too long, so I took it, but it was my turn."

"What did they do to you?"

"I had to sit on the bench for five minutes. But Mommy says I start Kindergarten in two months, and I better behave."

"Do you know what school you're going to?"

"Nope."

"You need to find out before our next family talk."

"Okay. Can I go play now?"

"No, it's Crystal's turn. What's going on with you, Crystal?"

"They made me eat bananas. Those are yucky."

"Did you tell them you don't like bananas?"

"No, but I told Mommy."

"What did Mommy say?"

"Her say, okay."

"Mommy said she would talk to them," Lonnie interjected.

"Lonnie, let your sister talk. I want her to be able to explain her situation to me."

"Lance can't talk, so can we go play now?" Lonnie impatiently asked.

"I think Mo and Nana are getting dinner ready. Let's go see. I love you guys. Remember that."

"Alright."

Despite Frenchy's woes, his friends remained a constant. They still gathered regularly for cards, which had a calming effect, making the pain he endured easier to handle. Pulling up with Grover, for their weekly poker game at Boppie's house, he noticed the fella's standing out front with somber expressions.

"Damn, I haven't even taken your money yet. Why the sad faces?" Frenchy joked.

Love's expression sagged. "Man, this is a tough pill to swallow. Scratch is gone."

"What do you mean gone?" Frenchy bellowed, grasping Love's words.

"They found him dead in his cell. Nobody knows what happened."

"What do you mean nobody knows what happened?" Grover belted.

"According to what I heard, he was fine at 'lights out,' then dead the next morning. No one is saying how," Love explained.

Suddenly, Frenchy heard a ringing in his ear, and could no longer focus on what was being said. It had been nearly 3 months since their encounter and Scratch should have long since been released.

Boppie observed Frenchy's despondence.

"Are you alright, man?"

"This can't be happening. When I was locked-up, Scratch saved my life. If it wasn't for him, I wouldn't be here."

"In all this time since you've been out, you never mentioned that," Boppie said.

Never experiencing someone close to him dying, the overwhelming grief was too much. His hands began to tremble, coupled with a stabbing pain in his stomach. *Is Scratch dead because of him?*

As the five Turks all looked down at their feet, with some holding their heads, none knew how to process their emotions. Memories of their early teen years, throwing rocks and catching lizards in the open fields of Pacoima, filled their minds. The brotherhood they all forged was forever engraved in their hearts.

With red-eyes fighting back tears, Pudgy's voice cracked.

"Dam, Scratch was my boy. I know he went out fighting."

Those words struck a chord with Frenchy, causing a flashback to his last conversation with Scratch. Lost among all the chaos and drama, was how Scratch somehow remembered his birthday after the attack in jail. With pride and respect for their fallen brother, Frenchy lifted his right arm in the air. One by one the others did the same, with silent tears filling their eyes. Then, together they all chanted.

"Turks are one."

* * *

The court date arrived for the divorce, and he felt heavy in his heart, knowing it was about to be final. The reality that he and Tipy would no longer be man and wife stung like a thousand bees. He was light-headed and woozy as reality began sinking in. He had talked to Boppie about giving him a ride to the Van Nuys courthouse, who agreed. Boppie arrived on time, and Frenchy got in the car with a subdued attitude.

"Hey, French. You don't look like you are doing so well," Boppie said.

"Man, you know."

"I want you to understand we will always be brothers. We were tight before Tipy, and nothing has changed."

"I appreciate that man. The past year has been treacherous. Scratches funeral was really tough me."

"Me too. You never answered my question about why you never mentioned the incident with you and Scratch."

"Like I said, it's been a rollercoaster. Between the coroner's office, jail, your sister, and everything else, can you really blame me for not saying anything?"

The two were silent as Frenchy gazed out the window feeling a sense of despair, praying somehow this whole thing could be magically reversed, but knowing that was just a pipe dream.

"What do you think about Kennedy getting assassinated?" Boppie said, breaking the silence. "Malcolm says the chickens were coming home to roost."

"I can't believe he was killed only little over a year after Marilyn. It makes me wonder."

"Well, Tipy said Marilyn Monroe was sleeping with both brothers."

"Yes, there's a lot of rumors out there. Of course, you can always count on your sister to be spreading one."

"Joyce is the same. She loves to gossip too. I think she misses us all living together."

"Man, we had some good times in that house. Just think 18 and 20 living in a place of our own. Our neighbors were trippin' with us being so young, but I'm gonna tell you this, those were the greatest days of my life. I would give anything to go back to that time. Let me give you some advice. No matter what, hold on to your family. Don't let anything tempt you to place them at risk. Anything."

"I hear you, brother," Boppie said.

Frenchy extended his hand for a soul shake. "Thanks for the ride."

"I'll always have your back." Boppie proclaimed, as each tightened their grip.

Inside, the courtroom felt like a zoo. Tipy and a lawyer convened at the plaintiff's table while Frenchy sat alone, staring blankly at the judge. He saw mouths moving, but nothing registered while he sat quietly throughout the proceeding. He was in a mental zone unlike any other, with darkness bellowing his crushed dreams. Then suddenly, a loud bang, almost like a gunshot, from the wooden gavel solidified the finality of Frenchy's nightmare. His body twitched at the sound, sending an electric wave of emotion from his head to toe. Tipy was no longer his wife.

1974 was a politically exciting year. President Nixon resigned after the Watergate scandal, and affirmative action was in full force. Frenchy had fulfilled his goal of working in communications and was producing radio programming for Capital Cities. He had successfully blocked out the past, establishing himself as a media magnate with his own chapter of an organization called Project BAIT.

Created to provide training for African Americans wanting to work in communications, BAIT was the acronym for Black Awareness in Television. Frenchy's Los Angeles chapter was located in Hollywood, producing television and radio projects that provided unique opportunities for the minority community.

Once again, he felt respected, airing his popular weekly show, 'Who Cares,' in Los Angeles. The Federal Communications Commission Fairness Doctrine required broadcasters to provide programming on controversial issues of interest to the community. Frenchy convinced Capital Cities that his radio show was perfect for this venue.

KPOL Studio, on the corner of Sunset Blvd and Wilton Place, is where they recorded and aired the show. It was a two-story facility smack dab in the middle of Hollywood, with CBS Television as a close neighbor.

Frenchy, now 34, blazed groundbreaking trails with his love for media. He enjoyed working with intellectuals of color both young and old. On his team, a youthful lady, Paisley Todd, caught his eye. She had a spark and energy level that impressed him from the beginning. This beautiful woman was only 24. They first met two years ago and she added tremendously to the organization. Paisley was an actress, who had played minor roles in films such as Cooley High, Mister Brown, and Halls of Anger. But it was her mind that captivated him the most. They were slowly becoming a partnership.

Paisley had a knack for developing stories, articulating them, and tuning in on all the fine details. At the same time, Frenchy did the technical sound, camera, editing, and budget. So, they made a perfect team.

"I have a book author coming on Sunday at 7 am," Paisley explained to Frenchy.

"What's his name?"

"Robert Slatzer."

"What's his book about?"

"It's a conspiracy theme about the death of a movie star."

"So, we are getting away from meaningful content to Hollywood tabloid gossip?"

"No, Frenchy. This is an interesting story."

"You're lucky I trust your judgment, Paisley."

Sunday morning, Frenchy was setting up the studio, getting out the headphones, and checking everything was ready. Paisley arrived wearing a solid beige skirt and jacket with a white blouse underneath, creating a professional look with her silky hair in a classic bun. It was understandable why she dabbled in the acting and modeling fields. Yet, her talent lay in interviewing because of her connection with people.

"Good morning, Paisley. Do you have your questions and script ready?"

"Of course I do. I checked out the book last night. We can't go wrong with this, no matter what."

"What is it about?"

"It's called 'The Life and Curious Death of Marilyn Monroe."

"What did you say?"

"The Life and Curious Death of Marilyn Monroe."

A dark shadow came over Frenchy's face as he gritted his teeth.

"We can't do this show!"

"Quit joking," Paisley jested.

"I'm serious."

"What are you talking about, Frenchy? We have an entire hour dedicated to the author discussing it. One of our interns set this interview up."

"No! Find something else. I'm not kidding, Paisley."

"We begin recording in forty minutes. Our guest should be here in ten. Have you lost your mind? This would be a blow to our mission of helping students."

Thoughts of Marilyn reentering his life petrified Frenchy. His heartbeat increased at the mere thought. Yet, no one in his current world knew the story and never would if he could help it.

"Alright then, this show is all on you."

"What does that mean? You need to work the controls! I don't understand you. What has gotten into you, Frenchy? We have a show to do."

Letting out a long slow sigh, he decided to bite the bullet and just get it done. After all, it was only a one-hour show.

"Fine, get your headphones. Where is this person? He's late," Frenchy exhaled in frustration.

"He should arrive any minute. Here's a copy of his book," Paisley said, placing it near the control panel.

With that, Bob Slatzer was at the entrance ringing the bell. He was roughly 5 foot 7 with brown hair combed across his head, unsuccessfully trying to hide his baldness. But, unfortunately, the hairline part was so close to his ear that it gave his shameful secret away.

Paisley and her intern greeted Bob, then briefly prepped him on the show's format. The show's opening began with Paisley after everyone was seated and in place with headphones.

"I'm Paisley Todd, and welcome to Who Cares, a program designed for minority stories in the community, for the community, and by the community. We ask you, who cares, and the consistent answer is, we do. Today's story delves into the death of a woman that suffered a deadly fate in a man's world. We are talking about a woman you all knew and loved, movie star, Marilyn Monroe."

The show cut to a music sting as Frenchy hit play on the reel-to-reel tape deck, launching "Bumpin' on Sunset" by Wes Montgomery. The interlude played for about twenty seconds before Paisley returned.

"Marilyn Monroe died twelve years ago, and today we have Robert Slatzer, author of a book titled 'The Life and Curious Death of Marilyn Monroe.' Welcome, Mr. Slatzer."

"Thank you, Paisley."

"So, tell us a little about your book."

"My book provides details, documents, and background to the death of Marilyn Monroe. It makes the case she had no reason to commit suicide and brings up the possibility of murder."

"What makes you think she may have been killed?"

"There are many reasons, Paisley, and I'll share them all. But, first, I must say that the county of Los Angeles authorities should conduct a thorough and honest investigation to provide the public with answers. Opening an inquest would uncover all pertinent facts to establish if Marilyn's death was murder, accident, or suicide beyond a shadow of a doubt."

With that, Frenchy looked down at the book, feeling a familiar chill of darkness, thought escaped long ago. He picked it up and began to thumb through the pages. Shockingly, chapter one boldly revealed her affair with Bobby Kennedy and JFK in the opening paragraph. Instantly he slammed the book down, paralyzed with the returning feelings of gloom.

"Frenchy? Frenchy the music," Paisley's voice brought him back.

Instantly he adjusted the mixer and then went to break. Frenchy sat stunned during the rest of the recording, operating on autopilot. He picked up the book once again. In the back were twenty pages of certificates and reports, then suddenly, his eyes fixated on page 304. Frenchy blinked and rubbed his eyes while the words CERTIFICATE OF DEATH took him back twelve years. Slowly scanning down the document, the signature Lionel Grandison got bigger and bigger, causing him to fall into a catatonic state.

"Frenchy, are you okay?" Paisley asked.

He slowly looked up to see Paisley and Slatzer staring at him, confused at his demeanor.

"Yes, I'm fine. I was just looking at my signature."

"Your signature? Do you need some water?" Paisley asked.

Slatzer was equally confused, wondering if this was a medical emergency or something.

"I haven't thought about this in years. Well, I was working at the coroner's office when Marilyn died. I signed her death certificate."

Silence sprinkled the room like pixy dust. Slatzer lifted a single eyebrow and tilted his head while Paisley rubbed absently at her arms. The student on the other side of the room pulled his glasses down and looked over the rims.

"You never told me you worked at the coroner's office!" Paisley grimaced.

"Well, I buried that part of my life. No pun intended."

With the book still opened, Frenchy pointed at his signature.

"So, you worked with Dr. Curphey and Noguchi? I have zero information about the coroner's office. This could fill in a lot of holes that I have. We need to talk," Slatzer pleaded.

"Nothing personal, Mr. Slatzer, but I'm not prepared to discuss that situation."

"I only need you to answer a few simple questions for me. Please."

"There are no simple questions regarding the Monroe case."

"But did you agree with the finding of suicide?" Slatzer persisted.

Pausing for a minute, Frenchy bit his bottom lip.

"No, I didn't."

"Look, she was involved with the Kennedys, and there has been a colossal cover-up."

"I read her diary," Frenchy let slip out.

"You've read her diary?"

"Yes," he hesitated. "It disappeared after a couple of days. But I can't go back to that time. Sorry. I wish you luck with your journey toward the truth."

Frenchy then dropped the book on the table.

"It was a pleasure meeting you, Mr. Slatzer. We will let you know when the show airs."

Frenchy left the studio room and headed downstairs to the lobby, with Paisley and Slatzer following closely behind. He opened the door to Sunset Blvd so Slatzer could exit, noticing the sunlight blazing on the pavement, making the Hollywood dust glitter.

"It was a pleasure," Frenchy forced a smile.

"Mr. Grandison, will you please meet with me? I would love to hear more about the diary. I saw it too. Marilyn shared a lot with me, and this whole thing needs to be examined. Please, just to talk."

"I don't think so. You have a great day."

"Well, here's my card. Call me if you change your mind."

"Goodbye, Mr. Slatzer," Paisley bid.

The door squeaked as it lumbered shut. Paisley grabbed Frenchy by the shoulder and looked into his hazel eyes.

"We've been working closely together for two years, and I have never seen you like this."

"Marilyn Monroe's death was the worst thing that ever happened to me. This guy can only dredge up things I want to forget."

"You may want to forget them, but they may heal you too. I see pain in your eyes. Teflon man Frenchy has vulnerabilities."

"You got that right."

"What could it hurt to hear him out? I didn't think you were scared of anything."

"It's not that I'm scared. Marilyn Monroe is in the past and needs to stay there."

"Alright. If you say so," Paisley exhaled.

The rest of the day Frenchy spent editing the show. Listening more to Slatzer's interview made him curious about what else he knew about the Monroe case. Scrutinizing his business card closely, he realized the irony of Slatzer showing up at the station. The little voice in his head said, throw that card away and forget about it. Getting involved again could be the biggest mistake he ever made. But the power of fate had brought them together. *What could it hurt?*

A few days later, he agreed to meet Slatzer at his office at the old Taft Building on Hollywood Boulevard and Vine. Retrieving his diary notes from a hidden spot at Mo's house the night before, his heart began to race as he flipped through the pages. Instantly the life-changing nightmare of 1962 flashed before his eyes.

Walking up to the entrance, a bead of sweat dripped down his face as Marilyn's ghost had inexplicably found him again. He was still somewhat apprehensive about this whole thing and hoped Slatzer did not sense his emotion. But despite many reasons to be skeptical, Frenchy was still intrigued.

"So, you believe Marilyn was murdered?" Frenchy began.

"Yes, I do. There are so many questions I'm seeking answers for. It's bizarre how our paths crossed when I had nothing from the coroner's office. No one will talk."

"I'm not surprised."

"What exactly was your role?" Slatzer inquired.

"I was the lead investigator."

"You disagreed with the suicide ruling. Why?"

"I read her diary, and she was involved with some very powerful people. Her final entries were about Bobby Kennedy."

"I think he did it, or the Kennedy conglomerate. He was at her house the day she died, then helicoptered to San Francisco as an alibi."

"I knew he was in town, but not sure if he was at her house. The housekeeper never said anything about that. Neither did the doctor."

"Why was there never an inquest?"

"One man, Theodore Curphey. He wanted the case closed right away."

"If you thought it needed further investigation, why did you sign the death certificate?"

"First of all, I was only twenty-two years old, and my boss told me to sign it or else."

Slatzer ran his hands through his thinning hair, eyes anchored on Frenchy.

"This is a bombshell. You know that, don't you? What did Noguchi have to say about all of this?"

"I questioned him. He had a peculiar, uncharacteristic demeanor and wasn't his usual self, but we were all under extreme pressure. Dr. Noguchi was a straight shooter but not prepared to fight that battle."

"Do you think someone got to Curphey?"

"Curphey and his team of conspirators had a different agenda. First, they concealed the truth by switching reports, then side-peddled the Chloral Hydrate after strangely discovering it in her system. When I told Curphey she had no prescription for that drug, he brushed it aside like everything else. Did someone get to him? Curphey held the most powerful position in Los Angeles County. If someone did get to him, they were above everyone's pay grade."

"We need to take this to the Grand Jury!"

"Absolutely not. At least not with me involved."

"You are the missing link we need. We can do a publicity run and make some noise so they will be forced to re-open her case."

"Bob, I'm not being a part of that," Frenchy reiterated.

"Listen, this case is massive. I went to Marilyn's house after she died, and I looked at the broken window, and the glass was on the outside, which meant someone had shattered it from the inside. That's a big problem."

"I knew those doctors were lying."

"The weekend before her death, she was in Lake Tahoe at Frank Sinatra's party and was touting a press conference where she was planning to tell it all."

"I read about that in her diary. It also mentioned Teamster Union boss Jimmy Hoffa and Mafia king Sam Giancana. They were concerned she knew about the attempt on Fidel Castro's life in the Bay of Pigs."

"What you don't know is Hoffa had her house wiretapped along with the FBI and CIA. They all know what happened to her, and no one is talking. Why?"

"How do you know she was wiretapped?"

"Bernard Spindel, an expert in audio surveillance, and his partner Fred Otash were hired by Hoffa to bug the residence. I heard some of the recordings."

"That should mean you know what happened the day she died."

"I didn't hear the one on that date, but days before she died, there were heated conversations with Robert Kennedy. Then on Friday, August 3, and Saturday, August 4, 1962, she had brutal exchanges with Bobby. There was a colossal phone argument, and on the tape, Marilyn was answering a call, and he told her he was coming over that evening but never showed up."

"He wanted her diary," Frenchy added.

"Yep. But then, at some point, Bobby came to her house, and on the tape, she said, 'The diary is mine. You weren't the first to take me to some damn meetings, but come to the press conference, you'll get a good look for yourself."

"Wow! That was on tape?"

"I could hear Kennedy leave, then Marilyn made some phone calls. But Kennedy returned later with Peter Lawford, and someone was throwing things and slamming drawers. There was yelling, asking 'where's that damn book, Marilyn?' Then a loud noise and a scream that seemed to be Marilyn falling and then crying. They left without the diary, but she was still alive."

Everything Slatzer heard correlated with what Frenchy read in Marilyn's diary, which could not be coincidental. Frenchy dropped his shoulders and briefly closed his eyes. He then turned to Slatzer.

"I have to ask. Why is this so personal to you? Is this about money?"

"Money can never bring Marilyn back. My relationship with her is something few could ever understand. I was married to her once for a short while, and we loved each other very much."

"Married to her?" Frenchy asked, shocked. "What happened?"

"When the studio found out, they made her get an annulment. That's a long story, but we stayed best friends. So let me ask you something. Why isn't this personal to you?"

Stunned, knowing Marilyn's case cost him everything, Frenchy still wasn't sure if this was his fight. He had already conceded and accepted the loss.

"You know what, Bob, this is personal, and for the past twelve years, I tried to put it behind me in ways no one could understand. This tried to break me."

"Let me tell you something you weren't the only one whose life was ruined by the death of Marilyn Monroe."

"What do you mean?"

"There was another man, officer Jack Clemmons, who was the first watch commander on the scene."

"Clemmons, Clemmons. Yes, I remember speaking with him. He complained about how the case was being handled."

"Well, he got fired because he was making noise about the witness statements. His whole life was turned upside down. He lost his pension, house, and most importantly, his family."

Folding his arms while his jaw slackened, Frenchy remembered Clemmons candidness. He was one of the few on the same page as Frenchy.

"Clemmons was a good man. We were true public servants, and that should have never happened to us. Getting penalized for doing what is right is not what this country should be."

"That's why it's time to tell your story. And if you, I, and Clemmons all work together, maybe we can find justice for Marilyn and ourselves. Of course, sometimes, doing the right thing comes with a cost. But you can and will sleep better at night knowing you did the right thing."

Frenchy's heart rate increased as he contemplated something once unthinkable. He knew things happened for a reason, but could never connect his misery with any purpose. There had to be an explanation for why he lost everything near and dear to him. Suddenly an unexpected thought popped into Frenchy's head. It wasn't just him, Clemmons, and Slatzer. What about Scratch? He also was a causality of Marilyn's death. He owed it to his fellow Turk to let his death not be in vain. Moreover, he was now older, stronger, and wiser. The time had come for everyone to discover the truth about Marilyn Monroe.

"Okay, Bob. I'm in."

To be continued…

Marilyn Monroe was born Norma Jeane Mortenson on June 1, 1926. She was an actress known as a Hollywood sex symbol, starring in many commercially successful films during the 1950s, while becoming a pop culture icon. In her teen years, she attended Van Nuys High School in the San Fernando Valley, just several miles from where Frenchy grew up. Monroe was among 20th Century Fox's biggest stars and the controversy surrounding her death has lingered in the minds of the world for over sixty years.

Los Angeles Times

MONDAY FINAL

VOL. LXXXI   SIX PARTS—PART ONE   MONDAY MORNING, AUGUST 6, 1962   KTTV (CHANNEL 11)   92 PAGES   DAILY 10c

MARILYN MONROE FOUND DEAD
Sleeping Pill Overdose Blamed

Red Super Bomb Kicks Off Series

High Altitude Test Reported as Being in 40-Megaton Range

UPPSALA, Sweden (AP) – The Soviet Union exploded a big nuclear bomb in the atmosphere Sunday.

Swedish scientist estimated it to be in the 40-megaton range, second only to the Soviet 50-megaton bomb set off last Oct. 30. A Norwegian scientist said his instruments showed only that it was smaller than that one and US officials would say only that it was "in the megaton range."

new Soviet testing "is regrettable for world peace."

The big blast appeared to have kicked off a new round of Soviet military maneuvers in the far north de-signed among other things to test new nuclear weapons.

The Soviet Foreign Ministry refused to comment on the

Nixon Team at Helm of State GOP

BY RICHARD BERGHOLZ
Times Political Writer

SACRAMENTO — Moving quickly and easily, the Republican state organization changed leadership Sunday with Richard Nixon in tight control.

The 561-number state Central Committee without an apparent ripple of dissent, selected new leaders for two year terms and adopted a series of policy resolutions, closely attuned to the views

Unclad Body of Star Discovered on Bed; Empty Bottle Near

BY HOWARD MERTEL AND DON NEFF

Marilyn Monroe, a troubled beauty who failed to find happiness as Hollywood's brightest star, was discovered dead in her Brentwood home of an apparent overdose of sleeping pills Sunday.

The blonde 36-year-old actress was nude, lying face down on her bed and clinching a telephone receiver in her hand when a psychiatrist broke into her room at 3:30 a.m.

She had been dead an estimated six to eight hours.

About 3:15 p.m. Saturday she had called the psychiatrist, Dr. Ralph Greenson, and was told to go for a ride when she complained she could not sleep, police reported.

Her body was taken to the County Morgue, where Coroner Theodore J. Curphey said after an autopsy that he would give a "presumptive opinion" that death was due to an overdose of some drug. He said a special "suicide team" would be asked to investigate Miss Monroe's last days to determine if she took her own life.

Newspapers printed suicide theory immediately after death

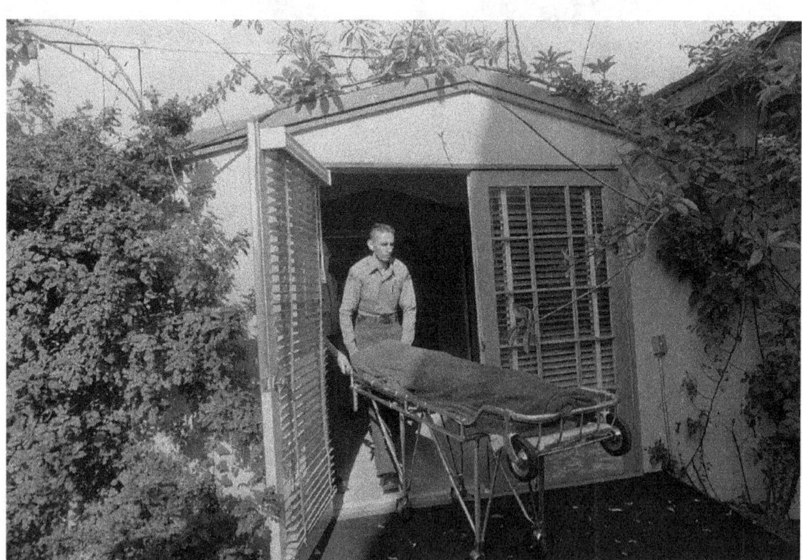

Danbacker retrieves Monroe's body for delivery to the coroner's office per Deputy Grandison's request

Los Angeles Police Department
FOLLOW-UP REPORT   ☐ MULTIPLE REPORT   DR 62-509 463

TYPE CRIME **DEATH REPORT**	ADDITIONAL MAJOR CRIMES COMMITTED—THIS INCIDENT		
DATE AND TIME OCCURRED 8-4/5-62 8P/3:35A	DATE AND TIME OF THIS REPORT 8-6-62 4:15P	LOCATION OF OCCURRENCE 12305 Fifth Helena Dr.	RPTG. DIST. 814
VICTIM'S NAME (as listed on orig. report) MONROE, Marilyn	LIC. NO. INVOLVED VEHICLE	CONNECTING PROPERTY REPORTS	

| Property Recovery | | TOTAL | PARTIAL | NONE | Additional Property | LOSS — THIS REPORT $ | |
| Property Disposition | | BOOKED | RELEASED BY DEPT. | | | RECOVERY $ | |

| Case Status | REPORT UNFOUNDED | CLEARED | ☐ RECLASSIFY TO: | MAINTAIN WANTS IN PROPERTY FILE? | YES |
| | COMPLAINT REFUSED | X INVEST. CONT. | | | NO |

PERSON(S) ARRESTED | LA OR 'J' NO. | SEX DESC. AGE HGT. WGT. HAIR EYES | HTA DATE | CHARGE | CRT. DIV.

(1) EXPLAIN INVESTIGATION PROGRESS AND STATUS. (2) DESCRIBE ANY CHANGE IN M.O. (3) WHEN VICTIM AND/OR WITNESSES LISTED IN CRIME REPORT HAVE NOT BEEN INTERVIEWED, GIVE REASON. (4) IF ADDITIONAL PROPERTY LOSS INVOLVED, ITEMIZE, DESCRIBE AND SHOW VALUE, LISTING ALL SERIAL NUMBERS. IF PARTIAL RECOVERY, LIST PROPERTY RECOVERED, USING ITEM NUMBER, DESCRIPTION (SERIAL NO., MONOGRAMS, ETC.) AND VALUE AS IT APPEARS ON INITIAL REPORT. EXPLAIN ANY CHANGES FOUND NECESSARY IN PROPERTY DESCRIPTIONS. REPORT ALL SERIAL NUMBERS AND INSCRIPTIONS DEVELOPED DURING INVESTIGATION.

ITEM NO. | PERSON REPORTING OR ADDITIONAL PERSONS INTERVIEWED | RESIDENCE ADDRESS | CITY | RESIDENCE PHONE | BUSINESS PHONE

Upon reinterviewing both Dr. Ralph R. Greenson (Wit #1 and Dr. Hyman Engelberg (Wit #2) they both agree to the following time sequence of their actions.

Dr. Greenson received a phone call from Mrs Murray (reporting person) at 3:30A, 8-5-62 stating that she was unable to get into Miss Monroe's bedroom and the light was on. He told her to pound on the door and look in the window and call him back. At 3:35A, Mrs Murray called back and stated Miss Monroe was laying on the bed with the phone in her hand and looked strange. Dr. Greenson was dressed by this time, left for deceased residence which is about one mile away. He also told Mrs Murray to call Dr. Engelberg.

Dr. Greenson arrived at deceased house at about 3:40A. He broke the window pane and entered through the window and removed the phone from her hand.

Rigor Mortis had set in. At 3:50A, Dr. Engelberg arrived and pronounced Miss Monroe dead. The two doctors talked for a few moments. They both believe that it was about 4A when Dr. Engelberg called the Police Department.

A check with the Complaint Board and WLA Desk, indicates that the call was received at 4:25A. Miss Monroe's phone, GR 61890 has been checked and no toll calls were made during the hours of this occurrence Phone number 472-4830 is being checked at the present time.

If additional space is required, use Continuation Sheet, Form 15.   *R E Byron 2730*   TOTAL VALUE $

DATE AND TIME TYPED | DIVISION | CLERK | INTERVIEWING OFFICER(S) | SER. NO. | DIVISION | PERSON REPORTING (SIGNATURE)
8-6-62 10:25A WLA JS | R L BYRON 2730 WLA D | X

FOLLOW-UP REPORT

Deputy Grandison saw numerous discrepancies in the initial police report as well as this follow-up report

CERTIFICATE OF DEATH
STATE OF CALIFORNIA — DEPARTMENT OF PUBLIC HEALTH

7053   17716

Marilyn Monroe

Female Cauc. Los Angeles, Calif. June 1, 1926   36

unk. unk. Gladys Pearl Baker — Mexico United States 563-32-0764

Actress 20 20th Century-Fox Motion Pictures

none Divorced

12305 -5th Helena Drive

Los Angeles Los Angeles

12305 -5th Helena Drive Los Angeles Calif. Mrs. Inez C. Melson

Los Angeles Los Angeles Calif. 9110 Sunset Blvd.

autopsy HALL OF JUSTICE LOS ANGELES 8-28-62

Entombment Aug. 8, 1962 Westwood Memorial Park

Westwood Village Mortuary

ACUTE BARBITURATE POISONING

INGESTION OF OVERDOSE

Probable Suicide

As Above

HOME Los Angeles L.A. Calif.

This is a true certified copy of the record
if it bears the seal of the County Recorder
imprinted in purple ink.

FEE
$2.00   SEP 24 1964

Ray E. Lee COUNTY RECORDER
AND DEPUTY COUNTY ... OFFICER
LOS ANGELES COUNTY, CALIFORNIA

Deputy Grandison signed this death certificate against his better judgment on August 28, 1962. Hours later he was arrested for a setup he never saw coming. His life was never the same.

Lionel "Frenchy" Grandison, seen here in 1974, rebuilt his life and career through communications while producing a groundbreaking weekly show at KPOL Radio in Hollywood.

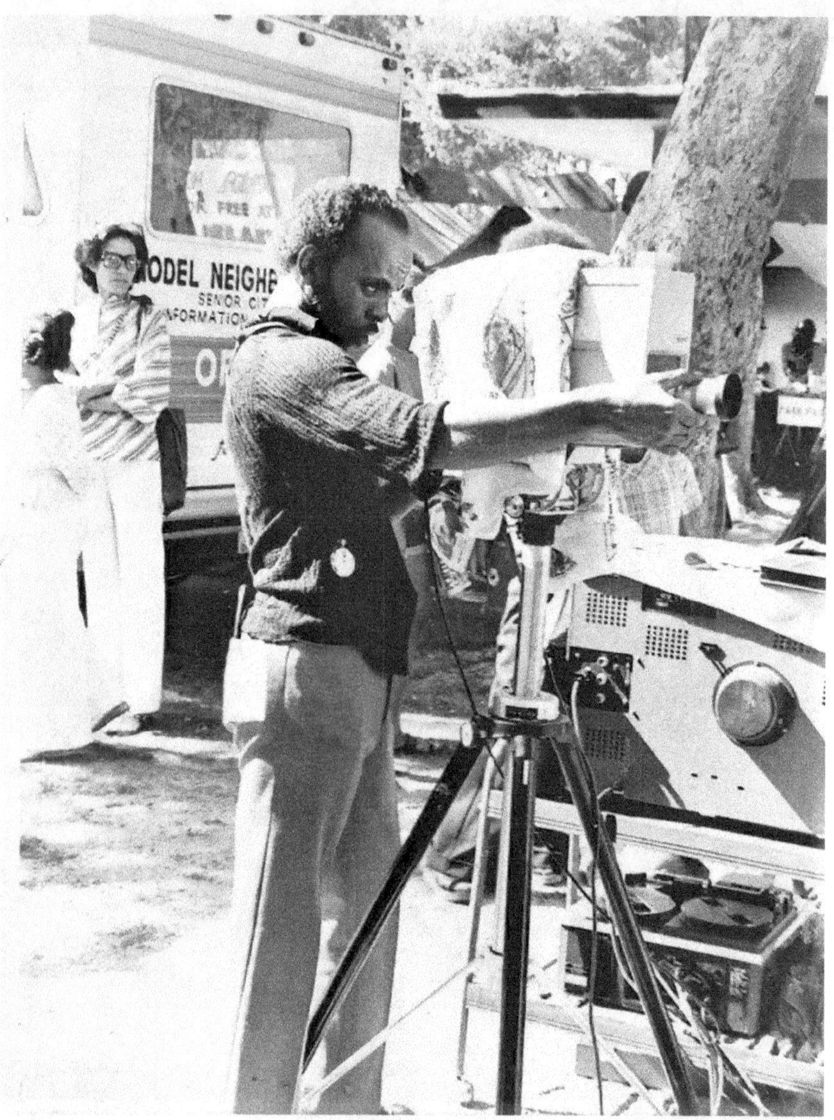

When Frenchy operated a chapter of Black Awareness in Television, he produced many community programs. He excelled in directing, camera work, editing, budgeting, and marketing.

After agreeing to share his story with Bob Slatzer, they went on a media campaign that landed them on network television and major publications. The effort to force a Grand Jury investigation sparked the District Attorney to revisit the Monroe case in 1982. However, the forces seeking to coverup the truth never dissipated. Whereas the people changed, the hurdles were taller and more dangerous. Part II covers the challenges of fighting a conspiracy after you get wrongly discredited.

Despite the divorce, Tipy and Frenchy co-parented well and remained friends over the years. He was always a major part in his children's life. This photo was taken nearly 20 years after the Monroe case.

This amazing photo of original Turks members (left to right) Frenchy, Grover, Love, and Pudgy was taken in 2018, over sixty years later.

I wrote this book in honor of my parents, Lionel Grandison Sr. and Alithra "Tipy" Louda. No two people in the world showed me unconditional love and support than them. My dad always told me I owed him a book ever since I could remember, and my mom openly and freely shared secrets and stories for me to tell. Well, dad, you have three books from me now and more in the making, and mom, your voice and humor are my lifelines. You thought Pacoima was boring but guess what? It's exciting!